REED

STORM ENTERPRISES BOOK 4

B J ALPHA

Published by Alpha Team Publishing

Edited by Dee Houpt

Proofread by Mackenzie Nice Girl Naughty Edits

Cover Design by Bee Bitter Sage Designs

AUTHOR NOTE

BLURB

Reed

Playboy. Bachelor. Billionaire.

I'm all those things, and life couldn't be better.

Until one night with a mystery woman sends my world into chaos and makes me crave more out of life.

I've never wanted a family of my own; let alone someone else's ready-made one, and when I find myself suffering the repercussions of that one night with her, I see an opportunity.

The woman I've become obsessed with holds the key to a business deal I'm desperate to win, and the baby in her belly is the turning point in that deal.

Am I prepared to lose the biggest business deal of my life over a one-night stand?

Or will I try my best to keep them both despite knowing it won't end well?

Gia Fanzio might just be the making of me, if I don't break us first.

Gia

You know how it goes, one night of passion with a hot

mystery man, and a few months later, you discover you're pregnant.

Imagine my surprise when the man who destroyed me for all others is an arrogant playboy, so absorbed in himself he struggles with even the basics of everyday life. Granted, mine is a little more complicated than most. I come with baggage—a lot of it.

Reed is determined to be a part of my family, and I can't help but fall for him while he tries.

What happens when his business deal corrupts everything we've worked so hard to build?

And worse, my life is at stake.

Our baby's too.

PROLOGUE

REED

MY FINGERS TANGLE in my tie to yank it open, letting me breathe again. The meeting was a shitshow. Of course it was. George Fanzio is a grade-A prick with little to no intention of following through with his promises. Now he claims a shareholder isn't playing ball with the sale of the site I'm desperate to purchase. When, in reality, we both know he's enjoying this little runaround he has me in. Three fucking years! Three fucking years, only to reach one stumbling block after another.

I want that fucking land, and the more he withholds it, the greater the challenge becomes.

A heavy sigh leaves me as I grab the glass of whiskey, knock it back, then slam the glass down on the bar and nod toward the bartender for another.

"Rough day?" a silky-smooth, feminine voice delivers from beside me, and my cock pays notice to her sultry tone.

As much as I can't deal with the exertion of sex right now, it would certainly divert my mind, and with a voice like that, I'm sure I could soon forget what a shitty day it's been.

So instead of giving George fucking Fanzio another minute's thought, I spin on my barstool to gift my attention to the voice in question.

My heart does a weird stutter when my eyes land on hers. Holy. Fucking. Shit.

A lump clogs in my throat as I blatantly scan over her entire being. Dark-green eyes sparkle with mirth, as if enjoying my obvious attention. She licks her lips; the little minx is begging for it, no doubt. Her dark hair is pulled up into a high ponytail, one I want to yank so hard her neck stretches, giving me access to sink my teeth into it and suck until copper spills onto my tongue, marking her as mine.

Wait … Where the fuck did that thought come from?

She licks her plump red lips again, and it's almost as if she has a direct line to my cock because it thickens in my slacks. Sliding her ass onto the seat beside me, she tilts her head.

All I can concentrate on is the natural beauty in front of me.

My gaze travels down her white blouse and stops on her heavy rack. Fuck yes.

I wonder if they're real?

Her nipples press through the thin fabric, and I want nothing more than to toy with them, kiss her peaked tips, and suck them into my mouth while feeling the weight of her tits in my hands.

My perusal continues, taking in her small form, but wide hips. Hips I could hold on to while I fuck into her, giving me the perfect view of those tits as she begs for me to suck on them and they bounce in my face. I'd mark them and bite into her until I've left her knowing who she belongs to.

Jesus, please let them be real.

Her olive skin shines like she's some goddess, and I find myself asking what the hell I've been doing, wasting my life on women who resemble the living form of a stereotypical Barbie when there are beauties like her out there.

Why the hell haven't I been searching for a woman like this? A natural woman with curves, and chaos in her eyes. So different from the pleading and desperate women I more often than not pay for.

"Are you finished?" The question is delivered with humor, and I jerk back. "Did I pass the exam?"

Her words stun me. She slides off the barstool and holds out her arms for me to appraise her while she does a slow spin on her black patent high heels, allowing me to view her perfect ass. One that's tucked tightly into a pencil skirt. The slit up the back taunts me, and I literally groan with the thought of bending her over and fucking her senseless. Maybe then her snark would stop, despite me finding it a welcome reprieve from the usual obedient shit I deal with.

The lump gathered in my throat thickens, as does my cock, and it's becoming uncomfortable. Eagerness has taken over, and I feel like I'm losing control. Something I hate.

It's rare I feel so unraveled, and I find myself attracted to the foreign feeling as well as wanting to punish her for it.

"You pass," I grunt out.

"Gee, thanks," she playfully bites back, returns to her seat, and faces me.

I take note of the briefcase beside her. Businesswoman? Not my usual go-to, but I like the thought.

Her delicate hand comes toward me, grabbing the drink I didn't realize the bartender had delivered, and I freeze when the beauty brings my glass to her lips and tips the whiskey back.

She releases a small gasp, then her tongue darts out and licks the remnants of the drink from her lips while I watch her in a lust-filled daze.

"So, what's your line of work? I'm a lawyer," she says, and my head rears back. "Family law, to be exact."

I scan over her again. Fuck me, that's hot.

"Me too."

Her green eyes roam over me before they come back to my face.

"Not family law," I tack on.

She laughs, and I want to hear the sound again.

"Do you have a room here?" She tips her face toward the ceiling, and I nod like an idiot. "Good. I've had a truly shitty day, and I need to forget." She sighs. Seems we've both had a shit day, and the implication is clear as day: she wants me to fuck her, and suddenly, my blood pumps wilder through my veins with a need to do just that.

Hell yes, I can do that. That's one thing I'm damn good at; I have a skilled tongue, an impeccable set of fingers, and a cock made for gratification, and not just my own.

"I can do that." I smirk back at her, not missing the way her chest rises, and her eyes flash with a touch of uncertainty. I should care about that small detail. But honestly? All I care about is getting my hands on the woman before me and making her night unforgettable, punishing that little body of hers for taunting me so blatantly. This woman who's asked me to help her forget her day, like she's helping me forget mine.

I lean into her to whisper into her ear. "I'm going to fuck you so hard you'll never forget me."

She shivers beneath me, and a burst of excitement flares through my body at her reaction.

Then her head turns until her lips almost touch mine. "Promises, promises." She pulls back and gifts me a wink, causing my eyes to narrow at her confidence, and my lips to turn up into a knowing smile.

Game. Fucking. On.

Stepping back, I reach into my pocket and throw a wad of cash onto the bar. Then, without warning her, I grab her briefcase and purse from the floor and take hold of her hand, pulling her behind me. The palm of her small hand and the softness of her skin against mine have me eager to claim her, something I've never felt before in my entire life. Rather than explore those feelings, I knock them to the side and concentrate on the here and now. To give her a night she will never forget.

Anticipation floods me as we head toward the door. "I hope you're ready for a night you'll never forget, sweetheart. But be warned, I don't do sweet and gentle."

"I'm counting on it," she quips back, adding to my delight.

The little minx is a tease. A very naughty tease, who's about to learn one hell of a lesson.

Reed Johnson cannot be controlled, challenged, or manipulated by any woman.

GIA

As soon as the elevator doors close, he's on me, spinning me to face the mirrors. Then he kicks my legs apart and pushes me forward, giving me no choice but to slam my hands onto the mirrored walls to stop me from falling.

The moment he stepped into the bar, I wanted to have sex with him. Handsome, sharp features make him look like a model who just walked off a runway. His dark hair has a kink to it, and I imagine it's normally slicked back to perfection, but given the hostility radiating from him and the way his chest heaved, I knew he'd been pushing his hand through his hair, no doubt in agitation. Something I see happen a lot in my line of work.

I've been trained to read body language to enable me to do my job better, and his body language screamed pissed off. Glancing around the room, I noticed all the women eyeing him, and I knew if I wanted him tonight, I'd have to make a move, and fast. The women were like vultures, no doubt hanging around in the hopes of snagging a professional man, uncaring if he's married or not.

"Are you single?" I pant out as self-loathing hits me in the chest at not asking before now.

"Of course," he responds with confidence, and I relax. "I don't do relationships." If I were anyone else, that would be a red flag, but what he's offering is precisely what I'm looking for.

"Me too," I moan as his hard cock presses against my ass, his firm hands finding my hips.

"Fuck, you're exquisite," he whispers, and presses kisses down my neck, and I tilt my head to the side to accommodate him better. "Is there anything you won't let me do to you?" he groans out, as if it pains him to ask. "Do you have any limits?"

His question shocks me speechless. Is there anything I don't want him to do?

It's been so long, I really don't know.

He nips at my neck, then follows it up with a flick of his tongue. "Answer me." His voice is deeper this time, dark and full of a commanding tone I find myself loving.

"N-n-n-no."

"Mmm," he muses, and licks a trail up my neck as he pushes his clothed cock into me again. "I want to devour you." One hand leaves my hip and holds my jaw in place. The dominance behind the action has my pussy clenching with need. "You'd like that, wouldn't you? Letting me destroy your little pussy while I play with you."

My gaze meets his in the mirror, and his green eyes are filled with smoldering lust, pupils blown wide, and the determination in them bores into me, making my breath hitch from the force of his stare.

God, I want him, maybe more than I've ever wanted anyone before, which is crazy.

This is a one-night stand, Gia, nothing more.

When his thumb grazes my bottom lip, my tongue flicks out, and I suck the tip into my mouth while our eyes remain locked.

A deep groan rumbles in his chest, and his body becomes

rigid as he presses down on my tongue while it continues to thrash against his digit punishingly. I delight in the way his body reacts to mine, almost like he's intoxicated with me, and the thought has wetness seeping between my legs.

I haven't felt like this in a long time, if ever. Maybe that's why the anticipation feels so heightened?

The elevator doors ping, and he detaches himself. My body sags with his loss, and he spins on his heel, clears his throat, and holds his hand out for me as if we both weren't just lost in a sexual haze.

My cheeks flush with need as I slowly turn toward him, slipping my hand into his large one. His fingers tighten to entwine us, and I will him to never to let go.

REED

With every step I take toward the penthouse suite, more exhilaration rushes through me, and when I scan my hand over the screen to access the hotel room, I practically sigh in relief at being able to step inside with her.

The way she held my attention in the elevator was profound. I've never felt so aroused in my entire life, and I'm ashamed to admit I came close to coming when she sucked my thumb into her mouth and played with it like she will my cock. I clear my throat to keep from spiraling. "Would you like a drink?" The door clicks shut behind us, and she lets go of my hand. I grind my teeth, the loss of her touch irking me, and having that reaction is somewhat disconcerting.

I never show affection and pride myself on the fact I have none to give, nor do I wish to receive it.

After unscrewing the cap on the whiskey, I pour myself a generous measure and lean back against the bar to give her my attention.

"No. I'd prefer to drink you down, though." She beams.

Jesus, this woman is going to be the death of me. I can feel it.

My cock has already soaked my boxers, thanks to her

teasing me in the elevator. I was seconds away from coming like a teenager, and I want nothing more than to punish her for it. I watch transfixed as her fingers slowly unbutton her blouse, exposing her full tits. She slips the material from her shoulders and onto the floor, rooting me to the spot, and my eyes lock onto the white lace holding her generous assets in place.

She moves onto her skirt, unzipping it at the back, and it drops to the floor. Her panties are on full display, and I clench my fists as I try but fail to see if her pussy is bare beneath the scrap of lace.

Her figure is fuller than my usual conquests, but much more enticing. So much so, my mouth waters. I want to kiss every inch of her. I want to suck her skin into my mouth and mark it with my own personal branding.

"Are you going to get undressed?" Her hands move behind her, as if to unlatch her bra, and I hold my hand up to stop her.

"Leave it on." She narrows her eyes, so I explain. "I won't be able to contain myself if they're real."

She chokes on a giggle, then shakes her head as a smile plays on her lips. "I'll leave it on, then."

Fuck me. I'm done for.

My eyes flare with a desire so profound I get lightheaded and have to clutch the counter to stabilize myself. I don't feel like myself anymore. It's like she's taken over my body and mind.

What the hell is happening to me?

"Shall I lose the panties? Or are you not going to be able to contain yourself?" Her lip twitches, and I fucking adore her playfulness. It's refreshing, despite wanting to mark her ass for tormenting me.

"Do it," I grunt out, and she shuffles the thin fabric down her luscious hips and over her heels, somehow maintaining a look of grace as she does. Then she dangles them from her finger.

"Now what?" She crooks an eyebrow at me.

"Now you're going to crawl to me and bring me those panties." I smirk and sip from my glass to act nonchalant, despite my heart racing so fast the lightheadedness from before is increasing.

She licks her lips as if contemplating my words, and for a split second, I think she won't comply.

When she lowers herself to the floor, my balls almost combust. Then she crawls toward me, each movement bouncing her glorious tits, and I bite back the groan itching to escape me. Instead, I empty my drink and place the glass on the counter. Her heavy tits swell over her bra, and I will myself to remain standing to watch the show she's putting on, but in my mind, I'm throwing her over my shoulder and marching us both to my bed. I ball my hands into fists so tight my knuckles ache. Her green eyes are hooded as she comes to a stop at my feet, looking up at me from beneath her thick lashes like I hung the moon and the stars.

Jesus, she's beautiful. My breath stutters at the unusual random thought. All the women I pay for are good-looking, but this one, this one, is fucking different.

I trail my finger down her cheek, and she leans into my touch, stealing my breath—another odd reaction for me. As punishment, I shove two fingers into her mouth, and my cock jumps, then her eyes widen. She sucks on them as I slide them in and out, mimicking the action my cock will make. "Good girl," I praise, then slip them from her mouth, and a gentle sigh leaves her now-plump lips. "Now, be a good girl and take my cock out. I want you to wrap your wet panties around it."

Her eyes flare and her cheeks redden.

What? Did she think I wouldn't know she's getting off on this as much as I am?

Her pupils burn with lust, and then, without needing further prompting, she unbuckles my belt. I can't help the hiss that leaves my lips when her dainty fingers graze over the trail of hair leading toward my solid cock. Then she pops open the button, lowers my zipper, and pushes my pants and boxers enough to allow my cock to spring free, I want nothing more than to push her hands away and take over, but I allow her to take her time, even though it pains me to let her.

When her soft hand reaches inside my damp boxers, I don't have it in me to be embarrassed by the wetness greeting her. I've never pumped so much pre-cum out of my slit in my entire life, and when she moans, more streams out and has me biting back the urge to thrust inside her.

"That's it." My hand finds her hair, and I cling onto her head like it's a lifeline. "Wrap those little panties around my cock, beautiful girl." My hips jerk in anticipation.

With the fabric wrapped around me, I throw my head back in awe and try to remain rooted to the spot. "Suck me into your mouth." I practically beg as lust thrashes through me.

Her hand works my cock up and down, and when the heat of her mouth encompasses my cock still tightly covered in her thin fabric, I tighten my hold on her hair. "Fuck, yes. Taste your dripping pussy on my cock."

Her moans send vibrations down my cock, and I relish it.

"Do you like how I taste?" I ask, yanking her greedy mouth from my cock.

"Y-yes."

My eyes roll as I push inside her drooling mouth again. "Good girl," I groan, painting her lips with the tip of my cock. The fabric prevents me from covering her in pre-cum, but I tell myself she is, and spittle drips from the corners of her mouth. "My beautiful little slut, tasting her panties." Then I thrust forward, and she swallows me down again eagerly. "Can you taste your pussy and my pleasure?" *Thrust.*

"Don't we taste good together?"

Thrust.

Her nails drag over my balls, and it takes everything in me not to pin her head to my hips and face-fuck her, but I'm enjoying this battle of dominance and submissiveness far too much.

"Lick your panties clean, beautiful girl. Lick all your mess away." My spine straightens as she works her tongue over my cock again and again, lavishing it with her desire to please me. "Fuck, you're so good at that, beautiful. So fucking good."

A moan vibrates my cock, and I can't help but to plunge farther into her mouth, causing her to gag, but she doesn't stop her movements, as if pleasing me is her only mission. "I bet your pussy is dripping, isn't it?"

She moans around me, causing me to grunt in need. "I can smell your little pussy coating your thighs like a greedy whore." My hand moves to cup her cheek, holding her still, then I withdraw my cock before plunging back in. "A beautiful little whore on her knees, sucking her panties from my cock."

Her tongue thrashes around her mouth and over my cock, faster and faster.

"That's it, keep licking. Keep sucking them clean while I come in them for you."

When her grip on my balls tightens, I have no choice but to release my pent-up frustration, so my fingers dig into her soft skin, and I slam inside her mouth.

"Fucking clean them," I grunt. Again and again, I work my hips while she continues to work me. My balls draw up, my muscles coil, and my body floods with such euphoria black spots distort my vision, and the beautiful girl staring up at me with my cock stuffed in her open mouth takes rope after rope of my cum.

The material surrounding it acts as a barrier to her

stretched mouth, and I loathe it. My teeth clamp down, and I shove myself deeper into her throat, determined to make her pay for the obstruction.

Finally, with one more thrust of my hips, I still. "Fuckkk."

Her tongue continues to work around me, then she sucks as if she's as desperate to taste me through the fabric as I need her to.

"Beautiful," I croon, the tone of my voice so foreign I don't recognize it as my own.

GIA

"Beautiful," he murmurs, and slowly withdraws his cock. I swipe the spittle from my mouth with the back of my hand, and he steps back. He unravels my panties from his cock—they're drenched—and uses them to wipe himself. Then he shocks the hell out of me by stuffing them in his pants pocket before tugging his boxers and pants up. "Bedroom." He gestures with his chin toward a door to my left, and I glance around the living space of the hotel room.

Clearly, he has money, from the Rolex watch on his wrist, to his Zegna suit tailored to perfection, along with the expensive cologne radiating from him. The man has taste, I'll give him that. The penthouse comes as no surprise to me, nor is it unfamiliar surroundings, having been brought up in luxury despite having no need for it.

But this man? He craves it.

He craves it all.

He offers me his hand, so I place mine in his, and a spark courses through me, taking my breath away. Glancing away from his startled eyes, I choose to ignore it and climb to my feet. My body shakes with a need only he can satiate, but I refuse to acknowledge it and the clear feeling of something more building between us. I turn away from him and head toward the bedroom; this is what I want and need from him. *One night of passion, nothing more.*

The moment I step inside the bedroom, the luxurious furnishings hit me, and my fingers brushing over the delicate silk sheets have nostalgia flooding my senses.

It's been a long time since I slept in sheets like this, and for the first time in a long time, I feel the loss of such privilege.

"You can lose the bra now." His deep, firm voice is laced in desire, and a wanton surge of need ravishes my veins at the sound.

When I lift my head to face him, I'm left stunned by his now-bare chest as he leans against the doorframe, watching me through hooded eyes. The man is a walking dream with bronzed skin and chiseled pecs; it's clear he looks after himself.

My ass finds the edge of the bed, and as if someone is commanding my body, I continue with the feigned act of brazenness. I inch my legs open, exposing the slickness seeping from my core.

He licks his lips, and those heated emerald eyes of his flare like a predator surveying its prey.

I remove my bra, taking my time and loving the way his Adam's apple bobs and slowly slides down his throat at my tits coming into view.

When I drop the bra to the floor, allowing my tits to bounce freely, he charges toward me and falls to his knees between my legs and buries his face in my chest. I begin to pant, and my fingers find his hair to anchor him to me.

"Fuck, you're incredible." With a grunt, he presses kisses over my breasts while kneading them with both hands, and his fingers graze over my nipples in a repetitive motion that has my toes curling. "So fucking soft and natural." He sucks on my plump flesh, and the sting causes me to arch my spine.

When one hand leaves my nipple, I want to cry out in

dispute, but he trails it down my thigh, and a shiver racks through me at his touch. Then he sweeps through the wetness at my center and strokes over my slick folds, and a guttural groan reverberating from his chest.

My eyes roll as he strums my aching bud, and my hips rise to meet his touch, desperate to feel the glory of his capabilities.

"Please," I beg, and he hungrily sucks my nipple into his mouth and toys with the pebbled tip over and over.

A garbled noise leaves him while he maneuvers his hand to slide his fingers inside me. "Fuck, you're tight, beautiful."

I clasp his hair harder, pulling him into my breasts. "Oh god."

He surges two thick fingers inside me. They pump in and out of my pussy, and I welcome the way he stretches me, wincing at the pleasurable bite of pain. "Please." My body sparks with exhilaration. "Yes!"

"Fuck!" As he pulls back to watch me, my orgasm ricochets through me. My head falls back and my hips rock against his palm while his fingers fuck me, and my tits bounce from the impact of his movements. Every morsel of my body is now commanded by him, and I wouldn't change it for the world.

I'm at his mercy, and I wouldn't want to be anywhere else.

REED

Fuck me. She's a masterpiece. A stunning, beautiful goddess put on this earth to make me question everything I thought I knew about myself.

If you'd have told me an hour ago that after my meeting went to shit, I would have the most beautiful, natural woman in the world in my bed allowing me to deliver her pleasure, I would have laughed in your face.

"Oh God, we don't even know each other's names!" She gasps and throws her head forward to face me, and her lips remain parted.

I chuckle at her assertion and the way she went from orgasming so epically to becoming concerned about niceties.

As I slide back on my heels to stare up at her, something tightens in my chest. I should tell her my real name; I know I should. Then she shakes her head. "It's okay. No strings, right?" Why the fuck does the idea of no strings suddenly irk me?

Pushing off the edge of the bed, I stare down at the woman that in one night has made me question so many things already, and anger simmers through me. She pushes the loose dark strands of hair from her face and scans me. "You're good with no strings, right?"

I bite back the need to tell her I'm not okay with it and smirk while shoving my hand into my pants pocket to take out my wallet. She watches on with narrowed eyes as I flick it open and pull out a strip of condoms. "More than all right with it." I wink like an asshole, rip off a condom, and throw the remainder on the bed, loving the fact her gaze has never left mine.

The room is alive with desire, an intoxication of pleasure, and I intend to cement my memory deep inside her, making sure she never forgets a single minute of the man who fucked her senseless. The man who rocked her core.

She's going to wish she knew my name, because I'm about to ruin her for all others.

I rip open the condom, push my pants and boxers to the floor, and kick them off, along with my shoes and socks. Then I roll the condom down my cock, delighting in the way her eyes flare with arousal.

"That's so hot," she rasps and bites into her lip.

When the condom is secure, I lift her by her thighs, and she squeals and wraps her legs around my waist.

I stare down at her, struck by her beauty. This indescribable feeling in my chest is different from anything I've ever felt with anyone else, more intimate, more meaningful somehow. My skin burns with a need to possess her, to make her feel the same as I do. So I lower her to the mattress and commit her every feature to memory. Her nipples graze my bare chest, and her nails dig into my shoulders, as if she's scared I'll pull away. A small flurry of freckles rests beneath her right eye, and her plush lips bow into the perfect shape.

Her lips tip up into a sweet smile that steals my breath, then she taps my shoulder. "Hot man. Can you move now?" she sasses, then bites into her bottom lip.

"Hot man, huh?" I grin back at her.

She nods.

With control I don't feel, I bend and capture her lips with a kiss that sends a wave of passion through me like no other. Then I guide my cock to her entrance, and our tongues dance as I thrust my hips forward, slamming into her. She throws her head back on a loud moan, and the tightness of her pussy encompassing my cock has me kissing up the column of her neck to pepper kisses along her jawline while I rear back and slam inside her again and again, each thrust rougher than the last. "Fuck, yes," I growl.

My hips work faster and faster, with a steely determination, and she clings onto me for dear life.

"Oh god. Don't stop. Please don't stop." The wooden bed frame slams against the wall with each surge.

Her pussy clenches around me, and I long to feel the heat of her insides against my cock without the barrier. Jesus, I've never wanted that before, and now it feels like something I can't live without. I long to feel the way she's about to contract around me as I mark her. "Fuck, you feel good, beautiful. So damn good," I grunt and push into her slick pussy.

My balls draw up, but I bite into my cheek to stop myself from coming, not ready to give in just yet. I slow my movements, then rear back on my heels and allow her legs to fall to the mattress.

"Holy fuck. I can see your pussy stretched wide around me," I choke out, and stare down at her small hole stretched around my thick cock as I slowly push in and out of her pussy.

"Feels so good," she moans, and her head thrashes from side to side.

"Give me your hand." Her head falls forward as she tentatively holds her hand out for me to take, and I guide us to where we're connected. "Do you feel that? That's me stretching your perfect little cunt."

Breath hitching, her pussy clamps around me, causing me

to hiss, so I release her hand and slide out to the tip of my cock, then slam back inside her harder than ever.

"Oh, fuck, yes," she moans wantonly.

Sweat beads on my forehead as I power into her, each surge deeper than the last, determined to leave my mark. "I'm going to pull out and come on you," I say, scanning her edible body and the way her tits sway with each movement.

She thrusts her hips, the desperation seeping from her. "Yes. Yes. Do it! Oh god, please."

Never in my life have I wanted to coat a woman's pussy in my cum—it's far too close to risking a pregnancy, and if there's one thing I don't want, it's that.

But with her, all my inhibitions are obliterated, my concerns blown to smithereens along with my intelligence, because her pussy tightens around me, and I want to own every inch of her as she owns me. I stroke my finger over her clit, and her hips buck, then I pull my cock from her pussy, rip the condom off, and continue to jack myself off over her wet folds.

The sight is my undoing, and the thought of her covered in my cum is too much for me to take. Every cell in my body tightens, the pleasure so strong it hits me like a tornado, and my cock pulsates, rope upon rope of hot, thick cum splashing over her pussy. I aim at her hole and want my cum inside her too; I want to coat her like no one has coated her before. I push the head of my cock inside her and continue jerking off while she screams her exhilaration into the room, only causing my orgasm to heighten. The most intense feeling of euphoria hits me. Mine. She's fucking mine now.

I want her tied to me forever. "Fuck, breed for me, beautiful," I whisper as my cum continues to pulsate from the tip.

"Oh god. I need you to fuck me again. Please, just do it. Do it all again," she groans and lifts her head off the pillow to stare at me.

My chest heaves as sweat pours from me, and with the tip

of my angry-looking cock just inside her pussy, I have no intention of fucking her again with a barrier between us. Her head falls back against the pillow, and when she pulls her legs back with her hands, opening herself up wider to me, and thrusts her delectable tits up into the air, I know I will love every second of filling her to the hilt.

This beautiful girl is mine, and I'm about to make sure she never forgets it.

Ever.

ONE

REED

2 DAYS LATER ...

SATISFACTION FLOWS through me like a drug, heightening the spring in my step as I head toward Owen's office. My god, I could actually whistle with how fantastic I feel.

Saturday night was by far the best night of my life; who knew one woman could make you feel so incredible, so whole, complete?

I'm kicking myself that I never got her name. She disappeared when the sun came up, which pissed me the hell off, but I have a trump card, and I'm about to walk into his office and insist he find the woman who rocked my world. Hell, changed my goddamn life, because for the first time ever, I want a woman by my side.

Have I gone insane? Possibly.

I want a repeat of everything I gave her and she gave me.

I want her.

One woman.

My obsession.

I swing open Owen's office door and beam in his direction when he spins to face me. I know what my three best friends are thinking with their eyes ping-ponging from me to one another, but I remain steadfast and throw myself into a chair to await the influx of questions about to descend on me for my unusually positive disposition.

"What the hell happened to you?" Tate scrutinizes my face.

"The deal with Fanzio go well, then?" Mase asks with a smile almost as wide as my own. At the mention of that prick's name, I grimace but shrug it off, determined to remain on target and not let the old goat dampen my mood.

Sure, George Fanzio might be a property billionaire who I'm relying on selling me land in some godforsaken town for me to expand my empire, but he's not what's important. She is.

Since my best friends and I started STORM Enterprises, we've had many deals, but none meant anything to me compared to this one. Maybe it's the thrill of the chase that has me so determined.

But I will get what I want; I always do.

"Actually, it went to shit."

Shaw's gaze bounces from the guys' to mine. "Well, why didn't you start with that, and why are you so happy when you've wanted this deal for so long?"

I wave Shaw off. *Fuck the deal.*

Blowing out a deep breath, I sit back in the chair, cross my arms over my chest, and with a huge smile on my handsome face, hit my best friends with the truth. "I'm in love."

"What the fuck?" Tate splutters his coffee like an idiot, while Mase, Owen, and Shaw all look at me like I've grown multiple heads. Who needs more when you have one as brilliant and good-looking as mine?

"Holy shit, that burns." Tate unbuttons his shirt, and I roll my eyes. "Fucking Jesus. Do I need the ER or something?" He turns from one side to the other, surveying his reddening chest while all I can do is wince at the thought of the stain on his shirt. Yeah, that's not coming out.

Owen points toward Tate's vacated seat. "Sit the fuck down, you wuss, and grow up. I need to hear this."

Tate mumbles something about needing a cold compress, but I ignore him and tell them what they're so used to hearing after I return from a meeting with Fanzio.

"The deal went to shit. He's not in a position to move forward yet. Yadda, yadda, yadda. So I went to the bar to drown in my misery."

Owen nods as I explain my current predicament.

"Then this woman sits down at the table."

"Gold digger!" Shaw barks, and I want to throat punch him for even thinking it. I know a gold digger when I see one, and she is not. Hell, I fucked gold diggers on the regular before her. "She has to be a gold digger. No woman sits down at your table without intent," he states.

"Oh, she had intent, all right." I smirk, remembering how forward she was. "Intent on riding my cock until it was raw."

Mase snorts, and Owen throws his head back on a loud chuckle.

"So, you fucked a gold digger. What's new? Why are you in love?" Shaw lifts his shoulder.

Annoyance reverberates inside me, and I shake my head. They're clearly not getting it. I feel something, and I never fucking feel a damn thing. "She wasn't a gold digger. Trust me, I know. She was a businesswoman. Had the hot-as-hell business attire on and a briefcase. A lawyer, actually." I smile —two intelligent people, fucking until our hearts were content. Not only does she match me inside the bedroom, but outside too.

"So, you fucked one woman?" Mase asks. He knows I struggle to get aroused by one person—it's why I use the

Indulgence service so much. It allows me to choose who I want, when I want them, and more importantly, how many women I want.

"I did. One!" I hold up my finger to emphasize the significance of the night. "Best night of my life."

Tate turns his attention from his chest to me. "When are we meeting this woman who managed to break you?"

He's not wrong; she sure as hell tried to break me. My cock has been perpetually hard since leaving the penthouse, and even though I asked security to locate her, I've had no luck. Hence my need for Owen to track her down. If anyone has connections to locate someone, it's him. "Here's the thing … I didn't get her name or number," I breathe out with a wince.

Tate gasps. "What?"

"I know." The tension in my forehead amplifies, and I rub at it in a lame attempt to ease it. "I fucked up. She said no strings, and I was good with that. I didn't expect that"—I motion toward the door—"she'd blow my fucking mind, and I have no idea who she is." I meet Owen's eyes, but instead of finding solace in them, I find anger.

"Oh, no you fucking don't. Owen has enough shit to deal with, like my sister. Oh, and he needs to do his fucking job. Not hunt down women who don't want a repeat of you," Tate spits out, shaking his head.

My eyes narrow, and I block out all the shit with Laya. Let's face it, his sister is nothing but trouble, and I'm more concerned by his comments regarding my girl. "You don't think she wants a repeat of me?" How the hell did he even come to that conclusion?

A scoff comes from Shaw, and my attention darts toward him. "She didn't leave her name or number. Pretty sure it's self-explanatory."

Wow. Don't mince your fucking words.

A weird tension fills the air, and my best friends frown at

me, waiting for me to tell them it was all a joke. That I haven't allowed one woman to wrap me up in knots based on one night alone.

Embarrassment hits me, and I dart my eyes away, and when they finally come back to the group, I clear my throat and shrug. "Not like there aren't a billion other women in the world falling at my feet." Even as I say the words, they feel like poison on my tongue.

I don't want any other woman.

I want her.

There's something about her; we had something more. She made me feel.

As the group continues talking like I didn't ask for their help, I agree. We have a lot going on, and finding a woman who doesn't want to be found isn't at the top of their list.

Nor should it be at the top of mine.

Nope, my priority needs to remain on George Fanzio and getting the deal of the century. I have to prove to my friends they can rely on me as a business mogul, that I'm not just the rich kid who threw money into his friends' pipedream, just to feel like I belonged somewhere.

While the guys all continue to throw jibes at one another, I push back in my chair and head toward the door. It's not until I'm about to go through it that Owen stops me with a hand on my shoulder. He scrubs a hand over his head. "Look, man, when all this shit with Laya is sorted, I'll look into the girl for you if you still want me to."

His eyes implore mine, and I notice the dark circles below them, and guilt hits me. This shit with Laya is slowly killing him. We all know he's been in love with her for years, but now she's married to a member of the cartel, and worse, pregnant with his baby. The need to protect her from the man she's unwittingly married to is taking its toll on him, so the last thing he needs is me adding to the workload.

"It's fine." My lungs feel like they're being crushed. "I

have a date tomorrow night." I lie, then quickly follow up with the more convincing response. "Two dates, to be precise."

Owen nods, but doesn't look convinced. I straighten my shoulders and step back.

"Now I have to do some digging, because George Fanzio is giving us that land, whether he likes it or not."

Owen's solemn face breaks out into a huge smile, and a burst of energy rushes through me at his response. This is what I need to do to show them what I'm capable of.

Show the world I'm Reed Johnson and no woman will bring me to my knees.

Not a single one.

TWO

REED

SIX MONTHS LATER ...

THE TWO BLONDES cackle beside me, causing my teeth to grind. Jesus fucking Christ, what the hell was I thinking bringing them here?

Originally, bringing them along to the Ridgeway community event was to help make my day more bearable, but that's going to be impossible.

Their smell is all wrong, their fakeness oozes from them, and every time their hands roam over me as if they own me, I feel like shoving them away.

That woman did a number on me six months ago, six long miserable fucking months, and to say I'm broken is an understatement. The only time I can get hard is with her in my mind.

The way her soft curves bounced below me, above me, and around me while I filled her like I've never filled a woman before. Then bam, gone from my life quicker than a priest coming in a whorehouse, and all I'm left with is a distant memory from a night that taunts me.

"I hope there's food at the party. I'm hungry," the one to my left purrs in a voice meant to be seductive, but it's not. It makes my skin bristle.

Annoyance simmers through my veins, and I pinch the bridge of my nose to try to not sound like a complete ass. "I've told you, it's not a party. It's a community event. Some charity thing for …" I forget what charity was in the email I received from Fanzio's office this week. "Some charity thing," I reiterate for good measure.

"I hope there's food at the charity thing." She nips at my ear, and I jolt. Just what the hell is wrong with her, trying to eat me like a piece of meat.

I lean forward and tap on the divider; relief floods me when Stanley, my driver, comes into view at the screen going down. "How much longer?"

He glances to his side. "We're almost there, sir."

"Thank fuck." I exhale, and relief rushes through me at lightning speed.

"Oh, goodie, the party is over there." The other blonde bounces, with glee in her whiney voice, and points out of the window. Pressure builds in my temple, and the tie around my neck feels tighter than ever.

Kill. Me. Fucking. Now.

———

What in the ever-living fuck is this hellhole?

I glance around again and grimace. I've seen nothing like this before; it's almost apocalyptic. People actually choose to come here? Derelict buildings surround a patchy scrubland. A games field, judging by the faded, painted lines and poor excuse for goals. Makeshift stalls surround the space, and I'm truly taken back by what they appear to be selling. It looks like someone raided the trash and emptied it on the table.

Balloons adorn the stalls along with a sea of wayward-looking adults, and worse, countless feral children run rampant, covered in dirt and food. Their laughter rings out like warning sirens in my head, and I spin on my heels as panic wells inside of me.

A small boy with what I can only imagine is a sticky substance on his hands wanders toward me, and I jump back, and my shoulders drop when he heads straight toward a stall.

Good God, do their parents have no shame sending them out like that?

A herd of rowdy kids runs toward me, and I hop out of the way as they bypass me and head toward a cupcake stall.

My mother used to say children should be seen and not heard. Then again, she despised her own child.

It surprises me they may actually want to eat something made by someone here.

Now I can appreciate why Fanzio wants to sell this place; it's a hygiene risk waiting to happen. It's more than likely crawling with vermin, probably diseases too.

I locate the hand sanitizer in my jacket pocket and douse my hands in it, then shove it back inside, making a mental note to shower extra thoroughly when I arrive home this evening. Preferably an aromatherapy shower to help de-stress me while my mind wanders to thoughts of her.

I snap my eyes open, not realizing I'd closed them, when thoughts of the woman who left me crept into my mind. "Are you okay?" one of the blondes asks, then reaches out to touch my face, forcing me to bat her hand away. I straighten my shoulders, determined not to show any sign of weakness to the women or these people, and take in the squalor.

My gaze locks onto a small child shoveling fries into his mouth with his bare hands, and the god-awful plastic cheese in spray cans covers his fingers. He slurps and turns to face me, offering a grin that exposes the food between his teeth.

Holy fuck, I think I'm going to puke.

My vision becomes hazy when lightheadedness hits me, and my chest tightens. Quickly, I work at my tie to loosen it, the material feeling like it's strangling me with each breath I take.

Jesus, when the hell did it become so hot out here?

As my attention flicks around the never-ending grounds, I grimace at the thought of entering one of the buildings. No doubt home to some wild critters that could attack you, leaving you with some flesh-eating bacterial disease.

"I want a cotton candy. Can I have cotton candy, Reed? Pleassse." The whine starts from beside me, and I dig into my pocket and extract a wad of bills before thrusting them at the blonde's enhanced chest to fucking shut her up. She bounces on her feet like a deranged animal, then claps in a childlike manner that sets my teeth on edge. For the first time in my life, I'm embarrassed by the people I choose to surround myself with, and worse, pay to surround myself with.

How did my life come to this?

She's the only thing natural to ever touch me, and she left me.

The sound of a door slamming has my eyes darting toward the 'Staff Only' exit, and without giving the blondes another thought, I head toward it. I need a break from this hellhole.

No wonder Fanzio wants to get rid of it, yet people actually protest to keep it open—absurd.

My mind can't comprehend their reasoning. Then again, when dealing with such simpletons, how the hell can you level with them?

My feet propel me toward the door at warp speed, a man on a mission for some clarity, for sure. Stepping into the open space, I breathe out a sigh of relief. There's only a handful of people milling around, making it possible for me to reset my spiraling thoughts.

A laugh echoes from the other side of what appears to be a warehouse, and I freeze. That laugh, I'd know it anywhere. It's haunted my dreams and plagued my thoughts daily.

Holy shit, this can't be happening.

She's here.

She's actually fucking here.

My eyes dart toward the laugh, and it's like the universe has finally granted me something worthwhile—her.

My pulse hammers, and I take measured strides in her direction while I scan over her face, pleased that nothing has changed about her. Not a damn thing. She's just as perfect as I remember. Even more so, perhaps.

She sits behind a table, stuffing soft toys into a box, then writes on it, and as if realizing my presence, her eyes latch onto mine from above the box. The smile, that only moments ago played out on her face, now falls, and I narrow my eyes at her disappointing reaction toward me.

The woman beside her turns to face me, but I don't give her my attention. Nope, that is directed at the beautiful woman who blinks several times, as if disbelieving I'm here. I smile brightly back at her. "Hello, beautiful."

GIA

My mind short-circuits as I stare up at him, and a loud chuckle erupts from his throat.

"Terra, could you give us a minute?" I ask my friend when she glances back at the man beaming down at me.

"Sure." Terra turns and walks away, and I don't miss the questioning look she gives me over her shoulder.

"What are you doing here?" I whisper-shout.

Amusement plays out on his handsome face, and the flirtatious grin and delight in his eyes make me fidget. He won't be thrilled by what I have to say to him.

"I'm a lawyer."

I nod, knowing this already. Fuck, he's hotter than I remember. His shirt stretches over his chest, and my fingers itch to explore the ridges hidden beneath the fabric.

Then he takes in the warehouse we use for donations before his eyes land back on me. "I want to buy this shithole and turn it into something profitable."

All the tiny pieces of hope I had in my heart are obliterated with his words, and my shoulders slump. Yep, he's an asshole. He's everything I didn't want him to be, but I need to push aside his master plans and focus on what's important.

I take a deep breath, then broaden my shoulders. "We need to talk."

"Or we could pick up where we left off?" His eyebrows dance, and my core fills with heat. *Oh, dear god, stay on target, Gia.*

Rubbing my temple, I shake my head and rise to my feet, allowing him to see what our last encounter left me with.

My bump.

His bump.

"We need to talk about this." I rest my hand on the obvious swell, then his eyes dart down to where I cradle my baby, and he rears back as if burned. His face pales and his breathing escalates.

Great, just great. He's freaking out.

A flurry of activity from behind him sees him being pushed forward, but it's almost like he isn't aware of his surroundings. Even when my son barrels toward the table with a bunch of his friends, he somehow remains frozen in place during the chaos, staring at me as if seeing through me.

"Mom, can we go on the Helter Skelter?" Bryce pleads.

"Please, can we?" Leroy adds with his hands in a praying gesture.

"Mom?"

"Can we? Can we?" Julian bounces up and down, knocking the box to the floor in his excitement. Any other time, I would ask them to calm down, but I can't think straight.

The walls feel like they're narrowing in on me, but the boys remain oblivious to the man staring daggers in my direction, and all I want to do is get them out of here so I can have a sensible conversation with him.

I bend down to grab my purse, then remember I gave all my change to the soft toy stall this morning. "Shit," I mumble, and chew on my lip. "Go find Terra and tell her I asked if I could borrow ten bucks."

The boys take off like their asses are on fire.

"Tell her that I'll pay her back later," I shout in their direction, and the door slams behind them, with no acknowledgment of my words.

Red-hot anger radiates from the man opposite me, and I swallow back the nervousness creeping up my spine. I've faced off in a courtroom with men like him and have never felt as intimidated as I do now, and I hate it. I may be a lot of things, but I'm not weak.

I blow out a deep breath, lift my chin, and say, "I'm pregnant and the baby's yours."

THREE

REED

SHE JUTS OUT HER CHIN, defiance flashing in those bright-green eyes of hers. "I'm pregnant and the baby's yours."

The loud chuckle that reverberates from my chest when I throw my head back is full of humor I don't feel inside. It's sarcastic and vicious, and judging by the way she flinches, it cuts her to the core.

Good.

I hope she sees the disgust on my face as my seething eyes lock with hers. Previously, it was full of heat and want, but now all I want to do is spit venom in her direction and deliver some truths I'm sure she can't handle, especially after ruining what could have been a perfectly good day. Nope, the universe intends on fucking with me, it seems. Because the woman I've been pining after like a damn idiot is nothing more than a gold digger after all, and if she thinks she can play me, she can think again.

"You're kidding me, right?" With a laugh playing on my lips, I shake my head at all the unjust in the world.

Her eyes widen and her lips part, but she doesn't say a damn word. She appears as shocked as I was only moments ago, but we both know it's all part of an act, and I refuse to give her any more of my time.

I lean over the table and ignore the way her familiar peach scent wraps around me. Even that pisses me off. "You've clearly seen an opportunity in me."

Her breath hitches when I lean closer.

"Look at you, in this shithole, and look at me." I step back to give her space, then hold my hands out. "You're clearly a liar, an opportunist." My voice becomes louder, my anger spilling over at her lies. "Lawyer, my ass," I spit out as the realization she is, indeed, a gold digger becomes more and more apparent with each passing second. A gold digger with a brood of kids. I grimace. "If you think for one minute, I'm dumb enough to think that"—I point at her stomach—"is mine, then you're insane."

Her nostrils flare, and I continue with my cruel tirade, determined to hit home the truth as hurt practically bleeds from her eyes. "You're a whore, sweetheart, nothing more, nothing less. I made one mistake of not paying for the reassurance of not having to deal with shit like this." I motion toward her bump again; if it's even real. "I won't make the same mistake again," I snipe out.

The clicking of heels approaches me, but it's drowned out by the rage thumping in my chest, banging to unleash further pain on her like she is on me.

When two sets of hands roam over my chest, I puff it out, especially when tears fill the woman's eyes, ensuring that if my words didn't hit home, the fact she thinks I moved on so easily should.

If only that were fucking true.

Bringing one set of fingers to my lips, I gift them with a kiss, despite wanting to push them as far away as possible, but I refuse to back down now. She needs to see she means nothing, that her lies will be buried alongside this building when I tear it to the ground, which leaves me more determined than ever to close this deal.

"Have a good day." I glance around the warehouse. "Come Monday, this place will be mine, and everything in it, just a memory." I wink and ignore the sharp gasp of air that leaves her when I turn and walk away.

Disappointment that she conned me so epically riddles me as I head toward the SUV, but I refuse to acknowledge it further. The green-eyed beauty who tortures my thoughts can remain just that, a memory. One I never want to relive, not after knowing the truth, and the way she's tarnished that night makes me despise her all the more for it.

I open the SUV, and a steely purpose overcomes me. I want that land, those buildings. I want it all. I'll show her, Fanzio, and my best friends who the hell I am and what I'm capable of. I'm done fucking around.

Nothing will stop me from getting what I want. Even if I have to destroy her to get it.

FOUR

MY FEET FEEL like lead as I make my way toward Owen's office. I've barely slept a wink all weekend, thanks to the bombshell the gold digger dropped on me on Saturday.

Hell, I don't even know how I got here.

The guys' voices all fall silent, and their focus descends on me.

"What the fuck happened to you?" Mase asks and tilts his head from side to side.

"Please tell me you didn't kill someone." Shaw pinches the bridge of his nose, and I jolt because my brother is incarcerated for doing just that.

I drop down into the chair, and my daze continues.

Something hits my head, but I don't move. Since the second my apartment door closed on me after returning from the "charity" event on Saturday, it's like I was given the pieces to an important puzzle that I'm struggling to piece together.

They were right; she is a gold digger, but why was she at a swanky hotel bar dressed the way she was? Was it all an act?

A way to lure men into bed. At least I know what I'm getting with the women I pay for.

"Reed." Mase snaps his fingers in front of my face, but I don't respond, uncaring to bat them away.

The bump looked real. Very fucking real.

And oh, sweet Jesus, she has kids. A lot of them.

"Tell him Lucinda has genital warts, and he might have them." Tate chuckles. "That'll freak him out."

"You do realize he can hear you himself, right?" Owen snipes back at Tate's childish antics.

"Shut the fuck up," Tate clips.

"I found her," I mumble, and the guys all sit forward. "The woman. I found her."

"And?" Mase asks, and searches my face with a furrowed brow, then his eyes travel down my body as if looking for something to explain my unusual behavior.

"That's good, right?" Tate grins from ear to ear, and I internally scoff.

"It's awful," I choke. "Fucking awful." I drag a hand over my head and blow out a deep breath. So fucking awful.

"Is she married?" Tate asks, and I flinch.

Oh shit, she has kids. Is she married? My eyes feel like they might pop out of their sockets. Oh God, I'm a home-wrecker.

"Worse," I admit meekly.

I swallow hard, finding it difficult to construct the words. "She's pregnant."

"Oh, fuck" slips from Owen, and I couldn't agree more.

Surely, it's not mine though, right?

She's a gold digger. She didn't correct me when I called her one.

She was living in a hellhole and has to borrow money from a friend. She isn't a lawyer.

She lied about it all.

It isn't mine.

It can't be.

"It's not so bad. I can't wait to have kids." Mase shrugs, and I flinch. Out of the five of us, there's only ever been Mase wishing for the perfect family life but never receiving it. But as each of my brothers has fallen for their women, so has their need to impregnant them.

Apart from me, that is. Until that one night.

That one fateful night when I lost myself in her soft curves, so much so, I didn't use a condom when I came.

Nope, I actually chose not to suit up.

It can't be mine. I can't be a father.

Absolutely not. She's a liar.

I spin to face Mase. "Oh, it gets worse. Trust me on that."

Tate's lip curls up. "How the hell can it get worse for you?" And if I didn't know her situation, I wouldn't agree with him more. He knows how I feel about kids, monogamy, a family. They all do.

"She already has a kid, maybe more than one. Who fucking knows, a whole damn family." A lot of them. They swarmed her like she was Mary goddamn Poppins. God only knows how many she has. Does she even know?

Tate chokes on a laugh, but my energy level and social battery are well and truly drained. "Oh shit, you might end up like the Brady bunch, Reed." He throws his arm out wide, with jest in his tone. "A whole family waiting for you to join them." He laughs to himself, but only he finds it humorous.

"Leave him the fuck alone, Tate," Mase spits out. "He's clearly in need of our support."

"It gets worse," I mumble. "It gets worse." My voice rises from panic as I'm about to admit everything about Saturday, the day from hell, and how it went to utter shit. "So much worse."

Owen steps forward. "Whatever it is, we got you." His eyes bore into mine, delivering the truth, and I swallow past the lump of emotion in my throat.

This is the only family I will ever need.

We have each other's backs; from the moment we met at boarding school, we've looked out for one another. Always will.

My eyes meet his. "Good, because what I'm about to tell you is un-fucking-believable." He nods with concern flashing in his eyes.

"She's a gold digger." Tate nods at my words. "Possibly a whore." Shaw grimaces despite using the services of women before now. "And she works in Ridgeway."

"The place you plan on buying from Fanzio?" Mase queries.

My eyes snap up to his. "The place I'm about to destroy," I state.

FIVE

GIA

ALEJO'S FEET rush to keep up with me as I stride toward my father's office with purpose. I'm about to cause waves, but I'm past caring; enough is enough. I broaden my shoulders. "Mrs. Mathers, are you sure about this?"

I lift my chin higher, and my heels continue their clacking on the marble floor. "Absolutely." I'm about to put him and those scumbags he works with in their places, and if that means taking Reed Johnson down a peg or two, then so be it. A glimmer of excitement rushes through me when I recall his words for the thousandth time since Saturday. *"You're clearly a liar, an opportunist."* I scoff at his audacity. The man is an arrogant pig, and whatever the hell I was thinking jumping into bed with him is beyond me. Frankly, it shows how desperate I've become. Maybe I should take a leaf out of his book and pay for the satisfaction. *"You're a whore, sweetheart, nothing more, nothing less. I made one mistake of not paying for the reassurance of not having to deal with shit like this."* I shudder at the cruelty of his words.

Bastard.

When I researched the man who threatened to take over the community center, I hardened my heart to the image of the lawyer staring back at me on the computer screen. The same one who has played the center role in my erotic dreams, day in, day out, for months now.

Reed Johnson is a billionaire. Of course he is.

He and four of his best friends created STORM Enterprises, a company delivering numerous services to the entertainment industry, particularly the security aspect. It appears Reed set his sights on my community's land to create another media empire. The only problem is, as a majority shareholder, I refuse to give in and allow my father to sell the land.

Reed will learn a lesson today; money can't buy you everything you want. I know that all too well.

Bypassing the reception, I head straight down the corridor toward his office. "Excuse me, you can't go in there," one of his minions calls out, but I ignore her and continue on. "I'll call security," she declares, and I will it to happen. Let the world see how my father treats me. Let them see the real George Fanzio.

Alejo's gaze shifts to mine, and I smile back at him. He hates the thought of getting into trouble. At twenty-three years old, he's been my legal assistant for two years, and I couldn't be prouder of how far he's come from the homeless teenager at the shelter I assist at to being well on his way in his dream of becoming a full-fledged lawyer.

Throwing open my father's office door, I lock eyes with the man I despise. His sadistic eyes flash with surprise before he masks it and huffs at my presence. The room becomes silent as the men take me in, and I ignore the way their eyes roam over me as I pull out a chair at the boardroom table and motion for Alejo to follow.

As my eyes scan the occupants of the table, I ignore the look of horror etched on Reed's face and the way his perfectly crafted jaw falls open at the sight of me. If I could take a photo of his slackened jaw, wide eyes, and pale face, I would win prizes for the most shocked face caught on camera.

"What the hell are you doing here, Gianna?" My father leans over the table, with malice in his tone, and I refrain from flinching, determined to remain strong under his presence. My stomach turns at the sight of him, and I fight the memories that haunt me.

"This is a board meeting, is it not?" I quip back and open my briefcase, sliding the file out and onto the table, ignoring the anger radiating from him.

The sneer on his lips deepens as he scans over my body and lands on my bump, and bile turns in my stomach at his attention.

A part of me wants to cover the bump despite it being too big to hide, and my fingers itch to rest over the baby, but I refuse to show any sign of weakness.

"I've told you before, and I'll tell you again"—I glower back at my father—"Ridgeway land is not for sale. You can have anything else. Hell, you have everything else. But not this." I shake my head and point at the paperwork. "I hold twenty-two percent." I tap the paperwork my father is familiar with but appears to have ignored in his quest to destroy my husband's legacy. Anger at his underhandedness flashes through me. "It's not happening." I push the paperwork in his direction. "Whatever deal you think you've signed off on is not legal. End it. Now!" I demand, and stab the file with my finger, while Alejo hands out the contract and proof of my shareholder rights to the other board members.

For years, I've left my father alone, allowing him to run his empire with no say from me. To be blunt, I want nothing to do with it or him. But trying to take my children's future, our community's future, from them in a bitter bid to control me is too much, leaving me no choice but to step in.

Alberto, my father's right-hand man, clears his throat. He's loyal to him to the bone, and he's also just as bitter, ruthless, and misogynistic, but he knows the legalities of the business by heart, so he knows I'm right. My father can't sell Ridgeway Common without my say-so.

The vein protruding from my father's temple looks fit to burst as he glares at me with such contempt I'd fear it if I wasn't used to it. I've spent years shying away from his scorn, but something inside me snapped when I was a teenager, and with the help of my husband, I got away from the man who betrayed me so brutally.

Kevan shifts from side to side, and guilt simmers in his stare. I hide my hands beneath the table and curl them into fists while glaring back at him. He was once my husband's best friend, but money and power can turn people's morals, it seems.

Taking a deep breath, I hold my hand out to Alejo, and he slips the small box into my palm. Then, in a move no one sees coming, I throw the box at Kevan's chest. "If you send me another marriage proposal, I'll be throwing a restraining order at you instead. Get it into your thick skull, I would not marry you if you were the last man on earth. And to think you called yourself Jaxon's friend." Tears swim in my eyes, but I blink them away. Saying his name in Kevan's presence feels like a dagger to my heart.

"Whose baby is that?" My father's voice slices through the air like a threat, but it's always the same; he can never even attempt to hide his disgust in me.

I stare straight ahead. "That's none of your concern. Are we done here?" I ask Alejo.

"Yes, Mrs. Mathers," he says, and Reed jolts.

"Another waste of fucking space. Like the last one, then," he states, and I let him have his dig.

"It appears so." I smirk toward Reed, who looks like he still hasn't recovered from the fact I'm *not* a gold digger, as he so eloquently put it. Nor am I a liar.

"I'll see myself out." I rise out of the chair, and my father does too.

"You conniving little bitch. If you think for one minute I'm going to let you get away with this, then you can think again," he roars, attempting to crawl across the table toward me.

"You left me no choice," I whisper, then head toward the door, feeling the weight of his words on my way out.

REED

I remain glued to the chair, my head swiveling from one person to the next. "What the hell just happened?" I exhale, flabbergasted at the events.

When she walked through the door with the grace of a ballerina, my jaw almost hit the floor. I was about to close the deal of the fucking century, but all of that was obliterated in a matter of minutes.

Her hair was in soft curls around her delicate face, and it took me a moment to register it was actually her. The bump was a giveaway, proudly pushing against her work blouse as I blinked through the haze of the whooshing sound in my ears.

She held her head high when she delivered her words with careful precision, and what hurt the most was she barely spared me a second glance. She's clearly done her homework and by now knows who I am. A ripple of anxiety waves through me, but I push it aside while looking around the room for answers. No one is saying a damn thing, the eerie silence filling the atmosphere, and everyone stares at the door she just exited.

Pissed at their lack of a response, I slam my fist onto the

table, and their eyes dart toward mine. "What the hell just happened?" I mean, it's clear what happened; in the bat of her long lashes, she tore up my proposal, destroyed my dreams—years' worth of plans gone.

Fanzio clears his throat. "My daughter is a bitch."

I jolt at the vitriol in his words and glance back at the door. Daughter?

Holy shit. She's his daughter?

That means she's more than likely telling the truth. She is a lawyer. She's not a whore. Not a gold digger, and oh my fucking god.

I loosen the noose around my neck as I become increasingly hot. Sweat beads on my forehead, and my chest heaves.

She's pregnant.

"We need to find the father of that baby." Fanzio babbles to his lawyer. "Find the father of the baby, and I'll get the shares. Then you can have the contract." Haziness floods me. "Are you listening, Reed?"

"I-I-I don't understand." My throat feels like I've swallowed razor blades.

She's pregnant.

Holy shit, she's pregnant, and it might be my child.

Oh God. I'm going to be a father.

"The father of that fucking baby has rights. I will buy him out!" Fanzio declares.

My gaze snaps up to his. "I'm sorry, what?"

"The father of the baby simply demands custody of the kid, or she hands over the shares." He shrugs like he isn't thinking of blackmailing his own daughter, and a gloating smile spreads across his face.

Kevan leans forward and toys with a ring on his finger with a far-off look on his face. Finally, he clears his throat and places the ring back in the box that Gianna threw at him. Jealousy creeps up my spine at considering George's employee.

"George, I don't think that's the best way to deal with Gia." He winces as he speaks.

"Shut the fuck up. This is all your goddamn fault. You're too fucking soft on her. Find the fucking father and get him to demand custody. He holds the shares over her head, simple. There's no way the little bitch would give up her precious family," Fanzio spits, and every vein in his withered face pulsates as he speaks. The venom flowing from him is raw aggression, something I've become accustomed to in his presence, but even I can admit his hatred toward Gia is bordering on vicious.

Why the hell does he hate his daughter so much?

As I sit back in my chair and contemplate his words, my racing heart steadies, and a smile slowly spreads across my face at a plan finally coming together.

If that baby is mine, then Gia can keep it; it's not like I ever wanted kids anyway. I can walk away, and we will both be happy.

Saturday may have been the worst day of my life, but Monday is sure as hell looking a lot better.

SIX

REED

MY MOUTH FALLS OPEN, and I scowl at the small house. There's no way in hell George Fanzio's daughter lives here. No fucking way.

I glance over my shoulder and tilt my head from side to side. This is the right address.

The street is crammed with parked cars, the houses are squashed together, and the tiny property she's registered to is rundown and not fit for living.

Why in the fuck does she live here? I glance around the street again as if someone will jump out and tell me this is a joke.

Because a Fanzio living in these dire circumstances has to be a joke. I shake my head in disgust. There's got to be more to it, and I will find out. Hell, I feel like every homeowner on the street is eyeing me up when I throw open my car door.

Stepping out of my car, I don't miss the curtain twitching at the house next door to Gia's, and I narrow my eyes at the old bat glaring in my direction. You would think she's never seen a Bentley Continental GT S convertible before.

A shudder runs down my spine—oh sweet Jesus, maybe she hasn't.

This is my worst nightmare.

The thought of being out of my comfort zone has a lump forming in my throat, so I swallow away the trepidation pumping inside me, and my stomach does strange flips.

Please don't be my baby, I chant as I take the handful of stone steps two at a time toward Gia's front door.

My chest relaxes on my deep exhale, and I press the doorbell, then clear my throat while waiting for it to be answered.

Noise behind the door has my spine snapping straight, but I lean in to listen for footsteps, and none arrive.

Stabbing the doorbell again, I grit my teeth. Along with a multitude of things, being kept waiting is not something I would normally endure without doling out consequences.

Sounds of laughter vibrate through the flimsy walls, and I feel like someone is taunting me. This shithole of a street, with nosy fucking neighbors, a broken fucking doorbell, and now, it's starting to piss rain. Fan-fucking-tastic.

"For fuck's sake. Open the damn door." I thump the door with my fist.

Just as I'm about to knock again, the door swings open, and my gaze drops to a boy with messy hair and an even messier face.

"Holy shit. What the hell happened to you?" I step back and grimace, but have to right myself before I go ass first down the stone steps.

Please don't come near me. Please don't come near me, I chant, then briefly close my eyes and will myself to have the strength to proceed.

As much as I want that contract signed, is it really worth all this?

The baby might not be mine.

"My mom's baking," the kid says, and I snap my eyes open.

A brown sticky mess coats his face, his chin taking the brunt of it, and, Jesus, he has it on his clothes too. "What is she baking, you?"

Then his word comes back to haunt me. "Mom." I pinch the bridge of my nose and consider how to deal with this, with him.

Movement behind him catches my eye, and I'm relieved to see Gia heading in our direction. "Bryce, what did I tell you about opening the door?"

The kid rolls his eyes, and her footing wavers when she realizes who's on the other side of the open door.

Her green eyes flash with pain, and she swallows thickly before she darts her eyes away. When she returns her gaze to mine, all signs of vulnerability are gone, and in its place is anger.

My hands twitch to pull her toward me, to slam my lips against hers, to own her mouth like she owns the part of me I refuse to dig deeper into acknowledging.

"Here. Take this." She thrusts a spatula dripping with the brown substance into the kid's hand, and his eyes light up before he spins on his heels and rushes down the hallway. "Don't run!" she throws out over her shoulder.

"What do you want?" Her pouty lips form a tight bow, and my cock thickens when my thoughts turn filthy.

I want to fuck her mouth so damn hard her lips become raw from sucking me. I want to stretch her mouth and make her choke, force her to take all of me.

"Reed? What. Do. You. Want?" She speaks slower, and my jaw tics at her attitude. Yes, I'd fuck that attitude right out of her after spanking her goddamn fine ass so hard she'll whimper every time she attempts to sit down.

"I brought you a gift." I pull the flowers and champagne from behind my back and hold them out for her, then shove them into her chest, giving her no choice but to accept them.

Her eyes narrow. "You brought me champagne?"

"To celebrate." I gesture toward the bottle.

She scans my face, and I want to jump in delight at how much her attention excites me. "I'm pregnant." Her monotone voice tells me she's anything but excited by my gesture.

"I know." I wave my hand toward her stomach. "It's hard to miss." I scoff on a laugh.

She flinches, but I follow it up with a change of subject and get to why I'm here. "Can we talk?"

"About what?"

My teeth grind. She's being fucking difficult, and I want a sensible conversation, one where we can establish a smooth path moving forward and maybe discuss a plan. A contract, even.

Loud squeals of laughter fill the silence from behind her, and I glance over her shoulder, unable to hide the sneer on my lips when I witness what looks to be half a dozen children fighting over a bowl.

Jesus, does she not feed them all?

Can she afford to feed them all?

Sickness wells in my stomach, curdling into a ball of dread.

Her long hair flicks from side to side as she shakes her head. "I need to sort the kids." She opens the door wider, and I shove past her before she can second-guess her offer.

"You can wait in there." She points to a room on the left. "I won't be but a minute." Then she leaves me in the hallway while she heads to what appears to be the kitchen.

My eyes wander to take in my small surroundings; it's like a fucking box. A small one. One that needs dropped in the fucking dumpster. Even the best upscales could do nothing with this Tardis.

When my attention latches onto some photo frames on a sideboard, I can't help but pick one up and scrutinize it.

Gia is smiling in the photo, alongside a shirtless man kneeling beside her and a small boy with a fishing rod in his hand. A wood cabin is in the background, and my throat becomes dry when I consider how happy she looks, how happy they all look.

As her footsteps approach, I snap out of my daze, place the photo down, and take two steps into the direction of the living space she pointed me toward.

A three-seater couch and a chair fill the space, and the only sign of money is the television hanging on the wall. I cluck my tongue at how small it looks, yet I suppose in this confined space, it fits just right.

"Would you like a drink?"

I turn to face her and can't help but appreciate how beautiful she is. God, she's stunning, and I'm certain she doesn't even realize it.

The tight, stretchy-looking dress she's wearing emphasizes the bump and her impressive rack, causing my mouth to water. Fuck, she's like a walking wet dream. Even while growing another human. My eyes fixate on her stomach, and I clench my fist, fighting the urge to caress it. *Where the fuck did that come from?*

"Reed. A drink?"

"No. I-I need you to do a DNA test." She rears back and her face falls. Fuck, I want to kick myself in the balls for putting that look of disappointment on her pretty face.

"Okay," she whispers, and shock hits me how easily she gave in. I expected a bit of a fight.

"Okay?" I raise an eyebrow.

"You're the only person I've slept with in years, so I'm pretty certain." She laughs, but it's forced.

I jolt. "Years?"

"Yep." She pops the *p,* then glares at me while crossing her arms over her chest and pushing her heavy tits higher.

Holy shit, no wonder she was tight.

Very tight. So tight, I questioned if she'd ever slept with anyone else previously.

Pulling my phone from my jacket pocket, I fumble, aware of her eyes on me. I quickly type out a text, informing my doctor we can follow through with my instructions as I'd planned. I'm about to shove my phone back in my jacket when what I can only describe as a brown wolf leaps toward me. "Holy shit."

"Chester, down."

The dog instantly responds, and my heart thumps with relief as my mouth falls open in a dazed shock.

"What in the fuck is that?" I sneer in its direction.

"That's Chester. He's visiting," Gia states.

"Visiting?"

"Yes." She crosses her arms over her chest again, emphasizing her tits and causing my mouth to water while the dog stares up at me like I'm his next dinner.

"Stop staring at me, fuckwit," I snap at the dog, but it doesn't so much as blink. "Is it broken?" I bare my teeth at it.

Gia bursts out laughing. "You're not a dog person, are you?"

I'm about to tell her I'm not an animal person, but the living room door is thrown open. "Mom! Why can't Milo sleep over?" The kid from earlier barrels into the room, but at least this time he isn't covered in filth.

Sweat beads on my forehead, and the walls feel like they're closing in on me.

The dog stands at attention, glaring at me.

"Bryce! Give it back, you've already had your turn!" a girl screeches, setting my nerves on edge, and I take a step back from the chaos, feeling well out of my comfort zone.

The dog licks his lips, and I narrow my eyes. "Go away." He touches my pants with his nose.

Oh, sweet Jesus, there's slime on my pants. I loosen my tie, but it does nothing to help the way my chest rises rapidly and my throat struggles to work.

"It's my turn," another kid screeches, and I squeeze my eyes closed, willing the noise to stop.

How the hell does she cope with this?

Thank God, I've no intention of sticking around to find out, I tell myself over and over a-fucking-gain as the kids get louder.

Oh god, Tate was right, it's like the fucking Brady Bunch on crack!

The kids' voices seem to be multiplying, so I breathe in through my nose and out through my mouth in a calculated move that does nothing to tamper my escalating predicament.

"Enough! Can you guys take this back into the kitchen?" she snaps out, and I open my eyes.

They groan their displeasure, and I thank God for her intervention.

It sounds like dozens of the little fuckers all have something to say about it though. "And Bryce, no sleepover, we already discussed this."

Jesus, I'm in literal hell.

Who the hell would want to sleep here?

SEVEN

GIA

AS SOON AS Bryce closes the door behind him, I turn my attention back to Reed. His handsome face is pale, pained even, and his chest heaves like he's seconds away from a panic attack.

I know the kids can be a little much with excitement, and clearly, Chester ruffled his feathers, but God, the man needs to take a chill pill.

"Reed? I think you should sit down."

He nods absently but doesn't move, his green eyes wide as they meet mine. "I think I'm having a heart attack."

A choked laugh escapes me, and I roll my eyes at his dramatics, but with the look of hysteria on his sharp features, I take a deep breath and walk over to the sideboard where I keep the only whiskey I have in the house.

I unscrew the cap and ignore the pang of guilt at opening my husband's bottle, then pour Reed a drink. He needs it more than my need to preserve it.

"Here." I push it into his hand, and he throws it back, then winces.

"Thank you." His ass finds my couch, and I sit beside him and bite into my lip while contemplating what to say. Slowly, the rise in his chest becomes steadier, and I can't help but sympathize with the asshole.

"Was it the dog or the kids?"

He swallows, then his green eyes meet mine. They shine with sincerity, along with a hint of embarrassment. "Honestly?"

I nod.

"All of it. Even the fucking house."

My protective instincts kick in and irritation slices through me. I've been more than accommodating so far, understanding even, but if he's going to come in here and start demoralizing my accomplishments, he can go to hell.

"I'm sorry." He's quick to respond, as if sensing the change in me. "I didn't mean to offend you." Searching my face, he tugs on his hair. "Fuck. I-I'm sure you're an amazing mom, Gia." My shoulders relax, and my face softens; he's trying. "But this"—he waves his hand toward the door—"is not something I'm good at." He stands and shoves his hands in his pockets. "I'm a lawyer."

I nod, because I already know this. I'm one too, despite the fact he hasn't recognized that, nor the vitriol that spewed from his lips at the community center.

"I like control."

I chew on my bottom lip, knowing how much he likes control. *Don't think about it, Gia. Don't.* I've spent months trying not to think about the way he makes not only my body, but my mind feel too.

"I don't do domesticated." His gaze locks with mine, holding me captive.

He doesn't want this baby.

He doesn't want to be a father.

As much as it pains me to do this alone again, I'd already

resigned myself to doing it when I couldn't locate the man I had one crazy night of passion with.

"The last thing I want is to become a father to a dozen kids."

I open my mouth to correct him, but Bryce throws open the door, making me grit my teeth. "Mom, there's a man at the door!"

Dear God, I want to scream. "If I have to tell him one more time."

"It's probably the doctor," Reed says.

Confusion hits me.

"I had him on standby." He smiles at me, as if proud, and I want to castrate the asshole. Still, I grind my teeth and deliver him a tight smile back.

"Excellent. Let's get this over with, then you can leave."

EIGHT

I'M LAID IN BED, staring at the ceiling. It's a Saturday night, and for the first time in as long as I can remember, I'm alone, not out with multiple women. Or bedding them, for that matter.

Nope, since Wednesday, I've barely slept a wink. Instead, my life has been hanging on tenterhooks, waiting for a report from the doctor to tell me if I'm the father of Gia's baby or not.

I already know I am. I can feel it, sense it, and for some strange reason, when she told me I've been the only person she's slept with in years, I believed her. Normally, I would've laughed in a woman's face, but this one, I believe.

Now all I can think about is: how many years? Who was the last one? Judging by the number of kids she has, she's gotten around a lot.

When I explained to Owen about her home life, he said he'd look into her more, because there's no way a Fanzio should be living how she does, but I told him not to bother. I refuse to show too much interest in her and her crowded family. Something about her intrigues me, and I find it terrifying. There's no way in hell I'm being lumbered with a woman and her gaggle of children, or the brown wolf-looking dog. She has no room in her house for that thing, let alone another baby.

Where is she even going to put it?

Unable to take my thoughts any longer, I roll onto my side and grab my phone from the nightstand to check my emails again.

Nothing.

Why the fuck do I pay this incompetent prick so much money?

My phone vibrates in my hand, and I stare at Owen's name as a pit of dread washes over me. Thumb trembling, I swipe across to answer the call.

"The results just came in," he breathes out, and I'm unable to talk. "Figured you'd want the results before he emails you with them."

I make a noncommittal grunting noise.

"Congrats, man, you're going to be a father."

"Fuck!" I launch the phone against the wall, causing it to shatter. "Fuck!" I scream louder than ever as anger with myself consumes me.

I shouldn't care; I've no intention of being a father.

Especially knowing what's at stake with Fanzio.

So why does my life feel like it's spiraling when I have the perfect get-out clause?

NINE

MY TIE FEELS like a noose around my neck, so I tug it loose and open my shirt buttons with the hope I can breathe more freely. Swallowing back another glass of whiskey, I savor the burn in my throat.

Whoever invented ties is a twisted fuck with a vendetta against businessmen. Yeah, it was probably a woman who wanted to secretly torture someone who scorned her by slowly depleting their brain of oxygen.

Why the hell does it feel like my life is over? When really, I'm getting what I want. If the baby is mine, then I can sign the contract for the land. Gia gets to keep the baby, and I can provide for them all. That way, we're both happy.

So why does the thought twist me up inside? Is it because my own father was so absent, and I loathed him for it?

A knock at my office door has my eyes narrowing. Please tell me it's not those women again. I already sent them a substantial lump sum to leave me the hell alone.

Owen steps inside, and his gaze roams over me. "What the hell happened to you?" He heads toward my desk, then spins a chair around for him to straddle while he stares at me head-on.

Great, a therapy session. Just what I fucking need.

The look on my face must tell him I'm unimpressed with his intrusion, because he chuckles. "Tell me what the fuck's happened now."

He and my best friends are aware of my predicament, but I haven't admitted I plan on signing over rights to my child to get the land I so desperately want.

"If the baby is mine, I'm going to blackmail Gia into handing over her shares of the land in order for her to keep the baby."

His jaw falls lax, then it tightens, his shoulders bunch tight, and his stare darkens. "You're giving up your kid?"

I laugh, but it's humorless. "What the fuck do I know about kids, Owen? I don't even like them."

His hands ball into fists, and my friend looks two seconds away from ruining me with them, but I don't care.

"I want the land." I change the subject before we go any deeper into my self-loathing. I've had abandonment issues since my childhood; I guess leaving a kid in boarding school and never returning does that to you.

Owen sighs. "You're really going to give up your child for some land?"

"It's a good business move," I retort.

"Fuck the business, Reed," he barks, causing me to jolt. "You're making a huge mistake, man, huge. You're going to regret it every day of your goddamn life, because what you're doing is far worse than what your father did to you and your brother. Your kid won't even know who you are, only that you're the bastard who sold them."

Sickness knots my insides at the thought.

I lift my head and glare back at Owen. "Maybe I'm just like him."

He shakes his head. "I refuse to believe that. Listen to

what's in here." He taps his chest right over his heart. "Not what's going off up here." Then he taps his forehead. "I mean it, Reed; you're going to destroy so many lives if you do this."

I swallow back the bile in my throat and consider the move I made earlier today. I've already set the ball rolling, and I don't intend on backing down.

"You're better than this," he asserts, pushing up from the chair. "So much better, Reed." As he turns and leaves the office, I can't help but feel like I'm making a huge mistake, but what's the alternative?

How the hell do I become the man I've no clue how to be? Especially when I don't want to.

TEN

"SO, the test proved he's the father, and you haven't heard from him?" Tyson asks.

Disappointment ripples through me, and I hide the sting of his words by blowing into my hot chocolate. "It's been over a week." I confirm.

"How do you know he got the email?"

A knock comes from the front door before I have a chance to respond, and Tyson takes off toward it.

"Who the hell are you?" Reed snarls out, the venom in it unmistakable.

Great. Just great.

He'd have to show up while Tyson is here, freshly showered, and wearing only his gray sweatpants. The man has an eight pack, along with a sleeve of tattoos that sends women into a frenzy. He has those warm-chocolate eyes you beg to devour you, and he finishes the look with short, cropped dark hair. He's the epitome of a hot military man. He's also my husband's best friend.

"Who the hell are you?" Tyson bites back.

Shit, I best defuse this. I scurry toward the front door to witness Reed and Tyson having a face-off with one another. Both have broadened their shoulders, their strong arms crossed over their chests.

I nudge Tyson aside. "Tys, can you take Bryce to practice?"

His eyes snap down to mine. "Is this him?" The sneer on his lips is clear, and I want to shrink away from the conflict behind it, but something about his protective stance has annoyance rumbling inside me. From the moment I told him I was pregnant, he's taken the big-brother role thing to heart— a little too much, truth be told.

"I'll be fine, I promise." I plead with my eyes.

His eyes narrow, then he turns on his heel and heads up the stairs with a heavy huff. "Change of plans, dude. I'm taking you to practice. Your mom can meet us there," he snipes out.

Great, and now he's making sure I have to go to practice too. Nice work. *Dick.*

Before I turn back to Reed, he's pushed his way inside and heading toward the kitchen, but he stops at the photos lining the hallway dresser and lifts the one of us at the cabin, causing a surge of emotion to overcome me.

Never in a million years did I expect the father of my baby to be looking at the father of my son like this. Nor would I have expected to be having another man's child six years later. Hurt slices through my chest at how things have turned out.

Guilt poisons my veins, and as my bump gives me a little kick, it's like a reminder to nudge the feeling aside.

"You have a lot of this man," he whispers, then places the photo down.

I clear my throat. "He's my … He was my husband."

Reed stiffens, then walks toward the kitchen. It's not lost

on me that he didn't head into the living room, given how that experience turned out before.

When he stops at the door to the garden, he turns to face me. "Are you divorced?" His sharp eyes sear into me, and my breath hitches, the intensity behind them almost cutting through me. *Wow. Does he think I cheated?*

"Widowed," I whisper, and every ounce of anger falls away as the sadness at confirming my status bleeds from me.

His shoulders sag, and I wonder if it was with relief that I'm single or knowing he didn't sleep with a married woman. "I'm sorry." His tone is sincere. "Really fucking sorry." As his eyes implore mine, I swallow back the emotion lodged in my throat. Then I do what I always do, I lift a shoulder. Having spent years dealing with people's reactions, I've become accustomed to shrugging it off as if it's an unfortunate event that I'm over. In reality, I never will be.

"Fuck, and he left you with all those kids." He exhales heavily and throws his arm out toward the door, with horror written all over his face.

My head rears back. "Huh?"

He shakes his head. "I'm not a knight in shining armor, Gia."

His sandalwood scent wraps around me in the small space, and a flash of his strong arms pinning me to the bed while he thrust his thick cock inside me has me squirming on the spot. The way his abs contracted with each thrust. *Oh, sweet Jesus. No, Gia.*

He clears his throat, and I tilt my head, my mind scrambling to play catch-up while he continues on. "I've had the results." He swallows thickly. "I can help out financially, bu-but I'm just not sure about anything else." Dragging his hand through his hair, he exhales heavily. "Fuck," he says, as if pissed with himself.

But not as pissed as me. He's not sure about anything else? I clench my teeth. Great, so I'm doing this alone. I hold my hand up to stop him from speaking, and his head rears back.

Clearly, the man is not used to anyone putting him in his place. "I don't need your help financially." He wrinkles his pompous nose and scans the small kitchen space, but I ignore him. "I've already raised one child without a father, and as much as I wouldn't have chosen to do it this way again, I'm more than willing to." I lift my chin and glare into his eyes, giving him no reason to doubt my strength.

"You said one? Is that one of the other kids' dad?" He motions toward the door, and the front door slams shut. I temporarily close my eyes.

His words replay in my mind, and I open my eyes. Oh no. He thinks … A loud laugh erupts from me, and my eyes water while Reed stares at me with an open mouth like I'm a madwoman. When I finally pull myself together, I swipe the tears from the corners of my eyes, then find Reed staring at my tits. Instead of acknowledging the heated gaze, I push it aside and put him out of his misery.

"I have one child, Reed." I hold up my finger. "One."

His handsome face contorts in confusion.

"Tyson"—I throw a thumb over my shoulder—"is my husband's best friend. He's in the Army, where he met Jaxon. He's a close family friend who's been an amazing support, nothing more. He stays over when he's on extended leave and helps with Bryce. Plus, he brings Chester with him, and when he leaves, he will drop him with his mother. Bryce loves dogs, and honestly, since Jaxon passed away, it's helped to divert his attention." Every muscle in his body relaxes on my words, and I don't know what he's more grateful for: Tyson being a family friend or the fact I only have Bryce and not a dozen children, which I'm sure he suspected.

"When did Jaxon pass away?" He winces, and I push the strands of my hair away from my face and lean back against the counter for support.

"Six years ago," I state.

He scans my face. "Fuck, and you've been living here." He shakes his head, and I swear I want to snap it from his judgmental shoulders. "And your son is how old?"

His questions surprise me, especially given he has shown no interest in my life or our baby's until now. To be honest, I assumed he wanted nothing to do with us, given his previous outburst.

"Bryce is nine, almost ten."

Staring down at his feet, he nods, then his eyes lock with mine, and I swear I can see into his soul. His vulnerability flashes across his face, and it remains there, allowing me to see him at his weakest, and I clutch my hand to my chest at the thought.

"I'm so sorry about everything I said to you, Gia." He swallows thickly. "Really sorry."

A lump gathers in my throat at the emotion in his tone, and as much as I want to tell him it's okay, I can't. I refuse to be a pushover.

Instead, I raise my chin. "It was uncalled for."

"I know that."

I lift my hand to stop him, and I'm surprised when he snaps his mouth shut.

"You don't ever call me a whore again." The way in which he used those words toward me cut me to my core.

This time, he rolls his lips, as if to disguise the smile, and I wonder if he's remembering how I begged for more of the words that fell from his filthy mouth. But I won't be drawn in to his playful demeanor. "I mean it, Reed."

"Understood." He nods; all signs of jest erased.

"And I'm a lot of things, but not a liar. Don't ever accuse me of that again." My eyes bore into his.

"Of course."

Without warning, a swift kick comes from within my stomach, and I settle a hand over the movement. "So, you're going to be a father." I tilt my head, waiting for his reaction. "And you don't know if you can be involved?"

He drags a hand through his hair and looks up at the ceiling, then after a deep sigh, his gaze lands on me, and the look of vulnerability makes my heart twist once again. "I've never wanted to be a father. I don't know how to be one."

His words cause a slice of pain to shoot into my chest, exposing a hole so deep it bares my very core, leaving me breathless.

"But I think I'd like to try to be there for you all. I just—" His Adam's apple slides down his throat. "I don't know how." The fact he said "for you all" tells me he means Bryce too, and that hole becomes deeper, but this time, with longing.

"Believe it or not, there's not an accurate guidebook to parenting, Reed. The real thing is nothing like what is written. I didn't have a clue about babies when I was pregnant with Bryce."

His eyebrows shoot up. "You didn't?"

"Nope. It took a lot of learning, and I got things wrong along the way. But I tried my best, and that's all a good parent can do, you know?"

He nods absentmindedly while I stroke over my stomach. Another movement has me smiling down at my hand, caressing the spot.

"Do you know what you're having?" He nods toward my bump.

"No. I've been in ignorant bliss, hoping to drag the pregnancy out."

His nose crinkles, and I shake my head at my lame attempt to explain.

"I didn't want to do it alone, so I was kind of hoping it wasn't really happening." I giggle at how ridiculous it sounds.

"It's definitely happening." He gestures to bump.

The baby delivers me with yet another swift kick, reminding me I need to feed us, and I rub at my stomach. "Would you like a coffee?" I motion toward the kettle and grab one of the cookies I made for Bryce this morning.

"Is it Luwak?"

My hand comes to a stop on the kettle, and my eyes ping-pong over his face. "Huh?"

"Luwak. Is the coffee Luwak?" He waves his hand toward the coffeepot.

"I-I'm not sure." I bite on my bottom lip. Is it Luwak?

He winces as if it will pain him to drink it, then he shakes his head. "It's fine. I'll have a coffee. Thank you."

As I turn to make his drink, I can sense his eyes on me, and heat creeps up my spine and over my face at the thought of having his attention.

Jesus, why the hell do I have to be in such a confined space with my hot baby daddy.

As much as I try not to think of that night with Reed, in all honesty, it's all I can think about.

Since falling pregnant, I've been ridiculously horny, and Reed's face has been the leading role in my nightly dreams that leave me waking up covered in a sheen of sweat, with wetness pooling between my legs. It's like he's opened a part of me I never knew existed, and now I'm begging for it.

Constantly.

REED

Holy fuck, that's fucking revolting. I spit the shit she calls coffee across the room, unable to help myself. "What the fuck is that?"

"Instant."

I scrunch my nose, never having heard of it.

"Instant what? Poison."

She laughs and wipes down the mess I created on the countertop. Her tits bounce as she does so, and I swear to Christ, my cock is seconds away from exploding.

Fuck.

This small space has to have frazzled my brain, because never in my life have I wanted a pregnant woman before now, and fuck, do I want her. Not only that, but I have a sudden urge to feel her stomach, caress it with my palms, hold it as I fuck her, knowing I put that there.

I created the bump that stretches her dress. Me.

That baby is mine.

Mine and Gia's.

In a matter of minutes, I'm throwing all thoughts of leaving my responsibilities behind, and all I can think about is making Gia and her son's life easier, more manageable. That, and sinking so deep inside Gia, she remembers who the fuck knocked her up in the first place, not that two-pump chump, Tyson. Me.

Her tits were big before, but they're huge now. I wonder if her nipples have changed too.

Pre-cum leaks from me in streams as I revel at the sight of her heavy chest.

"Your tits look incredible." Oh shit, did I just say that out loud?

She chews into that plump bottom lip of hers, and I eat up the small space between us to withdraw it from her mouth with a flick of my finger.

"So, you're single," I say. My eyes bore down into hers. "You're single, and you're having my baby." My tongue feels thick as I say it, but only because the need to claim her is so strong, so possessive that my entire being feels like it's being overrun with a driving force to control her.

Her cheeks pinken, and I love the effect I have on her, grateful it's so similar to my own.

She wants me.

"I am," she whispers, and before I know what I'm doing, all thoughts of the deal with Fanzio and of leaving her alone escape my mind as a need to stamp my ownership all over her and my child flash through me at a lightning speed.

My hand lands on the back of her neck to pull her toward me, and my lips take hers. I plunge my tongue into her mouth, not caring if she's a willing participant or not. This is about claiming her, showing her how out of control she makes me feel when I crave the control so greatly. I swallow back her gasp of surprise, and our tongues mix like a potent blend of euphoria. When I pull back, we're both breathless and our stares are riddled with curiosity and desire, stripping one another bare with the strength behind them.

My thick palm brushes over her heavy tit, and when she

arches her spine against my touch, it's game over. I'm taking her, contract be damned.

The sinful feel of her softness has my cock pumping pre-cum like never before, and I've no choice but to push against her, grinding the tip on her solid stomach, and a possessive growl lodges in my throat.

They're mine.

They both are.

All of them.

My lips slam against hers again, harder and more forceful than before, and I spiral over the edge of sanity for this woman. Never having felt so fiercely about anyone before her.

She's my undoing, but she may also be my making.

My balls ache with each brush of my cock against her softness. The way her nipples have peaked, begging to be pulled into my mouth, has pre-cum dripping into my boxers.

"Oh god, Reed."

I squeeze her tits and kiss up and down her throat, angling her head in each direction to allow me the best access. Her small moans of pleasure, the feel of her full tits, and the way her bump brushes against the tip of my cock has a need like no other flashing through me.

"Fuck, I'm going to come," I grunt and grind against her bump.

"Mmm," she moans into our kiss, and I plunge my tongue deep into her mouth and devour the sounds emanating from her. "I want you to." She nips at my lip, then follows the sting with a lick of her tongue. Holy fuck, she's hot. She's just as hungry for me as I am for her.

"Your tits are incredible." I groan at the feel of her plump flesh in the palm of my hand, my cock leaking more and more, and when I brush my thumb over her nipple, I squeeze my eyes closed at the sensation of my balls drawing up. "Fuck!"

"Yesss." She throws her head back, and I stare at her as my cock empties into my boxers while I toy with her nipple, imagining it whitening with milk when I pinch it gently between the tips of my fingers.

Where the hell did that thought come from?

"You like that? You like me playing with you?"

She moans, and I continue to thrust against her.

"You like me coming for you?" I thrust my hips up as my cock spills warm cum all over my boxers. "Fuck," I grunt, then slam my lips against hers. When my cock stops spurting, I pull back, breathless, but my arousal ramps up a notch, and I squeeze her tit greedily, unable to let her go just yet.

"Fuck. I can't believe I just came in my pants," I grumble and thread my hands around the back of her neck and pull her into a feverish kiss. Her pebbled nipples strain against her dress, and I hate it. Jesus, I need to see them, feel them. So in one swift movement, I slip the zip on the side of her dress down until it pools at her feet.

The sounds of our frantic pants fill the air, and her hands move between us, and I step back to allow her the space to work my belt buckle free.

Holy fuck.

My hungry gaze eats her up; I've never seen anything so mesmerizing in my entire life.

She's incredible.

Gorgeous.

Mine.

Her tits are swollen and heave over the top of where they're housed in a lacy red bra I love and hate. It's sexy and understated all in one, something for a pregnant woman, yet that taunts me in a way I never knew possible.

Her panties are exposed, but the bump between us hinders my vision.

Suddenly, all I see is our creation.

Our perfect damn creation.

I want to mark it, cum on it, and mark it for all to see.

The beauty of our creation is simply captivating.

We did this. We made this.

Ours.

"We did," she whispers, and her eyes mist over, and I realize I voiced my thoughts, but I don't have it in me to care. I want to sink inside the very woman I should be running from, but all I want to do is remind her of who she belongs to.

I stare into her eyes with all-consuming sincerity dripping from my own. "You're never leaving me, Gia, and I'm fucking staying." The confidence in my tone leaves no room for argument.

ELEVEN

GIA

"YOU'RE NEVER LEAVING ME, Gia, and I'm fucking staying." Truth bleeds from his eyes, and my breath rises at the intensity behind them.

"You need to be sure, Reed? Will you leave me when things get difficult?" The vulnerability in my tone is evident, but I won't hide it. Why should I? I already told him I didn't want to raise a child alone, yet I asked nothing of him and expected nothing from him.

He takes my chin between his fingers, his eyes a deeper green than ever before. "I'm never leaving you. I'm all fucking in." His tone is dark and laced in dominance.

Then he steps forward again, and before I know what he's doing, he's lifted me onto the countertop, spread my legs, pushed my panties to the side, and surged his dripping, thick cock forward.

I lean back on my elbows, and my head falls back against the cabinet as his grip on my thighs has me wincing from the bite of pain.

"Holy. Fuck!" Reed roars and stares down at his cock

stretching me open. His gaze shoots up to mine, then darts from my stomach, back up to my tits, and down to my pussy over and over as he snaps his hips back and forth.

This is what I need.

My clit throbs, but he doesn't even touch it before I feel the telltale signs of my orgasm approaching.

"Jesus, you're incredible, Gia." He buries his face in my breasts, pressing kisses on them, and when his hands tighten on me and his body coils, my release hits me. The jerk of his cock deep inside me becomes my undoing, and I freefall.

"Oh god!" I pant out into the kitchen. Reed bites my breast, my mouth falls open, and a scream erupts from me as my orgasm goes on.

The. Best. Sex. Ever.

"Holy fuck." Reed chuckles against my tit, then licks where he bit me.

When he draws back, he stares at it, then his gaze lowers to my nipple and licks his lips, causing my pussy to contract around him. He thrusts his hips forward, as if willing himself to go again, and he hardens again, but my cell phone cuts through the sexual haze.

"I need to get that," I pant out, but he makes no attempt to move.

My hand darts for my cell, and when I press the speakerphone, Tyson's voice blares out.

"Gia?"

Reed stiffens, then his jaw locks, and his green eyes turn dark. He slams his hips forward, taking my breath away with the rough action.

"Ye-yes."

"Are you coming to practice?" The sound of the crowd behind Tyson plays out like background noise.

"Fuck," I mumble, but bite into my lip to stop me from crying out again when Reed picks up his pace, his eyes flashing with determination.

"Are you on your way?" Tyson asks.

I gasp for air when one of Reed's fingers strokes my clit, and I clench around him, earning a smirk.

The bastard knows what he's doing.

"Soon," I grunt, and my tits bounce in rhythm with Reed's hips. The anger radiates from him as he pounds into me with malice.

"Hurry up, yeah?"

Reed grits his teeth like a rabid dog. Wild and possessive.

"Yesss!!" I end the call as my orgasm hits me, and when Reed's cock expands inside me, delivering me his warmth, it makes me feel like I'm floating in a sea of pleasure. Unknowing where I start and where I finish, I become boneless under his control.

REED

I can't believe I came in my pants like a fucking teenager, but at least I remained hard enough to fuck her senseless afterward. When I heard the fuckwits voice with my cock deep inside my woman, it spurred me on to fill her once again. The insane need to consume her forced me to become feral. Sweat drips from my forehead and my blood races as I slowly pull out of her swollen pussy.

She's filled with my cum, and it drips from her when I withdraw my cock. Like a magnet, my fingers are there swiping up the remnants of a sight so powerful my chest constricts and my bloodstream fills with pride. I bring my fingers to her bump, painting it with my possession, and write the only word that extenuates my feeling toward them both. "Mine," I whisper and coat her skin in my ownership.

She gasps as her startled eyes meet mine, then she shoves me away. I bristle at her breaking the moment, one so profound it's changed my life.

How can she push it aside so easily?

"I need to get to Bryce's practice." She drops her feet to the floor and begins to dress, pissing me off at dismissing us so quickly. "At some point, we need to talk about"—her eyes

meet mine and a flash of uncertainty crosses over her face—
"this." She gestures toward her stomach.

I nod and sigh when she simply covers my mark with her dress instead of wiping it off. A smile spreads across my face at the thought, and triumph rushes through me.

"My boxers are fucking drenched," I grumble, and tuck my spent cock into my pants.

My gaze never leaves her as she slides the long black dress into place, then adjusts it to hug her bump. I have the distinct feeling to pull her toward me to place a kiss on her forehead, nose, and then her lips, but instead, I finish buckling my belt. When she grabs her purse, I've already made my decision. I'm going to practice too, and I will find out what the hell this Tyson prick feels toward my woman and baby.

Perhaps he needs to be put in his place, and I intend on being the person to do just that.

TWELVE

GIA

WHEN I WALKED out of the house, I never intended for Reed to follow me, and when he headed toward his car, opened the passenger door, and gestured for me to get in, I stared at him with wide eyes. I don't know what I was more shocked at, the fact he took it upon himself to go to my son's soccer practice or that he expected me to get into his Bentley.

He must have realized the confusion on my face, because the next thing I know, he's grabbing my keys from me, scooping me up, and placing me on the passenger seat of my SUV and hopping into the driver's seat while I stare at him in shock. The man is a mind-fuck. One minute, he's freaked out at my very existence, and the next, he's taking over my life, literally coating me in his cum like a grand gesture and declaring me his.

After he buckles me in like a child, we drive toward the game, and as I look out of the window, the silence between us is comforting yet laced in uncertainty.

Reed remains stoic and stares ahead, his reflection in my window a reminder of his presence. My shoulders slump with a weird relief I haven't felt throughout my pregnancy until now.

I'm more than capable of doing this alone, and I'd resigned myself to the fact I would, but I won't lie. I'd like nothing more than a loving family for this baby, much like the one I had with Jaxon.

What if someone isn't allowed the same happiness twice in their lives? My stomach twists at the thought.

Reed clears his throat, and I turn toward him. He drags his hand through his hair, ruffling it. Something I'm sure would annoy him if he knew it caused it to look messy.

"I don't think I'm well dressed for soccer." He grimaces, then glances toward me, an awkward smile tugging on his handsome face.

Glancing over at his dress shirt and pants, I roll my lips—definitely not soccer attire. "You'll be fine." I try to give him a reassuring smile, but his eyes glimmer with vulnerability, and I hate it, especially when he's normally so strong and domineering.

So controlled.

"And my fucking boxers are still damp." He winces slightly, making me giggle.

As we pull into the parking lot, which is nothing more than a grassy patch of land in Ridgeway, his emerald eyes widen and his chest heaves, and I'm struck with the realization of just how much Reed is out of his comfort zone.

"You can just leave me here, and I'll grab a lift home with Tyson?" I suggest, feeling the need to put him out of his misery.

His spine straightens. "Absolutely. Fucking. Not."

I'm unsure if it's Tyson driving me home or the thought of leaving me here that makes him so possessive, but I decide to go with the latter in hope of him wanting more than a quick fuck in the kitchen.

I move to open the door, but his hand stops me. "I'll get

the door." He hops out of the SUV, rounds the front, and opens my door for me. "Do you need me to lift you down?" A line appears between his eyebrows, and I burst out into a giggle.

"I'm not an invalid, Reed." I bat his hand away and slide out of the car, then slam the door shut. "Besides, you just fucked me senseless. You weren't so concerned then." I grin up at him, and his hands hold my hips as he pushes me back against the SUV door.

He nuzzles into my neck. "I did, didn't I? And you've no idea how fucking hot it is to know you're coated in my cum." Wetness flows from me, and he licks a trail from my earlobe to my lower neck where he buries his face against me, breathing me in, and his sandalwood scent encompasses me. "Is my cum leaking out of you?"

I'm almost rendered speechless at his words. While the crowd seems to get louder, this man who consumes my body has me backed up against my SUV, whispering dirty words into my ear, clawing his passion from inside me, forcing it to the surface. "Ye-yes."

"Fuck." He pushes his hard ridge against me. "You've no idea how much I want to feel my cum seep from your pussy lips, Gia." Then he chuckles and pulls back to stare into my eyes. "I actually want to bury my face in your pussy and lick my cum from inside you. Can you believe that?" He shakes his head, as if bemused by his thoughts.

My mouth moves, but I say nothing. What can I say? That I want him to do just that, to taste himself from inside me.

"There you are." Tyson appears from the crowd. "You missed Bryce's shot at the goal. The kid almost had it." His eyes dart from mine to Reed's, with a knowing smirk I want to slap off his face.

Reed clenches his jaw shut and steps back, not even trying to hide the hardness in his pants as he crosses his arms over his chest.

"You might want to hide the stiffy. There're kids over there, pretty obscene to be aroused around kids," Tyson jokes, loving the way Reed shifts from foot to foot.

Reed grimaces, then looks over his shoulder toward the game. "Fuck. Gimme a minute."

He nods toward me and walks around the other side of the SUV while Tyson leads me toward the game, and as much as I want to watch Bryce, my mind can't help but wander to the man who has my heart captivated and my pussy clenching.

REED

Sliding into the backseat of the SUV, I'm relieved not only to have windows that are blacked out, but because we were so late, we are parked so far away from the game. I waste no time in unbuckling my pants, pushing down my boxers, and lifting my thick cock and heavy balls over the material.

There's only one way to get rid of my current situation, and that's fucking my hand to thoughts of Gia and her hot pussy wrapped around my cock as if she's made for me.

My hand pumps faster and faster at the thought of her pussy leaking my cum into her panties while standing in a crowd of people unaware of her predicament.

"Fuck, yes," I grunt with a shift of my hips, and imagine splashing my cum over her stomach and circling the tip of my cock around her pointed nipple. For some reason unknown to me before today, I want to taste myself on her, only on her. My balls draw up, and I hiss. The thought of her on her knees as I plunge into her wet mouth is my undoing, and my cock unleashes rope after rope of warm cum over my hand and down my shaft. "Fuck."

My chest rises and falls, so I relax back into the leather,

then shouts of encouragement snap my gaze to the crowd beyond the window, and I'm brought back down to earth.

I'm at a child's soccer game, dressed in clothes that resemble work attire, and worse, I'm covered in cum.

Fan-fucking-tastic.

Jolting, I glance around the car and grimace at the mess. Jesus, this is appalling. Discarded rubbish is strewn on the floor of the car, along with a bunch of kid clothes and, thankfully, a bunch of balled-up napkins.

This thing is a fucking pig sty.

But for once in my life, I'm grateful for the mess I'm surrounded by.

After wiping the cum from me, I stuff the napkins in one of the used McDonald's bags and try not to think about how long it's been there. Then I step out of the SUV and shake away the need to scrub my skin clean, and go in search of Gia.

Pushing my way through the crowd of supporters, I realize there are multiple games happening in this godforsaken place. A light giggle has me turning my attention to my right, the sweet sound something I'd recognize anywhere—my woman.

As if in slow motion, she throws her head back on a laugh, and her dark hair blows in the breeze as I take in her small stature beside Tyson.

Jealousy zips up my spine and slams into me like a freight train at his casual clothes and the way his T-shirt exposes his muscled biceps. I swear the moron is tensing them for added effect.

"Excuse me, sir?" My eyes travel over to a young woman looking up at me nervously. "Do you work here?"

She appears more like a teenager than an adult, and the way she wrings her hands in front of her shows me her worry. "Are you one of the investors?"

My brow furrows.

"In the baby changing room, the table is broken." She

points toward one of the dilapidated buildings, and I grimace. A baby changing room, in there? Good God.

A noise beside her has me noticing the stroller she has and the infant fidgeting beneath the blanket.

Jesus, she's not the mother, is she? My eyes search her face, but I'm snapped out of my stare when Gia approaches.

"Kimmy, I sent one of the volunteers over. He's going to get it fixed." Relief spreads over the young girl's face.

"Thank you, Gia." She nods in my direction and maneuvers the stroller around the crowd.

"Is that her baby?" I ask as the girl's small figure disappears into the crowd.

"It is," Gia replies, and I search her face for a sign of something more, and when she places her hand on her bump, I itch to join it. "Not every pregnancy is planned, Reed." Her eyes hold mine, and I want to tell her that ours is, that from the moment I sunk inside her and decided to fuck her bare, I willed this to happen, even if I hadn't fully realized it at the time.

And now I finally have something to live for, something I never knew I wanted.

"She just looks a little young," I mumble through the haze surrounding us.

"She is. Sixteen, to be precise." My mouth falls open, but Gia follows up with, "She couldn't help the situation she was brought up in. Nor can she help that the people who were meant to care for her were nothing more than monsters." Her words sit heavily in my stomach, and my mind whirls over what she's telling me. Every cell in my body tightens with a need for retribution for the young girl as anger for her strikes me hard.

"I got the bastard sent down, and as you know, nobody likes child abusers in prison." A knowing smirk plays on Gia's lips, and pride fills my chest.

She helped save that girl; she provided a service I chose

not to when choosing the course of my legal career, then I become even more in awe of the woman than I ever thought possible.

Her eyes dart to the side as if my stare brings her discomfort, and I hate that, so when they finally land on me again, I step toward her, brushing the wayward strands of hair from her face. She stares at me as if uncertain by my action, and truth be told, she should be. I've never felt the need for physical affection in my entire life before now. "Bryce's game is almost finished. Would you like to join us?" she whispers.

Looking out over the rugged ground, I wince. How the hell they play soccer on this terrain is beyond me. Instead of voicing my concerns, I smile back at her. "Sure."

———

Bryce is small compared to the other kids. So fucking small, I struggled to see who Gia was cheering on, but I give him his dues, he can run. He's like fucking lightning, and the only way the other kids can stop him is if they use their size to shoulder barge him to the ground.

Little fuckers.

One asshole, in particular, appears to have it out for him, and already, I hate the little shit.

When I asked Gia his name, she informed me it's Lenton O'Sullivan, who's the coach's kid. No shock there.

Well, Lenton O'Sullivan and his father need to watch the hell out. I refuse to stand for anyone taking advantage of my family, and that's what Bryce is. As much as I dislike children, Gia has one, so I guess I do too.

The whistle blows, and I can finally breathe again, and when Bryce is named man of the match, he's thrown up in the air with shouts of congratulations that make my ears ring out, but I can't deny how happy the kid looks with his circle of friends.

It wasn't until I met my best friends in boarding school that I started making memories, plans for a future, and not once did I consider having a family.

Why the hell would I?

I never had one to want one.

Bryce comes rushing over, covered in dirt that makes me step back. "Did you see me, Mom?"

"I did." She grins and takes his filthy cheeks in the palms of her hands and kisses his forehead, and I wrinkle my nose at the thought of the dirt now covering her too.

"Bryce, this is Reed. The baby's dad, the one I was telling you about," Gia explains, and Bryce glances up toward me.

"Are you going to live with us?" He scrutinizes me, and I can't help but wonder what the hell he thinks of me. I shove my hands in my pants pocket, hoping I look casual enough not to scare him away.

"No. He's not." Gia laughs awkwardly, and I snap my eyes toward hers.

Why the hell would she assume I don't want to live with them? If we're going to be a family, naturally it's the next step. When I said I was all in, I meant it.

"You did amazing, buddy." Tyson ruffles Bryce's dark hair, and I want to knock his hand away. Does he not realize the boy is practically my son now? He can't just touch things that don't belong to him.

The need to say something greater than "You did amazing buddy" prompts me to step forward. "I'm pretty impressed, Bryce."

His green eyes entrap mine as he looks up at me with hope.

"I think you deserve a treat." What treat, I've no fucking clue. All I know is he needs something from me. Something better than what that twat waffle offered, a messy hairdo.

"Can we go to McDonald's?" His eyes flare with excitement, and my stomach churns at the thought. Please God, no.

"Buddy, you went there last weekend." Tyson is quick to jump in, and I want to sneer at the fuckwit. Tate calls me a fun-sponge; he would have a field day with this guy.

Gia laughs uncomfortably as I will her to tell the kid not McDonald's, but at the same time piss off Tyson. "Sure. Reed can treat us." She winks, and the part of me that was dying seconds ago has sprung back to life.

I smirk in Tyson's direction while he mouths, *Fuck you* at me. I can only smile back in his direction with glee as I place my hands on Bryce's and Gia's shoulders and lead them away.

That's right, motherfucker, they're mine now.

THIRTEEN

I CAN'T HELP but keep checking the rear-view mirror as I drive toward the fast-food chain. "Are you sure he doesn't need a booster seat or something?" Nervousness rolls in my stomach as I consider I'm now driving my entire family in a vehicle that resembles a trash can.

Gia stifles a laugh. "I'm sure."

"My best friends' kids all have them," I add.

She shuffles from side to side, and her gaze lands on me, causing my cock to thicken once again. "How old are they?"

Her question whirls around in my head because it's a good question. How old are they? It takes a moment for me to respond as I consider when Shaw had his daughter, but I come up empty. All I know is the kids are younger than Bryce, a lot younger.

I throw out my hand. "There's a bunch of them, different ages."

"Mom." Bryce sits forward in his seat. "I've been saving the toys in the Happy Meals. Look which one I got last time.

The one all the kids at school want!" Bryce holds up a McDonald's bag, and I swerve the SUV from panic.

Oh, shit no!

My heart rate picks up, and my palms become sweaty.

No. God, no.

Then I grab the bag from out of his hand and scramble to open the window, shoving the bag through at lightning speed. Only when I close the window does my racing heart subside.

"Hey! That's mine. Momm!" he whines, and a ripple of sweat drips from me. "It was my favorite one." Of course it had to be his favorite. I grimace at the thought.

"I'll buy you a whole bunch," I state, and Gia's wide eyes search my face.

"You will?" The hope in Bryce's voice has me determined to please him.

"Yes. However many you need," I say, and Gia's jaw drops open.

"Wow. You're amazing, Reed!" he shrieks, and I grin from ear to ear, but when I glance at Gia, she is not impressed.

Great, I cheer the kid up and save him from trauma, and this is the thanks I get.

As I pull into the parking lot, I can't help the disgruntled sound of dread that escapes me. "Holy. Fucking. Shit." I groan at what might as well be a hundred kids and their families gathered inside the restaurant. My chest rises, and I shake my head. "Oh, sweet Jesus, this is awful."

A chuckle leaves Gia, and I turn my attention toward her. "It's not funny, Gia. That place is a breeding ground for germs." I motion toward the brightly lit building. "I'm going to come out of there with whooping cough or something worse." Digging into my pocket, I pull out the hand sanitizer, dousing my palms in the stuff like it's at risk of going out of production.

"Whooping cough?" She bites into her lip, as if trying to

rein in her amusement, and her eyes sparkle back at me. I can only nod, because my mouth is so dry it can barely function.

She turns her head over her shoulder toward Bryce. "Buddy, why don't you go inside and start ordering?"

"Okay. What do you want, Reed?"

His question stuns me. All I know is they make some odd-looking burgers out of processed products, and nothing about that appeals to me. I give him a tight smile. "I'm good, thanks."

"Your loss," he quips, and hops out and slams the door behind him before I have a chance to tell him that's doubtful, but at least I'm not the one about to get ringworm.

"You can't promise him multiple Happy Meal toys, Reed."

"Well, given that your son was about to dip his hands in a bag that had cum-laced napkins in it, I'm pretty sure you should be thanking me for my quick thinking."

She searches my face for a sign of sincerity, and when she realizes how truthful I'm being, she bursts out laughing and drags a hand over her face. "Oh my God!"

"I had to do something, so I promised him a bunch of burgers."

"No. You promised him the toys from the Happy Meals."

"Whatever." I shrug.

"Well, they release one toy a week. The previous ones are no longer available." She glowers back at me, and my face falls as realization dawns on me. I threw the damn toy out of the window, so now I need to figure out a replacement.

Great.

"Come on." She tilts her head toward the door, and I reluctantly follow behind, hating this place more and more with every step I take, despite not stepping through the door yet.

———

Oh God. I'm in literal hell.

A cesspit on a magnitude scale. There's garbage. Every-fucking-where.

Kids. Everywhere.

Hundreds of the whiny, sobbing, screaming, crying, loud little fuckers. Everywhere.

Adults who have lost all their faculties. Any sense of moral code has gone out the fucking window and into the abyss.

It's savage.

Absolutely brutal.

Why the hell would anyone choose to come here?

"This burger is so good. It makes me so happy I was man of the match." Bryce grins from ear to ear like I gave him a billion dollars, yet I struggle to function enough to respond. Ketchup drips from his chin, and I shift closer to the window and contemplate throwing myself out of it to get away from this nightmare.

"Would you like to try a fry?" Gia asks, holding said fry up to me.

"No," I snap.

"You said you'd get me the toys from the Happy Meals." Bryce's solemn voice surprises me, given he was just excited over a miserable-looking burger.

"Buddy, Reed can't get you the toys that are already out."

"He said he was going to get them. Why did you lie and become a litter bug?" His eyes narrow on me. "Why are you having a baby with him? He's not a very good example. We don't need him."

"Bryce. Don't be so rude," Gia snaps back at him, and as grateful as I am, I'm also momentarily stunned. After all, the kid is right, but I'm not about to tell him that, not with the death glare he has aimed in my direction.

I lean forward and steeple my hands on the table. The

table I insisted on Gia sanitizing twice before I would sit down at it.

"I'll get you the toys because I promised them. I'm not a liar, Bryce. I don't break promises." He swallows, and I continue. "I shouldn't have littered, you're right."

His eyebrows rise.

"That's not a good example, and I won't do it again, so thank you for the reminder."

Gia's hand moves beneath the table to my thigh, and something in her touch spurs me on.

"I'm very lucky your mom is having our baby, and more importantly, I'm lucky your mom has you too. That way, you can help us and remind me of where I'm going wrong." I laugh awkwardly on the last part, and so does Gia, while Bryce seems to be contemplating my words. He doesn't say anything for a minute, but when he does open his mouth, I wait with bated breath.

"You need a new car." This time, I throw my head back on a genuine laugh. He isn't wrong. Not one of my thirty-two cars is a family car.

I never anticipated a family.

FOURTEEN

WHEN WE ARRIVE HOME, Reed doesn't ask if he can come inside; he simply takes it upon himself to follow us, and I can't say I'm disappointed.

Chester barks when we enter, and Reed grumbles under his breath about him being a "Fucking wolf hound that needs a new home."

"He's a German Sheperd," I clarify.

He scrunches his nose. "Whatever. He's shedding hair all over me." He grimaces, swiping his hands down his pants even though Chester hasn't so much as approached him yet. "I probably need some vaccination or something."

I give him my attention, suddenly thinking about the baby. "Do you have allergies?"

"Lots," he responds. I feel the color drain from my face, and my stomach drops.

His eyes search mine. "Hey, are you okay?"

"I-I ..." I shake my head. "The baby," I whisper, and place my hand on my bump.

Reed's face whitens. "Shit. I'll call the doctor."

My ass finds the couch, and he starts tapping away on his phone.

"Jesus Christ, you pair are suited." Tyson strolls into the living room shirtless. "So what if he has a few fucking allergies and doesn't like dogs, get over it. The kid will come out sneezing, at worst."

"You don't like dogs?" Bryce asks, his face falling, and he stares at Reed as if he just told him the worst news possible.

Reed's spine stiffens, and he turns to face Tyson, pinning him with a thunderous glare. "I'll have you know, in actual fact, I happen to like dogs, and they like me." Reed puffs his chest out.

Tyson raises an eyebrow. "Oh yeah? Name one fucking breed you like."

Reed's commanding jawline tics as I watch on at the two men facing off with one another over a dog. "A bulldog is my favorite breed because I own one." Reed's handsome face turns smug, and he lifts his chin.

"You do?" Bryce asks, and he springs up from the couch.

"You do?" I really can't imagine Reed as a dog owner. Not when he's so … particular.

"I do." He crosses his arms over his chest. "Hence the fucking vaccinations to stop the itching."

Tyson huffs, then throws himself down in the chair. "Well, you can't get vaccinations to help you like kids, Reed," he taunts, and I narrow my eyes on him. He did not just say that, with Bryce in the room, no less.

"You don't like kids?" Bryce's eyes ping-pong between the two of them.

"Well, good thing I love them too, then, huh?" Reed counters.

Tyson scoffs and throws his arm out. "Please, we've seen how you act around kids. You've no clue how to deal with them."

I rub my temple as their petty argument goes on. "I take

my best friends' kids out all the time, actually." Reed glares back at Tyson.

"They must be desperate." Tyson grunts. "Surprised you get them home okay."

Reed narrows his eyes, and I swear I see the muscles on his back contract through his shirt. "Why are you here again? Because I'm here for Gia and *my* baby, and I'm just trying to understand what your place is here."

"That's something you won't ever understand," Tyson spits out, then stands, and they look like they're about to go to war. "I'd love to stay and argue, but I'm going on a date." He grins in my direction.

Reed's shoulders drop, and all the tension leaves his body in an instant.

"Is he staying tonight?" Tyson heaves a thumb in Reed's direction but looks at me.

"Yes," Reed answers before I have a chance to.

I shake my head. "That's not necessary."

"If our baby has allergies, I might be needed here. I'm staying."

I want to tell him that's a ludicrous argument, but I bite my tongue to stifle a giggle at Tyson's bugged-out eyes.

"Okay, on that dumb note, I'm out!" he declares.

"Don't forget to put a fucking shirt on. Nobody wants to see that shit," Reed bites out, and Tyson heads out the door, giving Reed the finger as he does. It's on the tip of my tongue to tell him every hot-blooded woman wants to see someone with Tyson's physique bare, but I think better of it.

Reed's phone pings. "The doctor says we don't need to worry, but he's made us an appointment for a scan." He smiles down at me with excitement glistening in his eyes that has hope stirring in my chest.

Please don't let us down. I can't lose another family again.

FIFTEEN

REED

SHE PUT me on the fucking couch. I stab my fist into the pillow again. The couch!

These sheets are not the Egyptian silk cotton I'm used to; it's a good thing her scent is covered in them, otherwise I'd insist on burning the useless fuckers.

The wolf dog stares at me; the damn thing hasn't shut its eyes all night, and I'm starting to wonder if dogs sleep with their eyes open. Is that a thing?

Rolling over, I wince at the sharp pain of the couch spring sticking in my back. My chiropractor will have a field day with me next week. That's if I can walk or even leave this house in one piece, given the way the fucking wolf stares at me like I'm his next meal. "Jesus, this is ridiculous."

A loud bark shocks the shit out of me, and I turn to face it.

"You want to eat me, don't you?"

It continues to glare at me.

"Well, I'm not your dinner, fuckwit."

It moves toward me, and like my ass is on fire, I spring up

from the couch. Like hell, I'm staying down here a minute longer with that thing.

As I leave the living room, the dog climbs onto the couch, circles it, then settles down on the pillow.

Slowly, I tiptoe up the stairs and turn right at the top. I'd watched Gia's ass head in that direction when she announced she was going to bed before shoving sheets in my hand like I wasn't welcome.

Well, screw that. If I want to be a part of her life, I intend to make sure she's aware.

Slowly, I push open her bedroom door and step inside. The bathroom light filters through from beneath the door, allowing me to witness the most gorgeous sight of her lying on her side, one leg thrown over the comforter and the other tucked beneath it. Her soft snores have me smiling, and I inch my way closer to her.

Glancing around the room, I take in the furnishings; it's neat, tidy, and has a homely feel that I'm missing in mine. My gaze latches onto the photo beside her bed, the same as the one on the sideboard downstairs, and my gut knots at seeing them together, happy and smiling, and here I am, the intruder.

When she moves, it draws my attention away from the bedside table. She wears a camisole top that has ridden up to expose her stomach, a stomach I'm desperate to touch and mark as mine. Small, silvery purple lines show the stretch of her skin, and I've never seen anything so incredible before. My mouth waters to trace the path of the lines covering our baby. Her heavy tits look like they're attempting to fight their way free from the camisole, and I lick my lips as I imagine how big her soft nipples have grown.

"What are you doing in here?"

I hadn't realized her eyes had fluttered open during my perusal, and suddenly, I want to show her everything I've been imagining. I want to touch her exactly how I crave and mark her precisely how I envisage.

So instead of using my words, I kneel on the bed beside her and slip the strap down on her top. Goosebumps spread out down her arm, and our eyes remain locked on one another's, the room filling with desire as she sucks in a sharp breath.

As my fingers brush against her skin, my cock jumps at the contact. I lean into her and press a soft kiss on the swell of her tit. Fuck, I wonder if she leaks milk yet?

My tongue darts out without thought, desperate to get in on the action, and she moans as I suck tenderly against her flesh.

"Oh god, Reed." Her fingers find my hair, and she tugs on the strands, pinching my scalp, and I suck harder to leave my mark.

I give her a gentle push, and she rolls onto her back, allowing me the space to settle beside her, and the movement exposes her full breast to me.

As my eyes roam over her delectable body, my heart hammers in my chest. I've never seen anything so magnificent in my entire life. This moment is profound, filled with awe, tenderness, and longing.

It's filled with everything I've never had or wished for, but I know deep inside I won't ever want anyone else.

She's it for me.

They're it for me.

They're my everything.

Her areola is swollen and dark, and the tip of her nipple is pebbled, begging me to suck on it. The bump protecting our baby is settled between us, and as the heat of her gaze soaks into my skin, I move my hand to caress our baby.

"Reed?" Her eyes are filled with unshed tears, uncertainty swimming in them.

"I won't let you down. I'm not going anywhere."

She nods, and my hand settles on her stomach. It's solid, and that thought makes me proud. A barrier of protection on the outside and our love on the inside means nothing can harm our little one.

I've got a lot to learn, but I'm determined to do it.

I span my hand wider, loving the feel of her soft skin, and the more my hand travels, the harder my cock becomes. When Gia whimpers a sound of contentment, I give in to the need to feel the softness of her nipple on my tongue.

My mouth wraps around her nipple, and she holds my head in place while I suck hard, gently tugging on her peak as if pleading with it to give me another sign of our child's existence.

She moans with each swipe of my tongue, and the sound makes my balls ache for release, pre-cum dripping from the slit and giving me no choice but to climb over her and settle myself between her parted legs.

My hands wrap around the fabric of her panties, and I tug them down while she leans up on her elbows to watch me. Then I release my cock from my boxers before throwing them to the floor.

I wrap my hand around my thick length, and she licks her lips, and as hungry as I am for her to taste me, I want inside her pussy. I want to fuck my woman as she lies completely exposed for me. As if sensing my thoughts, she lifts the camisole over her head, causing both her tits to bounce, and pre-cum slips down my shaft at the action, and I welcome it with a groan.

"Fuck, that's it. Play with those tits for me, beautiful."

Lips parting, she pushes them together, and I position my cock at her entrance. Her big nipples touch, and I hiss through my teeth at the feral need surging through me. I slam inside her, causing them to bounce, then I rear back and repeat the action.

"Christ, that's good," I groan through gritted teeth.

Slam.

"Don't stop, Reed. Again."

Her words spur me on, and I watch in rapture as her nipples point with pleasure. She caresses them and strokes over the soft skin, and I pound into her again and again.

"That's it. Take this cock in your little cunt, Gia."

Wetness pools between us as Gia's pussy welcomes my words, encouraging me further. "Drip all over my cock, beautiful." I move one hand to find her stomach while the other holds her hip. "You look so good swollen for me, baby." *Slam.*

Sweat drips from me as I thrust into her harder and harder, enamored by the way her pregnant body moves with each surge.

Fuck, she's incredible. "All swollen and round for me."

Thrust.

She moans louder and her pussy clenches.

"Feed me, beautiful. Give me your tits. Let me suckle from you."

She arches her spine and lifts one of her tits toward me, so I bend down over our bump and suck roughly on her peaked nipple. I swear I can taste something on my tongue, and a loud rumble leaves me, and my balls draw up. As she gasps, pleasure cascades between us while her hips pump in time with mine. I grunt and thrust inside her, then hold myself as deep as possible. My hot cum splashes against her inner walls, and I bite into her tit to stop myself from shouting out.

"Reeeed!" she screeches as I flood her pussy, taking her over the edge with me.

Pure euphoria engulfs me, taking my breath away in the process, and as I pull back to stare into her eyes, I know one thing for sure. Gia Mathers needs to be my wife. I just need her on board with it.

SIXTEEN

GIA

REED LIES BESIDE ME, pressing kisses to my breast. His thick palm spans over bump, and when the baby moves, his hand follows.

"Tell me about Jaxon," he whispers, and a chill runs through me. His hand stops moving, and he pulls me almost impossibly closer to him. So tight his warmth seeps into my skin, giving me the strength to tell him about the man I thought I would spend the rest of my life with.

"He was shot when he stepped in to help someone in a mugging." I swallow hard, then continue. "He was home on leave, but he'd only been here two days."

"I'm sorry," he whispers, then he stiffens and shakes his head. "That's a lie. I said I would never lie to you."

My mouth falls open, and I move to face him, but he shakes his head.

"What I meant was, I'm sorry that happened to you, but I'm grateful I get to have you."

His explanation softens the harshness of his previous

words, and when he presses a kiss against my breast, I surrender and rest my head back on the pillow.

"We met in high school." I stroke his head with the tips of my nails, something I find soothing. It's almost as if we both need to feel one another to believe we're in one another's arms. "He was a scholarship student, and I was the rich kid." I laugh at remembering how he used to joke with me. "He wanted to study law, same as me." As I smile down at Reed, he lifts his head.

"What happened?"

"Bryce." I smile. "Bryce happened, and when we found out I was pregnant, it changed everything."

Reed watches me closely, but I'm not sure why. "As teenagers with an unplanned pregnancy, the best plan was for him to join the military, so that's what he did. He made the sacrifice for our family, and not once did he complain about it." A proud smile spreads over my face at the recollection of how Jaxon stepped up to provide a stable family unit for us.

REED

"The best plan was for him to join the military, so that's what he did. He made the sacrifice for our family, and not once did he complain about it." A whimsical smile spreads over her face, and my heart beats faster.

How the hell do I compete with that?

The man sounds incredible. He gave up his future for Gia and their baby. When I so quickly planned to give up my child to keep my future.

Nausea rushes through me, and my hand stills on her stomach. She will hate me. I'm nothing compared to this man, and she deserves so much more. Hell, I hate myself.

"My father hated Jaxon, everything he stood for."

My chest tightens at the mention of her father, and when I hear her swallow and shift uncomfortably, something inside me snaps into protective mode to shield her from the feelings she's having. This is difficult for her, and she needs me to be strong for her and our baby. I go back to stroking over her bump, hoping it soothes her as much as it does me.

"He felt he was beneath me." She clears her throat. "I'd already moved out to live with Jaxon and his family, and no less than a few weeks later, I was announcing my pregnancy."

She said she was in high school when she met him, so she couldn't have been much older. "How old were you?"

"I was seventeen and still in high school."

"And your father allowed it?" I raise an eyebrow, because something tells me George Fanzio would have done his utmost to prevent his only child from leaving home for a life of potential poverty.

She shakes her head. "He tried to stop me. Cut off access to my money. I have the shares to the business my mother left me, and after Jaxon's death, he tried to cause trouble again. The only thing he's bothered about is his precious reputation and money. He's determined to get the shares one way or another."

I suck in a sharp breath at the mention of the shares, and this time, my movement doesn't go unnoticed.

Her eyes dart up to mine, a steely determination in them that makes my stomach tighten. "I won't back down, Reed. That center is Jaxon's legacy, and that's what it will remain. This community helped me when I needed it the most." She means when her father abandoned her. "When my father withdrew my private education and college funds, it was the community fundraising that enabled me to continue, then go on to further my education. Without that center, I would've never become a lawyer. We never would have owned our own house and had the stability for Bryce that we have today."

"That's why you helped that girl at the center?"

She nods. "It is. She's one of the many underprivileged who deserve the same education and welfare as anyone else. The center supports those less fortunate, and I intend to be there for them like they were for me. I work pro bono two days a week, and the rest of my shifts enable us to be financially stable."

Jesus, she's incredible. Mase once said I didn't have a compassionate bone in my body, and fuck, was he right.

Maybe I should change that? Do better for her and our kids. I place a tender kiss on her exposed skin. I'm in awe of this woman for so many reasons, and her kindness is just one of them.

"I'm in awe of you, Gia." I swirl a lock of her hair around my finger. "I need you to know I've stepped away from working with your father." Guilt lances through my chest at my own words.

"You have?" Her eyes glisten with unshed tears, and poison slithers through my veins at what I'm keeping from her.

But I push all my feelings of wrongdoing aside and give her the support she deserves. "You're my family now, and I want to stand by you and Bryce." My palm rests over our baby. "The baby too." And I mean every word of it.

I clear my throat and change the conversation, hoping she can't see the betrayal I feel seeping from my eyes. "What happened to your mother?"

She bristles, and I caress her skin, loving the way our baby presses against the palm of my hand. I wonder if the baby can feel me there? I wonder if it's a little foot or hand pushing against my fingers, causing my blood to rush through my veins with a fierce need to protect our baby. Everything about her stomach is amazing, and the fact that our little one is growing just beneath my palm has possession infiltrating my bloodstream.

They're mine.

Her solemn tone cuts through my thoughts. "She passed away when I was a child. My father hasn't been the same since."

"He's bitter." I crook an eyebrow and chuckle. Bitter would be an understatement to describe the man with so much anger inside him it's a wonder he hasn't given himself a heart attack.

"He's twisted," she says as her eyes meet mine, and my

eyebrows knit together, but before I have a chance to elaborate, she pushes the sheets from off her legs and heads toward the bathroom. "I have to pee really bad; your child is jumping on my bladder."

I watch her ass sway as she leaves, and my cock swells while my palm twitches to return to her stomach, already missing her touch.

I've never wanted a pregnant woman before, but now it's all I want.

SEVENTEEN

REED

AS SOON AS she walks into the bathroom, I throw off the sheets and follow her, and her startled eyes widen when I enter.

"Reed … what are you doing?"

I ignore her little outburst and switch on the shower. "I need to wash the dog off. I shouldn't have gotten into bed with you until I had."

Her eyebrows shoot up. "Now?"

"Hmm," I muse absently.

She giggles and shakes her head. "Can I finish peeing first?"

Her words still me, and my brow furrows as my gaze roams over her. I've never been in the vicinity of a woman peeing before, yet it felt natural to follow her in here. All I want to do is take care of her. Her swollen stomach housing my baby pushes her tits high, and I long to caress her, all of her. They're both mine, after all.

"Have you finished?" I whisper. The atmosphere in the room becomes thick with something indescribable.

"Yes," she whispers back, so faintly I almost don't hear it; her green orbs never leave my own. I reach for the toilet paper and break some off, then kneel at her feet. Her breath flutters over my face with the rise of her chest. "R-Reed?"

"Shh, it's okay, baby." I tuck her hair behind her ears. "Let me take care of you."

She swallows hard and scrutinizes me.

"Open your legs and let me take care of you." I nod toward her legs, and when she spreads them wider, I delight in the trust she puts in me. It feels like a turning point in our relationship, and my chest thumps with glory as I take the tissue and gently wipe at her entrance with a tenderness I didn't know I was capable of.

My breathing hitches and my cock twitches. Not because of some weird fetish, but because she's allowing me to intrude on something that is beyond private, something probably nobody has done for her before, and every muscle in my body swells with elation. She's allowing me to care for her and giving me the control to be the man I long to be. A caregiver, a homemaker, and a family man. Something I thought I was incapable of becoming, and it's the greatest gift she could grant me.

I wipe at her slick folds again, hating the moisture gathered on the tissue paper. Knowing I'm swiping away my cum from where it belongs irks me. "There you go, baby. All nice and clean." I lean forward, and our lips touch briefly before I pull back, and my cock is as hard as a fucking stone again.

I will not fuck my future wife on a toilet.

But in the shower is just fine.

GIA

What the hell just happened?

My lips tingle as he pulls away, and I touch my finger to them.

Did I get turned on by a man wiping away my …? My cheeks flame with embarrassment, but when Reed stands to his full height and I see his cock standing proudly and dripping with pre-cum, I almost reach out to bring him to my mouth.

"Shower." He tilts his head toward the shower, and I nod. My legs are wobbly as I get to my feet, and when he reaches past me to flush the toilet, I have to grip onto his bicep to stop myself from falling. He chuckles at my clear state of shocked arousal, then takes my hand, and I follow him into the shower.

He spins me so my back is to his front, then begins massaging my shoulders, washing away the tension of the day. When his hands work into my hair, I could cry out from the comfort washing over me. His fingers work into my scalp, and I moan when he lathers my hair, washing it for me. As the suds slide down my body, I can smell the conditioner he's squirting into his hands. "I always wondered where you got that scent from." He chuckles beside my ear, and goosebumps break out over my skin. "I've jerked off to the smell of peaches for months."

"Would you like me to make sure your pussy is clean?" he whispers in my ear, earning a shudder, and he smiles against me as his hands travel over my breasts and continue massaging me.

"Ye-yes."

"Good girl." He kisses the side of my face, then my neck, and I arch my back when his hands breeze over my full tits. "Place your foot on the shower seat."

I move quickly, doing as he asks, and he moves in front of me before kneeling beneath the showerhead.

Water cascades over his handsome face, and his muscles ripple as he jerks his cock once, twice, three times before a gush of pre-cum coats his fingers. When he lifts them to my mouth, I suck them inside, and my tongue swirls over his digits, causing him to hiss. Then he pulls them out, and I feel the loss instantly. He uses both his hands to separate my folds.

"Fuck, you're still dripping from me. I'm going to clean you up, Gia. Make you nice and clean so I can create a mess again. Okay?"

Okay? Is he serious? Every cell in my body is alive, every part of me coiled tight with anticipation. My pussy is slick from our arousal, and when his hot tongue slides through my folds and swirls in my pussy hole, I almost combust with the sensation. Again and again, he laps at me, eating his cum from me like a starved man, and the sounds that rumble from his chest are animalistic.

"Fuck yeah, keep fucking my face, baby. Keep feeding me my cum."

My core contracts, and I imagine it forcing the cum from inside me while I grip onto his hair to stabilize myself.

"Don't stop, Reed. Keep licking. Please don't stop."

"Fuck yes," he grunts.

My hips rise to fuck his face. "Lick it. Lick it away." My mouth spills the dirty words without thinking, my mind lost in the sea of pleasure he conjures. "Don't stop ..." My words hang in the air as my orgasm hits me and stars dance in front of my eyes. "Yesss!"

As he slowly lowers my foot to the floor, I cling onto the shower wall in a post-orgasmic state of bliss. Then he swipes at his mouth. "I never thought I'd enjoy tasting my own cum." He grins at me.

I rise onto my tiptoes and pull him in for a deep kiss, tasting myself on him, and when I pull back, we're both breathless. "You taste incredible." Something akin to gratitude passes over his face, and I make a note to give him more compliments, as many as he gives me.

"Are you sore?" he asks, and steps forward to hold my hips while delivering me with another kiss.

"Yes, but I want more. I crave you." I kiss him again and feel his smile against my lips. "I don't know how I went so long without sex."

He waggles his eyebrows. "I know, right? I bet it's been"— he looks at his wrist, as if to check the time—"all of ten minutes."

I swat at his chest. "I was meaning me not having sex in three years, and now I'm hungry for it."

He freezes, his body coiling tight, then he pulls back and stares down at me, and I scan his face, searching for the reason for the change in him. "Three years?"

I glance away and grab the shower gel, unwilling to do this here and now.

"You said Jaxon died six years ago. So, who did you have sex with three years ago?"

When I ignore him, he grabs the shower gel from me and places it back on the shelf. "Who, Gia?"

I take a deep breath and turn to face him. "I was lonely and a little drunk. It was a one off and has never happened again." I rub at my forehead and grimace at the way his chest rises rapidly. "It should never have happened." It shouldn't have happened; we both knew it.

"Who?" His voice ricochets off the shower doors, and I flinch.

I shrink away, knowing this will hurt him. "Tyson."

He stares at me in utter disbelief, and I didn't miss the way he jolted as I delivered his name on a soft whimper.

His Adam's apple slowly slides down his throat and back up again. His green orbs darken, and his nostrils flare. "You're mine," he states, and it isn't a question, but I answer anyway.

"I am."

He lunges forward and spins me to face the shower door. "You're mine, and that baby in you is mine!" he roars, and pushes down on my spine, then kicks my feet apart.

"Ye-yess." I tremble at his heavy-handedness, but arousal flares inside me at the possessive way he maneuvers my body to please him.

Jaxon's passion was always tender, and Reed's is out of control, possessive and borderline feral, but he has his softer moments too. He's the perfect combination of love and aggression. So when he slams roughly inside me with no more preparation, I moan in awe of the man filling me so brutally, providing me with something I never knew I wanted until I met him. Allowing me to embrace the darkness I've kept hidden.

My scalp stings when he wraps my hair around his fist and yanks my head back, and I savor it. Eyes rolling, I give myself over to him, then he slams forward, taking my breath away with the brutality.

"You're fucking mine!"

EIGHTEEN

REED

WHEN I LEFT Gia in bed this morning, it took everything in me not to slide between her legs and pump her full of my cum again, but given we barely slept all night, I figured she wouldn't appreciate me disturbing her again.

Knowing Tyson has fucked my girl makes me feel more possessive and wilder with rage than ever before. He's had a part of her, one I thought was solely for me, and the bastard who took her hand in marriage.

But I'll fucking show him. I can be everything Gia and my family need and so much more.

Instead, I'm stuck at work listening to my best friends' so-called advice.

"So let me get this straight. You want to borrow my daughter so you can show your new family that you like kids." Shaw's lip curls into a sneer.

"I need to prove I like kids." I shrug a shoulder.

"You don't like kids," Tate tacks on.

"I can like them for a day." How difficult can it be?

"Hate to break it to you, but you're going to have to like them for more than a day if you expect Gia to move in with you," Owen adds.

"Kids are cute," Mase says, and I shoot him a glare. Why the fuck does he always get so sappy around babies and kids? "They like me." He grins like the cat that got the cream. They like him because he's nothing more than a kid inside a grown-ass man's body.

"Kids can like me," I grumble back.

Tate leans forward, and his eyes bore into mine. "Dude. You told Eleanor that Santa wasn't real."

"Who?"

He groans, then slaps a hand over his face, dragging it down dramatically. "Eleanor, the kid you're trying to borrow." Tate throws his arm out toward Shaw, the father of the kid in question.

All I know is, he's the one with the oldest child. So surely, that's the safest option, and I have a point to make to Gia and Bryce, but also the prick who won't go away. I need them all to know I'm a family man. The only man they need.

"I need a dog too," I admit with a grimace.

The guys look at each other with wide eyes, then back to me. It would be comical how shocked they are if I wasn't so irritated by their lack of enthusiasm for my situation.

How hard can it be to take a dog and child to the park to meet Gia and Bryce? To prove to them I'm everything they need, and more importantly, everything they want.

"Aren't you allergic to dogs?" Mase asks.

"Apparently, not all dogs." I lift a shoulder. I don't have a rash, so it appears Tyson's dog is a viable option to be around. I just need something with a little more character to it.

When Gia explained that the wolf dog wasn't theirs, but instead Tyson, the cockhead's, she suggested taking my dog to the park this weekend. When she added for me to bring my friends' kids too for a picnic, I don't know what I was more surprised at, the fact I felt like this was some sort of test or the fact I'd have to sit outside and eat in an open space, where it's common knowledge bugs are every-fucking-where.

Why would anyone choose to eat outside in a park? Around animals and kids and bugs and dirt. Ew … A shudder ripples through me.

"Oh, and she has another man living with her. Tyson." I spit his name out like poison on my tongue. "All beefed up, and the kids fucking love him." I sneer. "He's just waiting in the wings for me to fuck up."

"How do you know?" Shaw asks.

"Huh?"

"How do you know he's waiting for you to fuck up? He could be her brother, like in Tate's situation when he punched the kid." He's referring to the time Tate unleashed hell on a guy in Ava's apartment and it turned out to be her brother. I wince at the memory.

"He's not her brother. She said he's her husband's best friend."

"There you go." He nods, as if that clarifies things. It doesn't, not for me anyway. They look like a family unit, and I'm the one intruding, the one on the outskirts looking in. Not needed. I have to make a stand in this dynamic, make sure this shithead knows his place.

"You're jealous?" Owen's eyebrows rise.

"No. I'm not fucking jealous," I snap back. "I'm just saying she has someone waiting for me to fuck up."

Needing to wrap up my plan, I turn to face Shaw, who stares intensively at me. "Can I borrow her or not?" I ask. We've wasted enough of my time already this morning.

Shaw sits back in his chair and narrows his eyes at me. "If you agree to do something for me, then I agree to let you borrow *Eleanor*."

I steeple my hands on the desk and sit forward in my chair.

"Go on …"

"Emi's asked me to go to a charity event organized by Luca." He curls his lip at the mention of his brother-in-law's name. Luca Varros is a Mafia capo who Shaw refers to as a controlling, ball-busting bastard. My poor friend has to jump through hoops to please him and barely has any control over his own life. When he accidentally knocked his now-wife Emi up during a one-night stand, he was forced into an arranged marriage by her brother. Good thing for him, he was smitten with Emi from the beginning. I nod along, and he continues to explain. "The last thing I want to do is go to a charity event organized by that demanding fucker. I'd rather pour bleach in the slit of my cock. So …" He smiles broadly. "You can borrow Eleanor and play the doting uncle for the day."

"Afternoon," I state, just so he knows I don't need the kid for the day.

He wafts his hand in my direction as if that piece of information wasn't important, despite it being vital to my plans. "In return, you attend the event as Emi's plus one." His smile somehow becomes bigger than before.

The other guys chuckle at Shaw's proposal, and I lean back to contemplate his suggestion. It will be like another work event. I can handle it, no problem. The kid, on the other hand, I'm not so sure, but I'll give it a go. Worst-case scenario, I'm never allowed to borrow her again. I tip my head from side to side; it's actually not a bad scenario.

"What will the excuse be for you not attending with Emi?" Mase questions.

Shaw balks. "She will just be grateful I don't put myself in a position to be shot by her brother again. We can tell him I'm sick and Reed offered to support her. He'll lap that shit up. Shows we're a team and all that."

Owen chuckles to himself and shakes his head as if the whole thing is ridiculous when, in reality, it's pretty genius.

"Deal." I smile back, mirroring Shaw's happiness.

Everything is coming together perfectly, and with that in mind, I push aside the concern in Owen's eyes as he stares at me, not prepared to deal with the shitstorm brewing in the name of George Fanzio.

Now all I need is a dog.

NINETEEN

REED

I CAN'T BELIEVE I'm doing this. An actual building specifically for dogs. I'm outside a dog pound, and my heart feels like it's about to explode out of my chest.

My phone beeps, so I glance down at the screen.

Shaw: Did you get one yet?

Tate: He had two last month. I don't know what happened to them.

What the fuck is he talking about?

Tate: Pretty sure I heard them howling in his office.

I smirk at his message.

Last month, is that all it was? The truth is, since seeing Gia again, I've not given any other woman another thought until now, and the thought of the two women Tate is referring to makes me shudder. I sure as hell never fucked them, despite their many advances. I haven't slept with anyone since the first night with Gia; that's how much she has me wrapped up in her.

My pulse races, and howling noises filter through the closed door. I can only hope that bulldogs don't howl, leave a mess, or make much noise in general. Hopefully, they simply sleep. A lot.

> Owen: Go inside and get the fucking dog, Reed.

I scan the parking lot for cameras. The fucker has probably hacked the surrounding security system to witness my meltdown.

After tugging my tie from around my neck, I stuff it into my jacket pocket and open my top button. Then I lift my middle finger into the air and spin on the balls of my feet, hoping whatever camera he's watching from picks up the action.

I must look like a lunatic to the outside world, but who gives a fuck. Right now, I feel like one.

> Mase: Send us a photo when he's home.

He? Home?

I give my head a shake. Mase needs therapy, for sure.

With a deep breath and with a confidence I don't feel, I throw open the door to the dog pound. A girl who resembles a teenager is behind the counter, blowing a bubble while she taps away on her phone. She barely lifts her eyes toward me when she opens her mouth again. "Hey, welcome to Dogs Are For Life. How can I help you today?"

Dogs are for life. Seriously? Who would want to deal with

a dog for life. It's more like a life sentence for the buyer for being good enough to purchase one.

I clear my throat and feign a smile I don't feel. "I want to purchase a dog."

"Please fill out this adoption paperwork," she says in a monotone voice, then pushes some papers toward me without giving me her attention, and I rear back at her rudeness. I'm hardly surprised they have so many dogs needing homes; she's not exactly selling herself or the residents. "Then we will be in touch," she adds on, and I jolt at her words. Be in touch?

Hell no. My nostrils flare and my jaw clenches. I need a dog today; she's fucking up my plans, and it just won't do. So, I lean over the counter. "I want one today. Now, to be precise." I stab my finger down on the counter. "Preferably, an old dog." They're saying dogs should be for life, so this way, its life is almost over, and I won't have to deal with it for too long.

She slowly brings her eyes up to face me. "What kind of breed are you looking for?"

My shoulders straighten. We're finally getting somewhere. "A bulldog."

Then she shakes her head slowly. "We don't have any bulldogs." She shrugs, then turns her attention back to her phone, dismissing me.

That's it? *We don't have any bulldogs?* Don't have any? I glance around the reception area and wince at the sound emanating from beyond the walls. This is essentially a dog shop; they have to have some, but I don't have time to argue. I dig around in my jacket, take out my black card, and slide it across the counter. "I'm sure you can find one." She lifts her head, and I drill my stare into hers.

When she shakes her head, annoyance shoots up my spine and my temple tics. "Something that resembles one, then." I nod toward the card and give it a tap.

"Resembles a bulldog?" she repeats slowly, and I nod again, with a mocking smile. Jesus, the world is full of idiots.

"I'll go grab one that resembles a bulldog." She gives me a tight smile, snatches my black card, and my shoulders relax. "But it's not a thoroughbred," she tacks on over her shoulder, like I should know what the hell that means.

When she eventually returns with a dog in her arms, my stomach sinks at the realization this thing will depend on me, and good god, it's unsightly. I step back because what the fuck? Is it meant to look like that?

Its tongue hangs from its mouth like he's attempting to take his final breath, which is perfect if you ask me. Although, the idea of it drooling freaks me out and causes my chest to rise, and when she thrusts it into my arms like I should know how to hold it, I can't help the gag that leaves me.

Before I know what's happening, she's scanned my black card multiple times, shoved bags and paperwork against my chest, and almost marched me out of the building despite me not receiving answers to a multitude of questions.

Thank fuck, I purchased a new state-of-the-art, family-friendly SUV. I sure as hell need the space for all this shit.

Somehow, I get the car door open, and thankfully, the dog has the foresight to jump into the car seat while I quickly move round the trunk and shove the bags inside.

Now all I need is Shaw's child, and everything will be fine.

I can do this.

TWENTY

GIA

WHEN I SUGGESTED TAKING Bryce to the park to meet with Reed and his friends' children, along with his dog, he practically jumped at the chance, and now I feel a little guilty. When he was bickering with Tyson, I thought he was all talk, but clearly, I was wrong; the man promised to never lie.

"Where are they?" Bryce whines from beside me while kicking his sneaker into the dirt.

"Give him a chance, Bryce. He has a toddler and a dog to bring. He'll be here." I hope.

He lifts his head to face me, and his green eyes clash with mine. "Does he even have a dog?" Jeez, even my son is skeptical.

"He does." I nod, then run my hand over my bump to soothe the anxiety creeping in. Reed is late, and something tells me Reed is never late.

Bryce's eyes suddenly light up. "Can we go on the rowing boats?"

I push his hair from off his face. "Buddy, let's wait and see what Reed wants to do before we make any plans."

"Ugh." He groans. "I hope he's going to be a cool dad for our baby." My heart squeezes at how Bryce has adapted to the fact he will be a big brother. He's really enthusiastic, and when I explained to him Reed was the baby's father, his eyes flared with hope, and it's not lost on me that the hope wasn't just for the baby but for him too. I'm praying Reed doesn't let us down.

"Can you slow the hell down? You're insane. Oh God, I'm sorry."

I spin around at the sound of Reed's frantic bellow, and my eyes widen at the sight. He's pushing a stroller with the cutest little girl strapped inside, giggling away and practically steamrolling through people as he jogs toward us, trying to keep up with a small dog running in our direction on an extendable lead that should most definitely not be extendable. He looks two seconds short of exploding or abandoning the dog and toddler, and I can't help but stifle the giggle bursting to get out.

"He's here!" Bryce declares. "And he has a dog, Mom!"

Bryce rushes toward the dog and falls to his knees to greet him. "Hey, boy. I'm Bryce."

Reed finally comes to a standstill beside me. He's pale and panting, a frantic expression dripping off him. "Hey?" I smile coyly.

"Hey." He steps forward and grabs the back of my neck, yanking me toward him, and slams his lips against mine. When he pulls away from our kiss, he's breathless and panting. "I missed you," he says, then his shoulders relax, and my heart does a silly flutter at his words.

The little girl takes this moment to bounce, making the stroller move toward Bryce, and I step away from Reed to bend down and greet her. "Hello, pretty girl. What's your name, honey?"

"El-Eleanor."

"Oh wow, that's such a pretty name." I glance up at Reed to find him smiling down at me, all signs of previous hysteria gone. "How old is she?"

His eyebrows pull together. "Not old enough to walk, apparently," he grumbles, making me giggle at his sarcastic tone.

"Reed. What's your dog's name?" Bryce asks, and Reed stiffens, then shifts from foot to foot, and I search his face for answers.

"Bubbles!" Eleanor shouts, and the dog raises its head.

Reed grimaces and swallows. "Bubbles. He came with the name."

Bryce tilts his head from side to side as he surveys Bubbles. "I thought you said he was a bulldog?"

"He is." Reed nods along.

I choke on a laugh. His face is serious, yet the only thing that resembles a bulldog is the numerous wrinkles in his face. If I had to guess, I'd say he was a pug mixed with multiple other breeds.

"Well, he's very cute." I pet Bubbles, and he licks at my hand, and when he rolls over, my eyes widen. "Reed, I thought you said Bubbles was a he?" I point toward Bubbles, who's clearly not a he.

Reed winces. "The paperwork didn't say, and I didn't think to check what was down there. Bubbles should have some privacy." He lifts his shoulder, then darts his eyes away to deflect from the conversation.

I choke on his explanation, then shake my head as I stand and tug on the sleeve of his T-shirt while I raise up on my tiptoes. "You're an idiot," I whisper in his ear with a smile. "A hot one." As I pat his ripped chest, his Adam's apple slides slowly down his throat. Our eyes remain locked, an undercurrent ripples between us, and when I slide my eyes down his body, I lock onto the way his cock is tenting in his joggers.

"Fuck," he growls, then turns to adjust himself, making me bite into my lip at the thought of him being aroused at my simple comment and touch.

I don't ever remember having this effect on my husband. The sexual tension between Reed and me is something new, exciting, and slightly forbidden, given how I'm pregnant already, and we're just starting a relationship. A thought hits me square in the gut, and my heart tumbles. Is this a relationship?

"Damn fucking right it is." My heart skips a beat when I realize I'd voiced my thoughts aloud, and Reed grabs my ponytail, wraps it around his hand, elongating my neck, and his mouth lands on mine. The kiss is forceful and erotic, completely inappropriate for a park, but when his tongue slides over mine, all thoughts of our surroundings disappear.

"Mom! Can we go on the rowing boats?"

Reed stiffens and pulls back from me. His lip twitches as my chest rises from the power of his kiss. "You make me lose my damn mind." He doesn't look too sorry about it and clears his throat, then spins to face Bryce and Eleanor.

"Can you row?" he asks Bryce.

"Sure." He grins back at him, and I grimace at the thought of my son's attempts at rowing. Maybe I should point out he's never actually done anything other than the actions to the children's nursery rhyme.

"Reed. I'm not sure he's—"

He swats his hand through the air. "He'll be fine. Won't you, buddy?"

"Yes!" Bryce exclaims, and jumps into the air.

"I wanna row the boat." Eleanor speaks clearly this time.

"Of course she fucking does," Reed mumbles so low I don't think I'm meant to hear him.

Bryce bends down to unclip Eleanor, then turns to face Reed. "Eleanor can come too, right, Reed?"

Reed's face is blank, but his chest heaves and his hands

ball into fists and just as quickly uncurl, so I step forward to help him out. "Maybe Eleanor should stay with me."

Reed nods, but when Eleanor's bottom lip wobbles, he exhales loudly and drags a hand through his hair. "Eleanor." Her little head snaps up to his sharp tone. "If you go on the boat, no crying, do you understand me?"

She nods and stifles a sob, and I want to laugh.

"Right." He broadens his shoulders. "Let's do this." He appears to be talking to himself, and I smile behind my hand at his seriousness. It's meant to be a fun activity, but he looks like he's planning a war.

Something tells me this will not go as planned.

REED

He could row the fucking boat, he said. Like hell he can. Barely two minutes in and his arms hurt him too much to continue, and don't even get me fucking started on the drama to get on the damn boat to begin with. As soon as Eleanor realized that dogs were not welcome on rowing boats, she turned into the kid from *The Exorcist.* Her head practically spun with the tantrum that erupted from her.

In the end, I slipped the poor attendant, who could probably sue us for damage to his eardrums, a few hundred dollars so fucking Bubbles could join us for the experience of me rowing the fucking boat, all while listening to Bryce and Eleanor's rendition of the nursery rhyme. I swear he's screeching on purpose, setting my teeth on edge as he destroys each decibel.

"If you see a—" A loud scream erupts from Eleanor before Bryce even finishes the end of the song, and I wince.

Kill. Me. Now.

I blow out a deep breath to try to remain calm. "Bryce. Can you stop with the song now?"

"She likes it." He motions toward Eleanor, who grins at him like he hung the moon and stars.

"Bubbles. I wuv you. I wuv you!" Eleanor makes grabby hands toward the damn dog. To say she's obsessed with her is an understatement, and even I feel for him, her, as she inches farther away. "Tum to me, Bubbles." She falls forward on a giggle, making the boat rock slightly, and the dog edges farther away from her. I can actually relate to the dog's fear of her. If I had the opportunity, I'd do the same. "Bubbles, tum here." She crawls in the dog's direction.

Knowing how gruff I can be, I lower my tone to speak to her. "Eleanor, Bubbles doesn't want …" She moves so quick I don't see it coming and launches herself toward the dog, and Bubbles makes a rash decision. "Oh shit." She jumps over the boat and into the water.

Even the dog would rather die than deal with her.

"Bubbles!" Bryce shouts as he stands, and panic sets in.

"Bryce, sit down!" I snipe out.

A loud cry rips from Eleanor as she becomes hysterical. "Bubbles!"

I pinch the bridge of my nose, wishing I'd gone into the office instead of attempting to play happy fucking families at this hellhole.

"Reed. You need to help her." Bryce's eyes dart to mine, imploring me to do something.

"There's no helping her. She's not going to shut up about the damn dog." I motion toward Eleanor, who's now lying on the floor of the boat covered in snot and tears while mumbling various versions of the dog's name, not one of them coherent.

Bryce's brow furrows. "I mean Bubbles. She's drowning!"

I scoff. "Dogs can swim, Bryce. They don't drown."

"Reed. Look." He points toward the dog, and sure as shit, it appears to be going under. Possibly to get as far away from Eleanor as possible.

"Fuck!"

Eleanor somehow gets louder at Bryce's declaration. "Bubbles die. Bubbles dead ..."

Bryce stretches one of the oars over the side of the boat as if the damn dog is going to latch onto it, and when he drops it into the water and turns to me with wide eyes, I shake my head at him.

Fuck my life.

"Reed. Do something!" Bryce's panicked voice has me snapping out of my trance, and I move quickly, throwing myself overboard to save the damn dog, who's literally blowing bubbles, all while wishing I was the one drowning.

TWENTY-ONE

REED

AFTER RESCUING THE FUCKING DOG, I deposited it at Gia's feet before swimming back out to the boat where I waited with the kids for the rescue boat to come pull us back to the dock all because Bryce dropped the damn oar. I didn't dare climb back in the boat, for risk of tipping it, and hearing the kids kick up the damn song again was enough to make me wish I hadn't made it back to them at all.

Being soaked through sure as hell meant the day was over before it even started. When I dropped Eleanor back with Shaw, he found it hilarious that I was drenched, so I pushed the dog into his chest without giving him the option of accepting the challenge and wished him luck with dog sitting for the night. Then I made my way over to Gia's house because I deserve some fucking TLC after today.

To say she was shocked to see me was an understatement; her jaw almost hit the floor. She probably expected me to go home and lick my wounded pride, but I wouldn't do that when she could do it for me.

I bypassed her at the door and went straight upstairs to

use her shower. There was no way in hell I was getting any of the green shit I was covered in on her and my baby.

Tipping my head back into the warm stream of water, I revel in the thought of cleansing myself of one hell of a day.

There's a soft knock on the bathroom door, and before I have a chance to respond, Gia slips inside. My eyes meet hers through the shower screen, and my cock thickens as she slides open the door and drops her robe to the floor, leaving her in her underwear. I lick my lips and take in her white lacy bra that holds her heavy tits up, then slowly travel my gaze down her swollen stomach toward her lace-clad pussy.

By the time my eyes are back on her face, my cock is at full length, and I pump it angrily and step out of the shower.

"On your knees, Gia." My voice is thick with pent-up aggression, and it's as if she's here because she knew I'd need this to help me unwind.

She remains focused on me and lowers herself to the marbled floor.

"I need to own you." My voice comes out on a deep growl.

She nods with not a glimmer of fear, as if she's accepting of me and my need to regain control, and the thought makes my chest expand with possessiveness. She's mine, and she's given me the green light to use her, to own her.

I step forward and fist her hair into a ponytail, forcing her head back. "Open your mouth and stick out your tongue."

She complies instantly, parting her soft lips, and my cock jumps at her tongue resting over her bottom lip as if begging for a taste of me. Pre-cum slips from my swollen tip and over my fingers at the erotic scene before me. "My beautiful girl is going to get her throat fucked hard and fast," I rasp, and she moans, spurring me on. "I'm going to leave your mouth dripping with my cum, like a needy slut."

She whimpers, her face flushes, and her heavy chest rises.

"Then I'm going to eat it from you. But first, I'm going to

fuck your throat so damn hard you'll feel like a piece of you is missing when I pull out."

Her eyes flash with desire, and my pulse races at the prospect of her being turned on by rough sex.

"Is that what you want? You want me to lick my cum from your slutty lips?" I lick my lips, imagining tasting myself on her. Something I've only had the urge to do with Gia.

"Beg me." I yank on her ponytail. "Beg me for my cock."

"Please." She licks her lips. "Please, Reed. Give me your cum."

"Take off your bra. I need to see those tits." I growl like a wild animal. Fuck, I want all of her at once. "I'm going to fuck them later, and you're going to thank me. Do you understand?"

"Y-yes."

"Good girl."

And Jesus, she whimpers at my praising her.

I suck in a sharp breath at the adrenaline thrashing through me and try to rein in the need to unleash inside her so suddenly.

This isn't going to last long; I know it isn't, but I will spend all night making it up to her.

As soon as she sticks her tongue out again, I plow into her mouth, making her gag when I hit the back of her throat. "Good," I hiss. "Good girl," I croon, and slide in and out at a leisurely pace, allowing her to get used to my length. Then, as my balls ache with need, I slide farther down her throat, where I hold myself. Fuck, she feels like heaven. She breathes through her nose, and I delight in the way the corner of her mouth leaks spittle as she holds me there like the good girl she is.

I watch in rapture as her throat swells with my cock stuffed inside her. Reaching out, I gently clasp my free hand around her throat, then slide out and back in. Each time, I become more and more hyped up to fuck her hard and fast, but I'm willing myself to remain in control despite my finger-tips tightening on her throat with each punishing stroke of my cock.

"You can take all this thick cock, can't you?"

Faster and faster, my hips work, and she hums around my length. I tighten my grip on the back of her head and throat, sliding in and out at a frantic pace. My orgasm slams into me, and I quickly withdraw, releasing her throat so she can stick her tongue out for me as I explode. I hold my cock to her open mouth and squeeze the tip as ropes of hot, thick, white cum coat her tongue and chin, making her a glorious, sticky mess.

"Fucking beautiful," I pant out as my orgasm subsides while Gia remains kneeling, looking thoroughly fucked and simply stunning coated in my hot white cum.

"Stand," I grunt, barely able to speak with how wound up I feel. I hold my hand out for her, and she rises to her feet, tongue still out and dripping with my possession. Using two of my fingers, I scoop some cum onto my fingertips, then paint one of her nipples with it before repeating the process with the other. "Swallow," I command, and my cock twitches back to life as her throat works to swallow me down.

I scan her delectable body, her swollen tits begging to be toyed with, and a need to satisfy my craving for her becomes heightened when the bump moves, reminding me I helped create that. "I need to fuck you now, Gia. Hard and fast."

TWENTY-TWO

"I NEED to fuck you now, Gia. Hard and fast." The raw aggression emanating from him has my panties sticking to my pussy. Never have I had a man so passionate and powerful look at me as if he can't contain himself, and I relish it.

I spin on the balls of my feet and head toward the bedroom, adding a little sway to my hips. Knowing how attracted he is to my pregnant body gives me confidence I rarely feel.

"Fuck," he growls as I walk into the bedroom. Then I slip my panties down before crawling onto the bed. "Stay!" he barks, and I feel the heat of him behind me seconds later. "Just like that." He scoops some wayward strands of hair off my neck and lowers his head to kiss below my ear.

"I'm going to fuck you from behind while I play with you." He bands his arm around the front of me, trailing it over my protruding stomach, then up toward my breast, which he squeezes roughly. "I want to suck on your tits and lick my cum from you." He pushes his hard length against my back, and I moan wantonly. Squeezing again, he caresses the tight bud of my nipple with his fingertip. "Are you going to feed me too?" he whispers, and I break out in goosebumps from the anticipation.

Why the hell does the thought of feeding Reed turn me on so much? The idea of offering him something only I can provide and the thought of him taking pleasure from that has arousal flowing down my inner thighs. "Y-yes," I whisper, and he chuckles.

"You like the thought of me wrapping my lips around here." He strokes my areola, and I push against him in encouragement. "And sucking until you splash your hot milk on my tongue, making me hungry to fill you."

"Oh god," I rasp, and push back again. My throat's painful after the way he took me, but I don't have it in me to care because the things he's saying sound like a seductive promise of things to come.

"Beg me to suck from your tits, Gia." He nips at my neck, and all words leave my mind. "Beg me to feed from your tit, Gia."

"Reed, please."

"Beg me to suckle on you, because only you can give me what I need. Only you," he rasps, and it sounds like a plea.

He slides two fingers inside me while the other remains playing with my nipple. "Oh god," I pant.

"Do you want my thick cock inside you, stretching your little pussy?"

"Ye-yes. Please."

"Such a good girl." He releases me, and I fall onto my hands and knees on the mattress. Then he takes hold of my hips and slowly slides his thickness inside me, a contrast to the way I was used in the bathroom, but as quickly as the thought came, it is slammed from my mind with the powerful surge of his thrust. One after the other.

"That's it. Take all that thick cock." I cling to the bedsheets while he bounces off my ass. "Stretch for me." A sharp slap fills the air, and seconds later, my ass cheek is on fire. The bite of pain mixed with the pleasure has me burying my head into the sheets to avoid screaming out.

"Fuck, your slick pussy looks good with my cock stretching you wide." *Slam.*

"Who put this baby in you?" *Thrust.*

"Y-you did," I cry out.

"Who fills you with his cum?"

He powers into me.

"You, Reed."

"Only fucking me, Gia. Only I get to fill you with cum."

One hand moves while the other remains bruising on my hip, and when he strokes over my clit, my orgasm builds at lightning speed. I shuffle against him, and he slaps my ass. "Mine to control!" *Slam.* "Mine to pleasure." *Thrust.* "What are you?"

"Yours," I whisper, and bite into my lip to withhold the scream fighting to erupt from me. He rubs my clit harder.

"Come!" he demands, and I do, tightening around him, and my body tenses.

"Mine!" He slams inside me again with a roar, and his cum floods me, causing exhilaration to flash through me.

He pulls out of me, and I sag against the sheets, but he grips my thighs and encourages me to part them, then buries his head between them.

Holy hell, he's …

His warm tongue glides up and down my slit, then enters me, and I clench in desperation. "Rub your pussy on my face, Gia. Make me eat our cum, baby girl."

Holy shit, that's hot.

I lift my hips to meet the thrust of his tongue, and when he slides his hands under my ass to encourage my movements, a strangled mewl leaves my throat.

My tits bounce as I moan while lifting my hips wantonly,

chasing another orgasm with greed while remaining high from my previous. "My baby momma looks good riding my face." He slurps, and the sound makes me combust. Lights dance and my body tightens, and when his wet thumb slips inside my ass, darkness consumes me, the pleasure so intense I give myself over to it.

REED

Watching my cum spill from her has the feral beast inside me salivating at the mouth. I want to taste more of myself from her, my pleasure mixed with hers. Two broken, lost souls becoming one.

I think she blacked out, but I'm not done with her yet. My palms band around her smooth skin, and I pry her thighs apart and lower my head, and when she realizes what I'm doing, she lifts herself up slightly on her knees to give me access. "Reed?" Her voice is sleepy, and I smile to myself. She's definitely still high on the pleasure.

"Shh, I want to taste us, baby. I want to taste us both on my tongue."

She whimpers on my words, and my cock throbs. Jesus, she's perfect. She loves my dirty mouth and rough hand.

"Lick you clean for me to fill you again." I groan in delight at our taste and swipe my tongue over her hole, gathering the excess of cum still dripping from her.

"Oh god, Reed." She pushes back on my tongue as I swallow our combined juices.

"Fuck, we taste good, baby," I grunt, and my cock twitches back to life.

She pushes back again, and I give her ass a sharp slap. "Hold on tight, I'm going to devour you."

"Fuck," she groans, and buries her head in the sheets when I stick my tongue in her hole and swirl it around while pressing my thumb to her tight ring. Her muscle allows me access when I push harder, and my eyes roll with ecstasy at imagining taking her there too.

The scent of our arousal and the sounds of her pleasure have me driving my thumb deeper, and my tongue becomes wild as I fuck her ass hard with my thumb while she fucks my face. Then I slide a finger in alongside my thumb, and she clenches around me. Her body becomes taut, and she freezes, and when a stream of clear liquid floods my mouth, my cock explodes with uncontrollable ropes of pleasure.

Holy fuck.

TWENTY-THREE

REED

USING MY ELBOW, I prop myself up to watch her sleep. The moonlight shining through the split in the curtains allows me to witness her beauty while she rests for our baby. My hands alternate between caressing her tits and her bump, and I will them to never change despite knowing they're going to.

I've never felt so enamored by someone before. So fiercely protective and utterly obsessed. There's no way in hell she can ever leave me; I simply won't allow it.

I've watched each of my best friends fall for their girls and never understood it until her.

How one person can hold me captive, I'll never understand it, but I couldn't be more grateful. She's stolen my thoughts, my power, and my heart, and the little baby moving inside their momma makes my chest swell with love I never knew existed inside me.

It's like I've waited my entire life for her.

My cock thickens inside her, and my hands roam freely over her bump and up to her soft, heavy tits. I'll never tire of this, feeling her delicate body against my solid one, and the thought of spending another night away from her and our baby, hell, even from Bryce has anxiety building in my stomach.

For some odd reason, I just lie there, my cock as deep as it will go while she remains asleep, and the feeling of us being so connected at such a vulnerable time has every cell inside me swelling with pride. They're mine to protect forever.

I place a gentle kiss on her shoulder, and she mumbles in her sleep. The need to reassure her has my body pulling taut as I nuzzle into her hair with a softness normally absent from me.

"Shh, it's okay, baby. I'm here."

Does she dream of him? And the two of them in this very bed. A surge of jealousy consumes me, and when my eyes lock on to the photo beside her bed, anger slithers through my bloodstream.

They're mine now.

And nobody will take them away from me.

Not even George Fanzio.

GIA

An arm tightens across my chest, and it takes a moment for me to realize who it belongs to.

Reed.

The man who, in the space of a little over two weeks, has taken over my life in every sense of the word. He's become a fixture in our baby's future, a part of my daily plans, and as he thrusts his hips against my ass, I realize he's consumed me too. His cock is wedged inside me, but something tells me he's still asleep, and I smile against my pillow at the thought of how obsessed he truly is.

His lips suck on the back of my neck, and I glance over my shoulder to witness his bright-green eyes sparkling back at me with mirth.

"I thought you were asleep." I smile back dreamily.

"My cock was stirring." He thrusts against me for emphasis.

"Do you wake up like that every morning?" I bite into my lip to stifle my growing smile, already knowing his answer.

"Of course. But I don't wake up inside anyone's pussy. Not like this." He thrusts again.

"That's reassuring." I giggle.

His eyes narrow. "For some reason, I like to be connected to you."

"I've noticed," I deadpan.

Then he nuzzles against me, and goosebumps break out over my skin. "We have the baby scan today." He smiles into my neck while his thumb strokes over my peaked nipple, making me slick with need.

"We do," I pant out, and he thrusts again.

He strokes over my tender bud again, circling it, then squeezes my plump flesh before repeating the motion. His movements are slow and calculated, and a need builds inside me only he can satiate despite showing no intention of.

"I can't wait for your milk to come in," he breathes into my ear, causing me to shiver. "I'm going to lick it from all around here." His finger circles the tip of my nipple. "While you beg my cock to fill you."

I push back against him, and he grunts.

"Then I'll open my mouth and let you see the milk on my tongue."

My eyes roll as I push against him, and he remains still, his solid length hitting me deep inside.

"Letting it drip from me." He pinches my nipple, and my pussy tightens. "All warm like my cum."

I erupt around him, and my body takes over the need inside me, and when his hot cum splashes the inside of my walls, I cry out in pleasure.

"Good girl," he croons from behind me. "Good girl for taking what you need and letting me fill you."

"Mom! We don't have any milk left!" Bryce bellows from the other side of the bedroom door, and I freeze while his words replay in my mind.

TWENTY-FOUR

REED

MY LEG BOUNCES uncontrollably as I take in the waiting room. I scan the area, regretting not insisting on a home visit. At the right price, you can make anything happen, even a home consultation with a baby scanner.

Gia strokes my knee as if trying to reassure me, but it's impossible. The thought of the germs surrounding me and those I love is all-consuming. My skin feels like it's prickling, and I try but fail to get lost in my mind while being surrounded by the hazards and chaos of a doctor's waiting room.

"Mrs. Mathers." My heart plummets on the nurse's words, and my body stills as a red haze of anger takes over me. She needs my surname. This is our baby. Ours.

Not his.

"Reed, that's us." Her voice is a delicate whisper, and all I can manage is a grunt. Then she takes my hand in hers and our gazes collide and every wrong is suddenly righted. "Are you ready to see your baby?"

"Our baby," I quip back, and she smiles.

"Our baby," she corrects with an encouraging nod.

"Come on. You'll love it. Seeing our baby on the screen is a gift." She tugs me to my feet, and I want to tell her I already do love the baby, and I love her too, but I keep my mouth shut. I don't want to freak her out; she'll think I'm crazy, that this is too soon, but I feel it deep inside.

They're my everything.

My heart pangs in my chest, and I swallow back the rare emotion in the back of my throat at the way she acknowledges our baby as ours, then gift her with an even rarer smile, one she mirrors, with her teeth sinking into her bottom lip.

Tugging her toward me, her bump clashes with my front. "Let's do this." I place a playful kiss on the tip of her nose and delight in the hitch of her breath when I pull back. "You can thank me properly for the gift after." I wink at her, then lead her by the hand to follow the nurse.

GIA

My eyes remain locked on the look of pure wonderment on Reed's face. He pulled out his phone and began reading off a catalog of questions I've never even thought of, and whenever the doctor began talking technically, Reed asked him to slow down while he made further notes to research later.

"And this here is the baby's head." The doctor points to the monitor.

"I think our baby is going to be a genius." Reed grins. "A real fucking genius, Gia." His face is alight with happiness.

A giggle bubbles inside me, but I keep it locked down. "How'd you come to that conclusion?"

"The baby's head is pretty big." He winces. "That's going to hurt." Then he leans forward and kisses my bump. "Don't hurt your momma, little one."

My heart swells at his gentle tone and endearment.

"Would you like to know the sex?" the doctor asks, his eyes darting from mine to Reed's.

I lift a shoulder and look at Reed. "You decide."

Reed looks like all his Christmases came all at once, and his body practically vibrates with excitement. Honestly, his enthusiasm is incredible to witness. "Absolutely." He grins back.

The doctor clears his throat. "Congratulations. You're having a little boy."

Reed blows out a deep breath, and my giggle erupts. Then he turns to face me, his eyes swimming with unshed tears. "This is the best moment in my entire life. Thank you, Gia."

I narrow my eyes. "Just don't let me down."

He swallows thickly. "I won't. I promise."

"Promises can be broken, Reed," I whisper, knowing how true that is, especially after Jaxon broke his promise to be with me for the rest of our lives.

"You're my family now, Gia. You and our boys." His words hold truth in them and sincerity pours from his eyes as I seek reassurance in them.

"Family," I murmur.

TWENTY-FIVE

REED

TAKING Gia to the scan in my brand-new, family-friendly SUV was somewhat life-changing. Not because of the vehicle, but because of the realization my bump is indeed a baby. Seeing him on screen for the first time and his heart beating caused something to change inside me. How the fuck could my father have treated me and my brother as if we're disposable? We're not, nor is my child. The knowledge of my previous actions burns beneath my skin, and I push it aside, willing it away like an idiot.

When I dropped Gia off at home today, I took her inside, along with the dozens of bags from shopping for our baby. I never considered shopping, always having opted for a design team to come to provide me with everything I needed, but being able to see things firsthand and choose items for our baby boy was surprisingly amazing.

As well as multiple outfits and blankets, I chose a baby-blue lion soft toy for him, which Gia was over the moon about, then I insisted on going to a shop which I'd googled to track down the McDonald's toy I'd thrown from the car window. After paying the moron at the counter way more than multiple meals at the place, I walked out of the shop happy with the action toy for Bryce. I only wish I was around tonight to witness his face when he received it. Instead, I'm delivering my promise to Shaw and acting as his wife's plus one at an event I've no interest in.

Emi looks stunning in her red fitted dress as I lead her through the crowd toward our table, but she's not my girl, and already, I feel awkward with another woman on my arm even though she's family.

I don't blame Shaw for not wanting to be here; we've barely been in the building for twenty minutes, and I already feel like I'm suffocating under the scrutiny of the press and Shaw's in-laws.

Outside was a shitshow of epic proportions. Having to pose for photographs is not something I enjoy doing, and I can't imagine my friend does either, but Luca and his family are huge benefactors to the event, so it was expected of Emi to be a part of photos.

We reach the table, and I pull out the chair for Emi to take her place. "When do we get to meet Gia?" she asks, sliding into the chair, and I take the one beside her.

Her question startles me. I've been living in a Gia bubble for a few weeks now, and the fact those closest to me are wanting to integrate her into their lives too has my chest swelling with pride to introduce her and Bryce to what is essentially my family. "Oh, you could bring her to Eleanor's birthday party at the end of the month." I crinkle my nose as she continues. "Eleanor would love to see you there too. You're all she's been talking about."

It's on the tip of my tongue to tell her I'd hardly call it talking; she can barely string a sentence together, but I don't want to burst her bubble of enthusiasm.

"Has Gia had a baby shower yet? If not, you could help organize one?"

The waiter places champagne on the table, and I throw it back. "I thought baby showers were for women."

Emi scoffs on a smile, then wafts her hand about. "Times have changed, Reed. Anddd, I think the men enjoy them more than the women." She giggles, and I blink at her. Yes, she's serious. Poor girl has, after all, been raised in a shroud of secrecy, all in the name of the Mafia. I highly doubt the men enjoy baby showers at all, but hearing her discuss baby plans has my attention like never before.

"How was the scan?" she asks while searching my face with all seriousness.

My heart thumps rapidly whenever I think of our baby growing safely inside Gia. "Amazing," I state, and she nods as if understanding, which, of course, she does. My friends all do, except Mase. He's the only one of the five of us not to have a family now, and out of all of us, he's the one most desperate for it. The thought sends a flash of determination through me. First thing Monday morning, I'm putting the pressure on. Mase needs his divorce settled once and for all. His bitch of a wife, Tara, needs to go, and my friend needs closure to allow him to move on and give him what he's always wanted.

"Oh God. My brother is on his way over here," Emi grumbles, and I smirk.

Luca Varros is the capo of the notorious Varros Family Mafia. He also forced Emi and Shaw to marry after she got pregnant on a one-night stand. At the time, I thought Shaw was full of lust, not love, because he gave in so easily to Luca's plans, but now, knowing how I feel about Gia, I can admit one night can change your life for the better.

I stand to greet Luca and hold out my hand, but he glares straight through me. Arrogant prick. He side-eyes Emi and gifts her with a smile as she stands, leaving me feeling awkward, so I drop my hand only for him to hold his out in greeting.

Jesus, he's a fucker.

Choosing to ignore his need for dominance, I greet him as if he isn't being an overbearing prick. "Good to see you, Luca." Lies. He squeezes my hand roughly.

"Mm," he muses, as if seeing right through me. "Where's Shaw?" he asks but aims the question at Emi.

She lifts her chin to face her brother. "He has the flu." Her cheeks redden, and Luca's eyes narrow.

Then he lifts an eyebrow. "And?"

Emi's mouth drops open and fire burns in her eyes. "And he didn't want anyone to get it. So he stayed home, and Reed was kind enough to offer to accompany me." He looks at me with sheer contempt, then his gaze flicks back to hers. "You wouldn't want to take the flu home to Camille and the children, would you?" Her lip twitches.

"No," he says, then finally drops my hand. One of his bodyguards speaks in his ear, and he nods. "I'll catch up with you later." He nods toward Emi. "Oh, and I'll send a doctor to check on Shaw."

Her eyes widen. "Wha-what? Luca, no, that's not necessary."

His lip twitches, as if pleased at her reaction. "I insist." Then he simply nods toward me, turns on his heels, and leaves.

"Great. Just fucking great. Shaw bows out of the event, I lie to my brother, and now we're about to be caught in a lie." She slinks back into her seat with a heavy huff, and I chuckle at my friend's demise. He can barely take a shit without Luca being informed, so how he thought he would get away with not attending this event is beyond me. Still, I got what I wanted, and that's all that matters.

Thankfully, my champagne glass has been refilled, so I take a smug sip as I consider how my plans are all slipping into place. Life is good. Very good.

So why the hell do I have this ball of dread welling inside me? Telling me everything is about to go horribly wrong.

TWENTY-SIX

GIA

LAST NIGHT, Reed didn't come over after work and said he had to work late. I've also not heard from him this morning, which is unusual, and I can't help the gnawing feeling in the pit of my stomach telling me there's something wrong and there's something he's not telling me. He's hiding something. Something vital that's going to break my heart.

If it was only mine in question, it wouldn't feel quite as bad, but there's Bryce to consider, and the baby too.

I'm putting a lot of trust in Reed, maybe too much too soon, but I'm so desperate for this to work. I refuse to acknowledge how quickly things are moving, despite those around me warning me otherwise.

"Mrs. Mathers," Alejo says, pointing his pen in my direction, "you seem happier lately."

I shuffle under his scrutiny.

"But not today," he asserts. "Can I help you with anything?"

My tongue thickens, and my eyes fill with tears at his kind

words. This is what the community is, what my work is all about. We support one another above all else.

"No. But thank you, Alejo." I pat his hand. "That means a lot." I take a sip of my water.

He beams back at me. "Well, if you need anything, let me know. I know people who can rough him up, if you need that."

I splutter on my drink in a panic. "That won't be necessary."

"Well. Just so you know."

A shadow crosses behind me, making me turn my head to face it, and Reed's eyes bore down on me and his jaw tics with the force of his glare.

"H-hi," I squeak, and shift in my chair.

"I came to take you to dinner." His stern voice cuts through the air, but his eyes lock onto Alejo, as if he's speaking to him, and I can't help the way my pulse picks up at the thought of him jealous.

Clearing my throat, I push back in my chair, quick to dismiss the growing tension. Reed takes a hold of my arm and pulls my back against this chest, then his tight shoulders relax when he bands his arm around my waist and rests it on bump, before nuzzling into my hair. "I missed you," he whispers, and all my previous anxieties drift away at his admittance.

"Mrs. Mathers? Do you want me to finish the files for you?" Alejo asks, and Reed bristles on his words, and I feel the change in the air once again. The tension is now tenfold.

Heat radiates from Reed, and his free hand moves to grip my hip with a bruising force. What the hell is happening?

I clear my throat and smile tightly back at him. "Please."

Alejo nods, then moves quickly to gather up the files we were working on while I turn in Reed's arms, and finally, his body softens.

"You're being a dick."

He licks his lips and smirks. "Just marking my territory."

I wrinkle my nose at his explanation.

"I'm not a dog, Reed."

He throws his head back to look up at the ceiling, then slams his eyes shut as if pained. "Ugh, don't even talk to me about dogs."

A laugh bubbles out of me at his dramatics. "Come on, then, take me to dinner." I pat his chest, and when his gaze comes back down to mine, the heat of his stare surrounds me, and every cell comes alive at the intensity behind it.

TWENTY-SEVEN

REED

AFTER DROPPING Emi off at home last night, I returned to my apartment to find Bubbles, the rat-bastard, had devoured my white leather couch. Stuffing was everywhere, making my normally immaculate apartment look like Christmas had come early and dumped a shit ton of snow in my fucking living room.

I turned my back on the mess and the yapping little shit and slammed my bedroom door, figuring I'd deal with it tomorrow. But once I slid into my silk sheets with thoughts of Gia on her bed springing to my mind, the little bastard started howling at my bedroom door like a deranged wolf with partial vocal cords. No wonder no fucker wanted it.

Then the scratching started, followed by the sound of glass shattering, giving me little to no choice but to throw open my bedroom door to check what the hell it had done. The dog pushed past me and jumped on my bed like she was competing in the Olympics, then did some weird circling motion before plonking itself on my pillow, reminding me of when the wolf dog at Gia's did the same thing.

Thankfully, the glass vase she destroyed in this ploy to take over my bedroom is easily replaceable, but the fact I had a dog in my bed wasn't. The thought of its hair all over me as I slept was too much to bear, so I did the only thing I could think of doing at 3:30 a.m. and grabbed the spare pillow to sleep on the floor. After all, it had obliterated my couch.

At 4:11 a.m., she joined me on the floor and woke me up by licking my face like I was its treat. How the hell can a little dog make a grown-ass man want to scream and cry? Plus, commit murder. I turned my back on her after delivering her with a tirade of expletives she deserved. Then somehow, I fell asleep, but when something warm splashed on my face, I shot up, expecting a water leak or something from my ceiling, not to be pissed on by a dog squatting over my face like I'm a damn fire hydrant.

My life is being destroyed by a shrunken bulldog with too much life in it.

I shot up, rushed to the bathroom, and slid on her dog shit in the process, then spent the entire morning vomiting from the trauma. Then I had to organize fumigators and a deep clean service for my apartment because there's no way in hell I can return there after the shitshow she's created.

Also, for some odd reason, I no longer like being on my own. Before Gia and our boys came into my life, I was happy with my solitude life, but now I realize I was just existing. I want to fucking live. Specifically, with them.

"I need to move into your house," I tell Gia, and place another forkful of salad into my mouth.

Her eyebrows shoot up, but she doesn't tell me no, not straight away at least. "Bubbles destroyed my apartment last night. It doesn't feel clean anymore." I shudder as I consider my words. It probably won't feel clean ever again, to be honest. Maybe we should get a new place before the baby comes anyway. "And it doesn't feel right being away from you guys." I admit, then hate how vulnerable I sound. "You might need me," I tack on.

Gia starts laughing, and I ignore her despite the way her tits bounce with each chuckle. "How long have you had Bubbles, Reed?" she queries while a knowing smile plays on her edible lips.

My fork stills midair. I don't want to lie to her, but I also don't want her to be aware of the lengths I've gone to, to prove myself to her and Bryce.

"Well, well, well. Fancy seeing you here." George Fanzio's voice cuts through the air like glass, sending the fun atmosphere icy in an instant, and something behind the way he delivered his words has me believing his appearance isn't coincidental.

The color drains from Gia's face, and her eyes close as if she's blocking us out. Annoyance rumbles inside me; is she ashamed to be seen with me? I quickly push it aside and do some damage control before he ruins my carefully constructed plans.

I stand and shake his hand. "George. Good to see you." Then I clear my throat and hold my hand out toward Gia. "Me and Gia are an item." I look at him pointedly, and his dark eyebrows narrow. "We're having a baby together." I smile proudly, and his eyebrows shoot up, surprise marring his face, whereas Gia bristles and shuffles uncomfortably, making me agitated at her lack of enthusiasm at my declaration. What the hell is her problem? Is she ashamed to be with me?

Discomfort swirls in my stomach, and self-loathing infiltrates my bloodstream. Does she think I'm not good enough for her?

She went to great lengths to be with her husband, and she speaks so proudly of him too, but me? She can't even admit we're an item. She doesn't think I'm worthy enough to be her partner. Am I not as good as Jaxon? Even the thought of him sends bitterness rushing through my veins, a potent jealousy I'm not used to, and I know here and now that I would fight to my death to keep her and our kids. There's nothing I won't do to get what I want.

"Gianna, you never mentioned that you and Reed were in a relationship the last time I saw you," George chastises, and his face turns from shocked to gloating, a sly smile playing on his lips. I shift from foot to foot, the weight of my secret weighing heavily between us. "And you're pregnant with his baby too?" His smile grows wider, and I swallow back the bile threatening to erupt from inside the pool of dread lurking deep within me. "How … perfect." He grins sinisterly. I've chosen to ignore the power George holds over me until now, and something tells me I need to figure this shit out sooner rather than later. By the look on his face, he's loving every damn minute of this.

"My baby has nothing to do with you," Gia spits back with such hatred, I rear back a little, stunned at her sharp, spiteful tone. This is not the Gia I know. She stares straight ahead, not even giving her father her attention, and frankly, I'm shocked at how rude her behavior is right now, and the fact she referred to our baby as hers is not lost on me. Not at fucking all. In fact, it's infuriating and another reason to feel not worthy.

"Gia!" I clip out, sharper than I intended, and her head snaps to face me, the venom in her eyes full of fire after a flash of hurt crosses her pretty face first.

"I've lost my appetite." She inhales through her nose, then exhales and throws down her napkin and pushes back in her chair, while I remain stunned at her outlandish and childish behavior.

George waves his arm in her direction as she gathers her purse and searches inside it. "She's always like this. But she has the nerve to label me the bad guy," he grumbles. "You need to learn to control her."

I'm too shocked at Gia's reaction to fully comprehend his words.

"I'm hardly surprised you chose to leave her at home last night and bring another woman to the event, because she has no clue how to behave in public. The problem is, she's been slumming it for far too long."

I wince at his words, and Gia jolts before throwing some cash onto the table, then she turns to walk away, but I grab her wrist to stop her. To say what, I'm not sure. I don't want to explain my actions here, not with George as an audience, any audience for that matter. I scan the room uncomfortably while I try to come up with something suitable to say.

This is why I don't do relationships. This is why I pay women for sex and nothing more. I don't like complications, and I have no clue how to deal with them.

Hurt laces her face, and tears swim in her eyes. "I can pay the bill," I grit out, despite that not being what I wanted to say.

What I want to say is, you're acting like a bitch. It's our child, not yours, and finally, she needs to stop acting like a goddamn child if she wants our relationship to work.

But I say nothing.

A muffled snort leaves her, and she lifts her chin to glare at me with contempt. "I'm sure you're aware by now I have money, Reed. I just choose not to spend it. I don't need anything from you, and I need nothing from him." She pulls her wrist from me and heads toward the door, taking a part of me with her.

"Good play." George chuckles and slaps my back, causing me to bite back a retort. "I wasn't aware you were so tactical, Reed, but I'm grateful for it." He grins from ear to ear before his tone falls serious. "Just make sure you deliver." He squeezes my shoulder, then walks away, but it's Gia my eyes follow as she pushes through the door, not looking back.

Something tells me I've epically fucked up, but worse, I know there's more to come.

TWENTY-EIGHT

REED

I FUCKED UP. I fucked up big time, but I will fix it.

I'm relieved to find the taxi pulling up when I place my SUV into park and throw open my car door just as Gia steps out. She pays the driver, and our gazes collide.

Her shoulders drop, and disappointment washes over her face as I head toward her, and that move alone causes irritation to rile through me once again.

"Go home, Reed," she snaps out, and turns her back and heads up the steps to her house, but I follow after her.

"Go home?"

She unlocks the door, and I push inside behind her. "Go home?" Throwing her purse on the counter, she turns to face me with her arms crossed over her epic chest.

"Who were you with last night?" she bites out, and I won't lie, the fact she's acting jealous sends a rush of elation through my veins.

"I went to an event, and I took Shaw's wife, Emi, with me. I was asked to be a stand-in." I fail to mention the fact I had to negotiate being a stand-in to borrow their child, but she must sense the truth in my words because her shoulders drop.

"You didn't tell me." Hurt laces her words, and my heart skips a beat at the thought. "What was I supposed to think?"

"I'm sorry. I should have told you."

She turns her head away, and I hate that she's pushing me out. "I have to deal with Tyson staying here, Gia. Under the same roof as you."

"He's a friend. He's like a brother to me," she bites out.

"A brother whose cock slipped inside you."

She cringes at my words. "I told you it was a mistake. We both agreed as much. You'll be pleased to know, I didn't even come." She shrugs, and my chest preens with pride, but I need to say what's on my mind before I kiss her senseless for her comment. Dumb fucker can't even make a girl come.

She strokes over her bump.

"You were rude, Gia. You spoke about our baby as if he's solely yours." My jaw tics with aggravation when I consider how she could take all this from me. She holds all the control, all the power in our dynamic, but the decisions she's making should be discussed first because he's my baby too. "That's our baby you're discussing."

Anger flares in her eyes as she stares back at me. "I don't want that son of a bitch anywhere near me and *our* baby." The way she spits *our* boils my blood.

"That's something we'll discuss at a later date," I grit out, refusing to hide my annoyance, and when she jolts, I know my words have annoyed her further, but what does she expect? Me to back down and let her have her way without discussion?

Her nostrils flare, and she lifts her chin higher. "It's nonnegotiable."

I choke on a humorless laugh. "Because your father didn't like your late husband does not mean he won't like this one."

Her eyebrows narrow, and genuine surprise coats her

features. "This one?" Hurt lances through my chest at the thought of her never considering me a viable option for her. Possibly our baby too. Was this always her intention? To never truly acknowledge me?

"Yes, this one. What the fuck do you think this is between us?" I step forward as hurt mixes with anger. "We're getting married, and I'm adopting Bryce. Our baby will have a solid family unit," I bite out.

Rage simmers through me when her mouth drops open and her chin wobbles, then she shakes her head, and fury threatens to erupt from inside my veins.

"You've got to be kidding me? You're not adopting my son!" She throws her arm out.

"Ours. He's going to be ours." I point at her.

"He's not yours!" she screams back at me. "He's Jaxon's son. Not yours!" She shakes her head, her chest rising.

Pain stills my heart as her words sear deep, slicing through me and twisting my emotions, and I stare back at her, motionless.

And there it is. The confirmation I needed. He's Jaxon's and not mine. He's another man's child and will never be mine. Despite everything I'm trying to do, I'll never be enough.

My eyes lock on to the photograph on the sideboard of them as a family. It's almost as if he's taunting me from beyond the grave. I drop my head forward to block out the image of the three of them, a happy family unit without me, and swallow back the lump of hurt gathered in my throat.

"He's not going anywhere near my children, Reed." Her voice wobbles, and I snap my gaze back up to hers.

Tears flow down her pretty face, but there's more than that; it's determination too.

I knew Gia was strong, but this side of her is like fire, and I've gotten burned. Her flames devour me and scar me deep, and in this moment, the sheer brutality of them threatens to extinguish every thought and feeling I have toward her.

My strength is my own, and I've let my emotions take over. I've allowed her the strength to possess me, granted it wholeheartedly, but not anymore.

"We'll see about that, Gia," I snipe back. Then I do what I promised I would never do. I turn and walk out the door.

The sound of her cry wavers my footing, but I replay her words in my head as I stride down the stone steps. *"He's not yours! He's Jaxon's son. Not yours!"* And that thought gives me the strength I need to walk away.

TWENTY-NINE

REED

"LET ME GET THIS STRAIGHT. You left her?" Emi asks, staring at me with an open mouth. I throw the drink back, slam it on the table, then motion for Shaw to pour me another.

"She said Bryce was Jaxon's son," I grind out. "Not mine."

"Hate to break it to you, but he is," Tate grunts, earning a glare from Owen.

"If someone said Romeo belonged to that cunt, I'd slice the fucker up," Owen states, and who can blame him? He took on his wife's baby and adopted him when he was merely weeks old.

Emi shakes her head. "That's different. Jaxon was nothing like Romeo's sperm donor." She's not lying. On all accounts, Jaxon was a good man, and as much as I'm grateful Gia never suffered at his hands the way Laya did at her husband's, it's also impossible to live up to him.

"Why does she hate her father so much?" Mase asks as I swirl my glass while staring aimlessly at the amber liquid.

I clear my throat. "He didn't like Jaxon."

Mase scrunches up his nose. "Got to be more to it than that."

"He's trying to sell off the land and demolish the buildings Gia is working to keep open to spite her," Shaw tacks on, and I'm grateful my friend listens to my moans of contempt.

"Why would he do that?" Mase asks.

"'Cause he's a dick." Owen shrugs. "Everyone is aware of what a dick he is. He speaks to people like shit, and his reputation precedes him."

Mase winces at Owen's words, then asks, "Did you research him?"

Owen lifts his shoulder and shakes his head. "People talk." He drags his hand over his head and exhales. "Do you want me to look into him?"

"I think you should. There's more to this," Emi instructs, shocking the shit out of us all. "Besides the fact you know he's an ass and can be difficult, he also has a vendetta against Gia. I mean, the girl fell in love with a good guy, refuses to spend Fanzio's money, and wants to be left alone to raise her kids. She needs commending, not hurt. There's more to this, Reed."

A sliver of nausea runs through me, along with guilt I hadn't asked more about her relationship with her father, too concerned with discussing anything remotely to do with Fanzio. It was easier to not discuss him at all.

"You need to make this right. That poor girl has nobody. She's pregnant while raising her son who doesn't even have a father, and now, he, alongside her, will think you've left them, Reed." Her eyes implore mine, but it's her words that lance through me like a bolt of sickening dread. She's right. Bryce and Gia deserve better. They deserve a man to stand by them, not one who walks away when things get difficult.

"She won't be alone; it sounds like she has help. Right, Reed?" Tate's lip quirks, and I want to punch him in the throat so badly as he references Tyson, but my mind keeps replaying the fact that I left her, left them all. Pushing back in the armchair, I finish my drink.

"You need me to take you?" Mase asks.

I drag a hand over my head. "Yeah." Then I sigh heavily, feeling the weight of the day on my shoulders. This has to have been the worst day in my entire life, even worse than the day I brought the little shitbag home, and I never want a repeat of it again. "Please." I nod at him, and he gifts me with a smile.

"Everything will be okay, man." He squeezes my shoulder, and I wish I could feel an ounce of his confidence right now. "Just show her you're not going anywhere. That's what I'd do." He stares back at me with conviction, and I see the truth behind my friend's eyes. He'd give anything to be in my position, a family of his own instead of the one crumbling around him. Something passes between us, and I straighten my shoulders while lifting my chin, promising him without saying it that I'll do whatever it takes to help him too.

Starting first thing Monday.

His bitch of a wife is going down so he can finally start a new life and have a chance of the family he's always dreamed of.

Now I need to win my family back, and more importantly, I need to keep them.

THIRTY

GIA

I DON'T KNOW how long I took to fall asleep; my tears stopped falling because my body was spent after attempting to curl into a ball, a little bit difficult given my growing bump.

Warmth spreads through me and his scent wraps around me, along with his thick arms, as I melt into the heat of his solid chest.

I'm dreaming, right?

He nuzzles into my hair, sniffing me before exhaling and sending a shiver over my body. Then he hooks his fingers into my panties and sweeps them to the side before guiding his solid cock to my entrance.

Oh Jesus … I clench at the thought of him stretching me, and when he thrusts up inside me, my eyes snap open at the intensity of his force.

I attempt to move, but his heavy arm tightens around me, then he slides his thick hand up my camisole, and he holds my breast in his palm. "Don't tell me to stop," he grunts, and pushes his thick cock inside me. "I just want to feel you close to me." Tenderness laces his tone, and I find myself nodding, allowing him to remain positioned inside me, but I don't know if it's for him or me.

"I'm sorry," he rasps against my ear, and I don't know what he's apologizing for: his words, his actions, leaving me? "I'm sorry for everything," he whispers, confirming my thoughts, and all I can do is nod.

———

I don't know how long we lie with his warmth wrapped around me like a blanket protecting me. His cock is lodged firmly inside me, and his heavy breaths float over my hair.

My pussy tightens around him, and he chuckles. "You need to stop doing that, baby. It's making me want to fuck you, and I only intended to tell you how sorry I am while I hold you."

I lick my lips. "Mm-maybe I want you to show me."

His arms tighten around me, then he slowly pulls out of me, and I hate the feeling of his absence. He pushes me onto my back, and I whine at the loss of his touch.

"Shh, it's okay," he whispers, and positions himself between my legs, so I rest up on my elbows to peer over my bump. He strokes his cock at my entrance, and I watch transfixed at his large fist pumping up and down, and his pupils flare with arousal. He licks his lips, and he his abs contract, his breathing getting heavier as he stares at my wet pussy. "Your pussy is fucking begging for my cock, Gia." His eyes swim with possession.

Then he guides the head of his cock up and down my slit, coating it with my arousal as he toys with the entrance to my pussy hole. With each stroke, I buck beneath him, and his chest rises with what I can only imagine is the need I feel. "Can you feel how much I need you, Gia?"

I nod frantically, lifting my hips.

"Can you feel how much my cock wants to stay inside you?"

"Please."

"Tell me what you want, beautiful. Tell me what you need."

"You," I pant. "I need you, Reed."

His gaze lifts to meet mine, and we stare at one another, the strength behind his eyes screaming at me how much he needs me, pulling at my heart and twisting. I belong to him, and him to me.

He lines up his cock, our eyes remain locked, and this time, he slides in slowly, taking my breath away with the way my heart beats faster at his stare, the way he leans over me and presses his lips to mine, careful not to squash bump in the process. The tenderness behind it and the slow motion of his hips moving so passionately tell me everything I need to know.

"I …" He gazes at me. "I'm not good with words, Gia."

My throat clogs, and I simply nod.

"I want to show you."

He's all in.

His heart, body, and soul.

This man has the power to destroy me.

The ability to control me.

And I give it to him.

A tear slips from my eye as I register the movements for what they are. He's making love to me. My beautiful, powerful, emotionless man is making love to me.

He watches my face before placing a soft kiss on my lips, then cups my jaw and turns my head to the side to kiss up and down my jawline until our lips meet again. He grunts when I slide my tongue into his mouth, and when he pulls back, breathless and eyes full of awe, I take his strong jaw in my palm and guide him back to me.

Our kiss is delicate. Unlike any of our kisses before, there's no fight for control and no me submitting. It's like we're creating love for the first time, and the thought of our baby between us while we become consumed with one another makes my eyes fill with tears of triumph, and I turn my head to blink away the weight of emotion striking through me.

My eyes clash with the photo on my bedside, and I still.

REED

Slowly, I rock my hips, showing her with my actions when words aren't enough.

I've never been a man to show emotion, words or actions, and while it's something that others have picked up on, it's never bothered me until Gia. Simply because I want to give her more, so much fucking more. More than I can give, yet I still wish it to be possible.

Her body works in tandem with mine, like we were meant for one another. Her legs wrap around my waist as if to lock me in, and I move at an orchestrated, leisurely pace deep inside her. I gently kiss down her face and back up again, resting on my forearms to not crush her bump or cause her discomfort. She swallows under the heat of my stare, but I don't waver. My eyes never leave her face, even when she turns away from me.

Then she freezes, and I still, thinking I've hurt her somehow. I scan her face, then follow the line of her sight, and sickness zips up my spine at a rapid speed like poison infiltrating my bloodstream.

She's thinking of him.

My heart plummets and my breath stutters.

She's watching him as I make love to her, and the thought causes my chest to feel tight and my throat closes, and I quickly withdraw from her. "Fuck!" I roar into the room. "Fuck," I repeat on a frustrated grunt, and I shuffle to the end of the bed away from her, away from the pain. Trying to regulate my breathing but failing, I bury my face in my palms, the hurt cutting so deep it twists inside me.

I'll never be him.

I'll never be enough.

"Reed?" I hear her move behind me, but I'm too lost in my thoughts to acknowledge her. "Reed. It's not what you think."

A scoff erupts from me.

Not what I fucking think?

I shouldn't have come here. I shouldn't have tried to put things right when they're so desperately wrong.

Her soft hands rest on my shoulder, and her bump presses against my back. "Please let me explain."

I shake my head, hoping to banish the thoughts in my mind. "I'll never be enough, Gia," I whisper into the room. "And you know what the sad thing is? I accept I'm not good enough, as long as you'll still have me."

She flinches, slides off the bed, and kneels at my feet. Then she pulls my hands from my face, and my jaw tics at the thought of her witnessing my vulnerability. "Is that what you think?" She shakes her head. "You're wrong, Reed. So fucking wrong."

I stare back at her tear-streaked cheeks and hate the sight of her hurting, so when she maneuvers herself to straddle my lap, I allow it. I'd give her anything if it means accepting me.

"I became emotional because I feel the connection between us, Reed," she breathes out, and positions my cock at her entrance. "I looked at Jaxon"—my body freezes, but I remain transfixed on her face, waiting for her words as she slowly sinks down on me—"and I realized I've fallen in love with another man." She takes my entire cock in her slick pussy, and my breath catches. "I want you, and it's terrifying."

"Fuck," I choke out as my body becomes one with hers. "I don't think I've ever been loved before," I state.

She giggles and rocks against me. "I'm sure you've had a million girls declare their love for you." Her eyebrows lift, and I smile back at her.

"Not true love. Not like this," I say, but don't allow myself to say the words I desperately want to, too scared to give everything I feel away. So instead, I opt for the easier option. "I've never felt this way before, Gia."

"I know, baby." She holds my chin in the palm of her hands, then brings my face to hers and kisses my lips softly. "I've got you."

GIA

His lips are my undoing. They're soft and vulnerable, and when his tongue lashes out to take back the control, I moan against his touch. He grips my ass cheeks and thrusts up inside me, his thick length hitting the perfect spot. "Yes," I beg. "Please don't stop." I throw my head back, and he kisses the column of my throat, then down my chest until he reaches my sensitive breasts. They're heavy and tender, desperate for his touch, and when his tongue sweeps over my peaked nipple, I combust around him.

"Holy fuck," he grunts, chasing his orgasm. "Again, baby. I want you to come again with me sucking on your tits."

His filthy tongue is an aphrodisiac to my wanton soul, and wetness spills around us, but his movements never slow. My tits bounce in his face, and he groans, sweat coating his forehead. Every muscle on his crafted body contracts under his movements, and when I feel a release of milk from my nipple, my body becomes taut, my pussy clenches, and Reed growls as he sucks against me harder. His body wrings tight, his breathing escalates, and finally, his warm cum splashes deep inside me, spilling between us as he pushes inside me again and again to drain himself of every ounce of his cum.

He pulls back to face me, and the wonderment in his eyes allows me to see straight into his soul. He loves me, and though he hasn't said the words aloud yet, there's not a doubt in my mind that they're coming.

Reed Johnson may be my greatest downfall; I just hope he can always build us back up.

THIRTY-ONE

REED

SHE LIES TUCKED under my arm with her head on my chest, and my fingers tangle in her hair while she drapes one leg over my waist, allowing me to feel every move that our son makes.

"When my mom died, the man I knew my father to be became someone else." I listen intensively, grateful she's giving me this insight into her life. "He'd always been absent, cold even, but it's as if he hated me for her leaving us."

I knew George was a widow, but I never realized to ask questions about Gia's family, especially given that she only classed Bryce as family, and the community too, I guess. "How did she die?"

"Cancer."

I swallow back the lump gathered in my throat at the way her voice wavers. "I'm sorry."

"It's okay. I was twelve. A long time ago now."

My fingers toy with her hair. "Still doesn't stop the hurt, though, right?"

"No, it doesn't." She lifts her head to face me. "What

about your parents, Reed? Do you have a relationship with them?"

A snort leaves me. "No. My father was a jackass and died about five years ago. For someone always surrounded by so many people, he died alone. A lonely old man."

"That's … sad."

I shrug, not feeling the least bit sad about his death. Feeling nothing at all, like always.

Out of all my best friends, I'm the one who comes with the most influence, money, and prestige, and I grew up hating what it cost to receive it. That's the only feelings I've become accustomed to over the years—hate and the physical pleasure from sex. Nothing more, nothing less.

"I have a half-brother Isacc; he's a fuckup, thanks to our father. Our father couldn't wait to shove us both in boarding school. That's where I met the guys, and I'm grateful for that, at least. But I don't have one fond memory of my father, not one. He just was never there, and I spent a long time hating him for it.

"Isacc didn't thrive on the structure of school, like me. He was the bad boy, and our father constantly threw money at him, and it left him spoiled and made him think he was invincible to the world, when in reality he had a harsh lesson to learn." I clear my throat and shake my head, appalled at my brother's indiscretions.

Gia must sense my unease because she doesn't push me further, and I'm grateful for it. I'm sure I will share the story of his downfall sooner or later; I am, after all, his lawyer.

"What about your mother?"

A disgruntled sound bubbles out of me. "She's a bitter, twisted old woman. My brother's mother passed away in tragic circumstances, and she took great pleasure in making sure we weren't going to support him, as if it was his fault our father strayed countless times and created him. Whenever it was the school holidays, me and my father would spend an afternoon with him, and she constantly reminded me that he's nothing, a worthless bastard child that nobody wanted."

I laugh, but there's no amusement in my tone. It's bitter like how I feel. "The funny thing is, I had a family, and they didn't want me either." I shake my head. My kids will never feel the way I did growing up. They have an incredible mother, and I may not know much about parenting, but I know the kind of parent I want to be, and I'll do my utmost to protect my family from the likes of mine. "I never want you to meet her."

"Oh." The disappointment lacing her tone has me wanting to elaborate.

"She has a cruel tongue, Gia. I can guarantee you, she'll have nothing nice to say to you. You deserve better than her judgment, and I'd never put you and Bryce in a situation where you'd be uncomfortable, and trust me, you'd be uncomfortable." The hypocrisy of my words isn't lost on me. That's the exact same as Gia not wanting her sons around her father, and my blood runs cold at the way things went down back at the restaurant.

"I'm sorry about what I said at the restaurant."

She places her finger over my mouth. "It's okay," she whispers.

I gently remove it and shake my head while entwining my fingers with hers. "It's not. I'm sorry, and you're right. If you don't want our children to see your father, then that's up to you. You're their mother, a damn good one, and I support you." I feel the tension drain from her body. "And as much as I wish I was Bryce's father, I'm not." I swallow thickly, hating the words as I say them. "I won't push for his adoption, but I need you to know I want it." I stare into her green orbs, and they fill with tears. My heart pounds, and I long to tell her how I feel but can't quite make the words come out, so I hope she can decipher what I'm trying to say. "I want all of you, Gia. You've stolen my heart, little thief."

She lifts up, and I think she's going to kiss me, but her lips rest over my heart, and I wouldn't change a damn thing about it. "You're a little thief too."

———

The sun streams through the curtains, and I reluctantly lift my head from off the pillow and glance at the clock—10:30 a.m. Fuck!

My eyes latch on to the spot where the photo that normally sits beside Gia's bed is, and it's absent, as is my girl. Her side of the bed is cold, and my body fills with a need to be near her to make sure she's aware of how much she means to me. So, with that thought in mind, I throw the sheets back and grab my boxers and pants from the floor, then slip them on before heading to the bathroom to freshen up.

When I make it down the stairs, I glance at the sideboard and find the photo's missing from there too, causing my heart to constrict. She's fucking trying, and that means the world to me.

The smell of pancakes fills my nostrils and has my stomach growling. A smile tugs on my lips as I enter the kitchen, but it soon dies when Tyson comes into sight. He sits at the counter drinking coffee with a sly smirk on his face when he sees me. Then he trails his eyes up and down me before flicking his gaze back to Gia.

"Pleased to see you got your head out of your ass," he grunts, and stares at my girl's back, and my body tightens at the thought of him staring at her ass. She is, after all, in my white shirt. Does she even have panties on?

A feral sound leaves my throat, then I quickly mask it with a cough, and when douche canoe chuckles, I snap my gaze back to his. "Why are you here, anyway?" I grit out while Gia thrusts a coffee in my hand.

She tilts her head to face me with a serene smile, ignoring my souring mood. "Do you want pancakes?"

"Are they organic?" I ask while glaring at Tyson.

"They are." I gift her a nod while smiling smugly in Tyson's direction. There you go, motherfucker. She's accommodating my needs.

"I came to take Bryce to summer camp," he declares, with a grin mirroring my own.

Mine slides off my face in an instant, and my spine straightens at the thought of him continuing to play a father figure in Bryce's life when he has me. "Well, I'm taking him."

He crosses his arms over his chest. "He's already there." Then he glances at his watch. "Camp started at eight a.m. today." As he clucks with his tongue, it makes me want to rip the smug look off his face.

"Well, then, you're not needed here any longer," I clip out, and wave my hand toward the door.

"I have a late meeting at the center, so he's going to need to be collected from camp." Gia's eyes ping-pong between mine and twat waffle's.

"I can do that. What time?"

"Six." They speak at the same time.

"That's fine. I'll go into the office for a couple of hours, then collect him."

"Thank you." Gia lifts onto her tiptoes and places a kiss on my cheek. I band my arm around her waist and hold her while my eyes remain locked on Tyson. Turning her, I lower my lips to hers, all while watching the prick from over her shoulder, staking my claim on the woman who's captured me. He rolls his eyes, and I lift my finger behind Gia's back, flipping him off.

"Okay, lovebirds. I'm out!" he declares, and I smile into our kiss. That's right, fuckwit, you're not needed here.

THIRTY-TWO

I'VE SPENT the last two hours working on Mase's divorce, and finally, I have some news he's going to want to hear, so I made the call and told the guys to gather in my office.

With my arms crossed over my chest, I beam in Shaw's direction, and he leads the guys into my room. "Oh god, he got laid." He surmises. I mean, he's not wrong, but that's not the reason for my glowing disposition.

"Are you back to fucking multiple women?" Tate asks, and I glare back at him.

"My wife is pregnant. Why the fuck would I want any other woman?"

Owen's eyebrows shoot up. "I wasn't aware you tied the knot. When the hell did this happen?" They all stare back at me as if I'm insane.

"Semantics." I waft my hand toward them, and Mase stares back at me with wide eyes while the others start laughing.

"So, what's the news?" Owen asks as he perches his wide ass on the meeting table. Jesus, the guy is built.

"Mase." I tap my pen on my chin and spin in my chair to face him, and he shifts from foot to foot under my stare. "I have news." He gulps, and the fear in his eyes makes me want to rip his wife apart for putting the look of vulnerability on my best friend's face. He was once the life and soul of our party. He had a promising career in his father's empire, and everything went to shit when he agreed to marry her. Her manipulation, her cheating, all her cruel taunts about him not being able to give them a child have taken a toll on the man before me.

"I've been working on your case." He nods along to my words. "The judge has thrown out her dispute."

Tate sits forward. "What's that mean, exactly?"

"It means in a matter of days, you're going to be a free man, my friend." I grin at him.

Mase's mouth falls open, and his eyes widen.

"Holy shit, man, that's incredible!" Tate booms, and rushes toward him, then grabs him in a bear hug while Mase remains stunned to the spot. Tate pulls back. "Too bad thirsty Thursday is almost dried up now." He's referring to the bet we used to have on Thursdays of who can get their cock sucked the most. More often than not, I would win, based purely on the number of girls I would get to do it, whereas poor Mase never participated, being a married man.

Owen grins from ear to ear, and Shaw slaps Mase on the back, congratulating him.

Tate stills, and judging by the smile encompassing his face, I know whatever is about to come out of his mouth will be amusing, because his eyes dance with glee. "You know what this means, right?" We all wait for him to elaborate. "The Indulgence app Reed loves is going to get some hammer. We're hooking you up with the best goddamn escorts in town." His eyebrows waggle, but I remain shocked at his words.

"Loved," I snap, and they stare back at me. "You said, Reed loves when referring to the app. It's loved. Past tense."

Tate rolls his eyes. "What-the-fuck-ever. You can give him some pointers."

I throw my head back in the chair, with a groan and pinch the bridge of my nose, while the guys start asking Mase about what kind of woman he wants to fuck first.

This case has cost hundreds of thousands and been in the pipeline for years, and all they're bothered about is getting Mase laid.

As long as he doesn't fuck up and fall for an escort, I tell myself as I gather my phone and keys, ready to collect Bryce.

———

Shouting comes from the locker room, and I find myself moving faster. Jesus, is this the prick who's teaching the kids during summer break?

My early years at boarding school come rushing back, with the booming voice ricocheting off the walls of the corridor.

"Reed. You're a useless piece of shit," the track coach spits out while I kick my sneaker into the ground. "Your daddy didn't want you and now the team doesn't want you. No wonder your family left you here." My coach's words fill my veins with disappointment. He's right. I'm useless. "No fucker wants you." A shiver runs down my spine at the thought of being alone.

I shake away the memory and move closer. "You're a sniveling little girl. You know that? A coward. You'll never amount to anything." There's no way in hell this guy is getting away with speaking to kids like this. I've been on the receiving end of this shit, and I wouldn't wish it on anyone, least of all a child.

"Do you have anything to say, Bryce?"

My blood freezes and my breath stills.

Bryce?

My nostrils flare with an uncontrollable rage.

No. Fucking. Way.

I throw open the door to the locker room so hard it bangs against the concrete wall, making the douche coach jump back, but not before I see how he was towering over Bryce. When Bryce's eyes lock with mine and his tear-streaked face comes into focus, something inside of me snaps.

I stride toward the piece of shit so fast he doesn't know what's coming, then I land blow after blow against his jaw, causing blood to splatter across the linoleum floor and up the wall.

"Oh shit. Reed!" Bryce's startled voice filters through the red haze, and I finally pull back to take in the coach. His face is red and swollen, and he groans as he rolls on the floor in a dramatic fashion.

"You're fucking fired," I clip out, and point down at him, and my fists twitch to continue the onslaught.

He coughs up some blood, then he winces. "You can't fire me," he splutters.

"Just you fucking watch, and I'm pressing charges," I grit out, my heart racing with a wild fury struggling to remain hidden.

He sits up and wipes the blood from his mouth. "You're pressing charges?" A strangled scoff bubbles from him, and his eyes fill with glee.

Oh, no, he fucking doesn't. If he thinks he can blackmail me, he can think again.

"I'm an attorney, asshole. I eat scum like you for breakfast. What you just did was child abuse, and trust me when I say, I'm going to ruin you."

He stumbles as he gets to his feet. "Hated the little bastards anyway," he grunts, and I take a menacing step toward him, and the sad little sack of shit darts for the door.

When it clicks shut behind him, I stroke over my bloodied knuckles while surveying Bryce, who sits studying me.

"We don't have a coach now." His voice is solemn, but it's his words that strike me. Was he okay with being spoken to like that in order to keep a coach? I glance around the locker room, taking in the broken doors and graffitied walls. Jesus, this place is abysmal. I rub at my temple to ease the budding tension.

Christ, is Gia okay with her son being here? An idea strikes me, an easy solution to all the problems right before my eyes.

"Would you like to move schools?"

Bryce rears back, as if stunned. "Fuck no. My friends are here."

"Mind your language," I chastise.

"Sorry," he grimaces, then clears his throat. "My friends are here, and they're good people. I like it here. Just he's a bit of a d—" He swallows. "Dope." And I can't help the laugh that escapes me. I'm pretty sure he wasn't going to call him a dope.

I mull over his words. His friends are here, and I know how important they are in one's life, I'm not about to change that for him.

"Okay. No changing schools." I stroke over my bottom lip and survey the hellhole. "We need to invest, though; this place is a shithole."

"It is." Bryce nods and glances around the small space.

"And you need a new coach. A decent one. I'll find one for you." I nod along to my own words and start making a mental list of everything that needs to change.

Bryce stands. "Well, we need one real quick. We have camp again tomorrow. What are we gonna do?"

"Going to do. Not gonna."

He rolls his eyes, and I ignore him and open the cufflinks

on my shirt, roll up my sleeves, then straighten my shoulders. "I'll do it," I declare with a newfound vigor.

His eyes widen, and a garbled sound leaves him, making me narrow my eyes. Is he becoming sick, possibly due to the trauma of the asshole screaming at him, or worse. "Did the coach ever touch you?"

Bryce stares back at me, his pupils bulge, and his mouth drops open. "W-what?"

"The coach, Bryce. Did he ever." I scrub a hand over my head, then kneel so I'm level with him. "Did he touch you?"

"Ew. God no. I'd have kicked him in the nuts. Oh, and also, he likes my mom."

I wobble on my heels as lightheadedness hits me. "What?"

"Yeah, he kept asking her out on a date." He continues while my anger returns and seems to multiply. "My mom said to Tyson it was sleazy, asking a pregnant woman out."

"I agree." I nod profusely. If he thinks he's getting away with no charges being brought against him, he can think again. I will dig up every sordid little detail of the sorry sack's life.

But first, I need to remind Gia of who she belongs to, because the thought of anyone else touching my girl has me wanting to rip some fucker's limbs from their lifeless, bloodied body. Then I need to take my girl on a date.

GIA

"Do we really have to go to court?" Kimmy nibbles on her lip.

I cover her hand with mine. "No, hun, we don't."

Relief floods her face, and I understand more than anyone could ever know.

"It's just a phrase we use, these documents that I'm creating"—I point to the paperwork—"will protect you and your baby's identity. I will present them to the courts. In-between time I'm working on moving you to another state." I bend down and grab the file from out of my briefcase, ignoring the shooting pain that lances across my stomach. "I've already started making inquiries."

Her face lights up, and I smile back at her just as broadly.

"You can have a fresh start, you and this little one." I tap the buggy next to her.

Tears swim in her eyes, and her bottom lip wobbles, then she throws her arms around me, knocking me back into my chair. "Thank you, Gia. I know you've been through a lot too, but thank you for everything you do for us."

A throat clears from behind us, and we both freeze. "I'm sorry to interrupt." Reed's guilty face comes into view. "I knocked." He holds his hand out toward the door.

I quickly scan him, knowing he wouldn't interrupt a meeting for no reason. He of all people knows the importance of confidentiality. "Is everything okay?"

He shifts from foot to foot, then drags his hand over his head. "Everything's fine. I just had a little altercation with the coach." He holds his bloodied hands up.

My eyes bulge. "Altercation?"

Kimmy leans back in her chair and watches the exchange with amusement.

"I don't like how he speaks to Bryce." He shrugs, and my jaw drops open. His eyes flare with desire, and when I roll my lip into my mouth and my tongue darts out to moisten it, the air thickens between us.

"Do you need me for anything else?" Kimmy asks, and I'm snapped out of my daze.

My cheeks redden as I realize she witnessed the change in the atmosphere, and I dart my eyes away from hers. "No, hun. We're done for today."

She gets to her feet and brushes her hands down her diner apron. "Well, thank you for working later today, it saved me having to swap my shift."

"You're welcome." I begin to pack up the files.

"It was nice to meet you again, Mr. Johnson."

"You too." He smiles at her tightly when she passes him, then heads out of the door.

"You interrupted a meeting, Reed." I lift an eyebrow toward him, and he steps toward me. "It was very rude," I chastise with a playful tone.

"It's because I want to do rude things to you." He grins at me wolfishly, then places his hands on my hips as he draws his lips to mine.

I pull back quickly, already intoxicated by his presence. "Where's Bryce?"

"Tyson has him. I dropped him off at home."

The way he says home makes my stomach flutter with a

thousand butterflies, despite knowing it was simply a slip of his tongue.

He kisses me again, but this time hard, and his fingers tug and tangle in my hair, holding my head in place as he devours me. "Fuck, I missed you."

I tilt my head to stare up at him. "You saw me earlier today."

He shakes his head with a bemused expression. "I know, it's ridiculous. But I'm addicted to you."

I chew on my bottom lip, magnetized by his admission and the way he stares into my eyes as if I'm his entire world. His universe.

Then he grinds his solid cock against me, and I whimper, with my nipples pebbling against my white blouse. "Are your nipples leaking for me to suck on, Gia?"

My throat becomes dry as I contemplate his words. "I ... I ..."

Stepping back, he disconnects us, and I feel his loss instantly. "Let me see." He drops down into my vacant chair, and my fingers itch to run my nails along the exposed skin beneath his shirt. I glance back at the door. "I locked it." His lip twitches.

My fingers tremble with need as I unbutton the blouse, and wetness pools in my panties at the way his hungry eyes bore into me. The green in them has darkened; they're full of a threat, a promise of power and control.

When I drop my blouse to the floor, his nostrils flare and he licks his lips like a starved animal preparing to devour its prey. I unclip my bra, and when the lacy fabric falls from my breasts, a growl emits from deep inside him. He surges forward, lifting me as if I weigh nothing, and spreads my legs so I'm straddling him. My skirt has risen, exposing my panties, and when he pushes them to the side and his thick finger slides through my arousal, I quickly unbuckle his pants.

He hisses when I slide my hand into his boxers, and when I wrap my hand around his velvety length, he groans as I pull him out. Then he pulls my ass cheeks apart as I lift to position him at my entrance. I lower myself down on him with a moan of pure, unadulterated bliss as my muscles wrap around him.

"Give me your tit to suck, baby," he grunts, and I lean back enough to expose myself further to him. With one hand, I guide my swollen nipple to his waiting mouth. "Good girl," he rasps before wrapping his lips around my bud, then he greedily sucks it into his mouth. Holy hell, my body trembles, and I bounce on his firmness, riding him hard and fast while he suckles on me as if I'm feeding him.

He removes a hand from my ass cheek and pops off my nipple. "Suck," he growls and holds up two fingers before shoving them roughly into my mouth, giving me no real choice at all. Thrusting them in and out until I gag, his smoldering gaze flares with intent, and he hardens inside me with the abrasiveness of his action.

When he slips them back out, his eyes are ablaze with desire. "Feed me." His tone is sharp, demanding, and full of power, and I lift the other nipple to his mouth, as if offering myself on a platter for him, and he sucks hard. The bite of pain behind it sends a wave of euphoria through me, and my slickness coats us both, my eyes rolling at the overwhelming sensation.

His palms expand until the tips of his fingers are toying with my asshole, and when one of his fingers slips inside, I clench around him. He slaps his free hand against my ass cheek. "Let me in, baby. Relax." I want to ask him how the hell can I relax? I've barely done this before, but he feels good. So good, and I'm too lost in the sensation to speak.

His finger moves deeper inside me, and he grunts his approval, enjoying this as much as me. My pussy clenches, my body tightens, and when my orgasm hits, a flood of milk spurts from my nipple. Reed thrusts harder with a growl, then he holds himself deep and sucks on me like his life depends on it. He's hungry, greedy, and feral for me, so I throw my head back in sheer ecstasy.

"Fuck," he roars, and my body relaxes as he slides his fingers from inside me.

Our heavy pants fill the air, and I slowly raise my head to look at him. A cocky smile spreads across his face, and I swipe the bead of milk from the corner of his mouth and push it past his open lips. "You taste fucking delicious, you know that?"

I giggle at his words, bite into his bottom lip, and shake my head, and he raises an eyebrow.

"You need to taste yourself." His eyebrows dance, and I bury my face into his shoulder and laugh.

"Stop!"

He chuckles against me, and the sound fills me with happiness. When he pulls me back to face him, my cheeks heat. He gently strokes over my lip with the pad of his thumb. "Delicious, baby." Then he replaces his thumb with his lips.

"You're filthy, Reed Johnson."

"I am." He smiles proudly, then pulls his shoulders back and grins. "And you love it."

"I do." I nod. "That thing you did with your finger." The redness on my cheeks deepens. "I didn't think I'd like it, but it was …" I'm at a loss for words.

He narrows his eyes. "Wait. Are you telling me you've never had your ass fucked?"

My mouth drops open at his bluntness, and I stumble on my words. "Nnn-no. Jaxon and I…" He jolts beneath me, like he does whenever I mention Jaxon. "We were young and didn't experiment with a lot of things you've probably done." Heat spreads up my face and over my ears.

His pupils darken as he studies me. "Fuck. I can't wait to spend the rest of my life with you." He whispers it so low I don't think I'm meant to hear him, but that doesn't dispel the giddiness brewing inside me at his words.

"Come on, let's get you cleaned up." Tapping my ass, he lifts me to my feet, and I hate the way his cum slips from me and down my thighs, leaving me a sticky mess. But when he sinks to his knees, I watch in rapture as he places my panties over my wet pussy, then he kisses me through the drenched fabric. "I want you to stroke over your pussy all the way home." The heat of his breath whispers through the material, and I grip onto his hair to keep myself upright.

"Then when you're all needy, I'm going to slide my thick cock into your tiny ass." His voice is thick with want, and I pant at the promise in his words.

Never before have I wanted my ass fucked, but now, it's all I can think about.

THIRTY-THREE

REED

SHE'S NAKED AND BARE. Her desire is as exposed as her body, and with each pump of my cock in my fist, her pupils spark with need.

Knowing she's never partaken in ass play was a shock and a gift wrapped into one delicious package that allows me the pleasure of taking her for the first time. If I could give Jaxon my thanks, I would.

"I'm going to take your virginity, Gia." My words are like a rebirth; she's giving me something she's given no one else, even her husband, and fuck me, I'm grateful for it.

Her finger works quicker over her swollen clit, and I roam my gaze over her delectable body. The silky locks of her hair are fanned out over her pillow, and her heavy tits heave with every movement. Our bump sits high on her stomach, thanks to the pillow I have thrust beneath her back, showing me her perfect little asshole dripping in my cum that escaped her pussy.

I kneel onto the mattress, positioning myself between her legs as I continue to pump my cock, loving the way my pre-cum drips from me in streams of need and covers my fist. My craving for her is obscene, but I don't care to hide it. She knows how much I want her, need her, and this will just be another way to show her.

She was right when she said I've done lots of things, but not once have I felt satisfaction from one woman. Not once has my desire been heightened to the extent Gia commands it.

And now, as I press the head of my thick cock around her swollen pussy, the surge of ownership ravishes my veins. She's giving herself over to me, all of her. To me.

Sliding the head of my cock down and over her asshole has my heart thumping wildly. I want to make this experience pleasurable for her, so slowly, I push inside, watching in awe as her small asshole opens to accept me. Unable to help myself, I thrust forward slightly, careful not to hurt my beautiful girl, the mother of my baby, my everything. "Good. Good girl," I croon while trying to maintain a level of control I don't feel.

I lick my lips, and her body attempts to reject my cock, her muscles contracting against the intrusion of me stretching her. "Let me in, baby. Keep playing with your clit while I sink inside your tight little hole."

As she clenches around me, it causes me to hiss, and a soft moan leaves her lips.

She whimpers when I push deeper, the head of my cock now past her barrier. "Fuck, that feels good." And she looks damn incredible. I brace a hand onto the headboard to steady myself, to rein in the need to fuck her hard and fast and fill her until she's dripping in my cum like a needy little slut.

"Reed?"

Her eyes dart from my face to between her legs, and I'm pretty certain she can't see a damn thing, and I hate the thought. Maybe next time I should record it for her so we can watch it back together while I stretch her from behind. "Fuck yes." I push deeper.

"Squeeze your nipple. I want to lick your milk after I'm done breaking your ass in for my thick cock."

"Oh god." She moans at my filthy words, and her lips part.

"You like that?" *Thrust.* "You like being my little slut?" I pull back and slowly slide back inside. "Begging for me to pump you with my cum?"

I lean over her, then take a hold of her jaw and press hard. The action sends pleasure zipping up my spine, and my cock sinks deeper inside her. As her jaw widens, I deliver a slow stream of my spittle into her mouth, and her eyes gleam with submissiveness. "Good girl. Now play." I release her jaw, and she swallows, then nods before trailing her hands over her tits, squeezing them together as she strokes her thumbs over her nipples. I groan in delight at her actions, reveling in the way her hips lift toward me and her spine arches with each graze over her peaked nipple.

"Such a good little slut for me," I growl and spear her with another inch of my cock again and again. I pick up my pace, struggling not to sink as deep as possible, careful to only stretch her and not fill her completely.

"Oh Jesus," she moans.

With a sharp hiss, I thrust again inside her ass, stilling as I rest my full length there, allowing her to become accustomed to the stretch my thickness causes.

"I need you to move, Reed." She moans, and I slide out of her with attentiveness I don't feel. "I really need you to move," she repeats, louder this time.

"Fuck, Gia. I'm trying to be gentle here," I grit out through clenched teeth.

"I want you to fuck me," she screeches and wraps her legs around my waist and digs her heels into my ass.

"Fuck!" I bite out and rear back, then slam inside her hard, causing her breath to still.

"Yesss!" She tips her head back, and her muscles spasm

around me, pulling me in as I surge into her ass harder and harder.

Sweat beads on my forehead as I work my hips faster and faster. Taking her ass rougher than I ever planned to. "Holy fuck, yes. Soo fucking good, Gia," I drawl out, and bite into the side of my mouth.

She continues to play with her tits, and I fucking love her for it. Fuck, do I love her, and when her milk makes an appearance, my balls draw up at the sight. My cock is almost painful, and my jaw drops open along with my slit, and I unleash my thick, hot cum deep inside her ass.

"Jesus. You're everything," I groan, darkness consuming me.

THIRTY-FOUR

REED

I'M ALMOST THIRTY-FIVE, and I've never been on a real date before, not really. My conquests or chosen escorts might have accompanied me to a nightclub, but there was an expectation of sex at the end of the night, with no feelings involved. Don't get me wrong, I'm hoping I end tonight with sex, but if I don't, as long as I'm in Gia's bed and it's her I wake up to every morning moving forward, I'm happy.

When I first told Gia I was taking her on a date, her head reared back, and her stunned expression was priceless. Of course, I had no choice but to take her parted lips in mine and tell her to go and get ready.

Even Tyson the Dickwad was on board with me taking her out. He grunted his approval and nodded like a puppet when I said I needed him to watch over Bryce and the out-of-control hounds from hell. Bubbles has taken to the He-man wannabe. So much so, I'm kind of hoping he takes the dog with him, pretty sure it could be used as a service animal.

This past couple of weeks with Gia have been the best weeks of my entire life, and I'm itching to make it permanent.

"I can't believe you organized all of this." Gia smiles widely, and my heart thuds in my chest as I entwine our fingers together. Then she scans the room again, and my eyebrows furrow. This is the third time she's done this in the span of only five minutes.

The restaurant is high-end, with crystal chandeliers that the candle lights flicker off of and a violinist playing Mozart in the corner of the room. The tone is romantic and elegant, but the way Gia fidgets from side to side and her eyes dart around the room gives away how uncomfortable she is, and I hate it.

I could be anywhere with her. I don't need any of this, and neither does she.

"Sir, the Pinot Noir 1945 is available," the server says, and I cast my eyes over Gia and her glass of water.

"I'm good, thank you."

My eyes narrow, and she bites into her bottom lip, and my cock hardens. Her green eyes twinkle as if knowing my thoughts.

"You can have a drink, Reed. I'm happy to drive home."

"Absolutely not." I hold her eyes. "I don't need a drink. I'm just happy to have you."

"You already have me. Smooth talker." She sticks her tongue out at me, and I chuckle. "Thank you for bringing me here, Reed. I love it." Glancing round the room again, she smiles whimsically.

"Do you?" I lift my eyebrow and lean forward. "Because I'm starting to regret it." Her face falls, and she darts her eyes away from mine, so I instantly regret my words. I tug on her hand to draw her attention back to me. "Let me rephrase that. I'm regretting choosing here. You deserve better."

She scoffs on a laugh, then takes in the other customers again. "Pretty sure, you don't get much better than this."

"Anywhere with you being comfortable is better than this." I motion around the room with my hand.

She pulls her top lip into her mouth. "This is the type of place my father would bring me to as a child." Her eyes meet mine, and there's so much sorrow in them I could drown in it. My spine straightens, and a newfound determination kicks in.

"Okay, we're leaving."

Her eyebrows shoot up, and I push my chair back, throw my napkin on the table, and stand. "Reed? N-no. It's fine." A spike of adrenaline floods my veins.

"Come on." I hold my hand out for her, and the moment her shoulders relax, and relief floods her face, I know I've won, and when her hand slips into mine, I feel like everything is how it should be.

"Reed, is that you?" a sneering voice has my stomach plummeting, then I spin to face the one woman I truly cannot stand.

My mother.

GIA

Reed's body locks up tight, and his hand almost chokes mine.

My eyes roam over the woman before us, with silver hair pinned back into a tight bun. Not a hair out of place.

She has pearls around her neck, and her chin is held as high as her heels, but she barely reaches Reed's shoulder.

"Who is this?" Her gaze travels over me and latch onto our entwined hands, and I want to hide behind Reed, thanks to the vicious glare she's throwing my way. Her stare lands on my stomach, then her eyes snap back up toward Reed's face. "Is she? Is that yours? You've got to be joking!" She's getting louder now. "I bet she's a gold-digging whore!" I jerk at her words, so familiar and just as cruel. Is this where Reed got his assumptions from?

"Don't speak to her like that," Reed snaps back, and my mouth falls open.

His mother's sharp eyes feel like lasers burning through me as her lip turns up, and she eyes me from top to toe.

"Yes, Mother. I have a baby on the way, and don't look at my fiancée like that!" Fiancée? My gaze darts to his, but his steely eyes are narrowed in on this mother.

She gasps and throws her arm over her chest dramatically. It's so theatrical I have to will myself not to giggle.

"You're just like that bastard you call a brother," she hisses, and Reed flinches. I squeeze his hand in support. "You'll lose everything, just like him."

Reed lowers himself to speak nearer her ear. "Don't call him that."

"You're a letdown, just like him." Then she flicks her gaze over to me. "He won't stick around. He'll want another whore soon enough. Just like his father, jumping from one to the next, leaving all the little bastards behind in boarding schools."

Reed's nostrils flare, and he holds his hand out toward his mother. "Here is a prime example of how not to parent. This is why I prefer to say I don't have any. Now, if you'll excuse me. We have somewhere better than here to get to."

Her mouth falls open, and I think she's going to chastise Reed for his scorn, but she doesn't. "Better than here?" A scoff erupts from her, drawing attention to us. "This restaurant has a waiting list a mile long. You'd do well to get anywhere better than here." I jolt at her words. I should have known the restaurant would have a huge waiting list, and guilt ravishes my veins.

Reed's smile curls into a cunning smirk. "A million percent better than here."

Then, without so much as a goodbye, he strides forward, leading me out of the restaurant door while my feet hurry to keep up with him.

When the evening breeze hits us, he finally comes to a stop and turns to face me. The way his hand trembles as he tucks a lock of my hair behind my ear has me wanting to comfort him. "I'm so sorry about her, baby." His gaze flicks over my face as if searching for a sign of something.

"It's fine." And it really is. I'm used to people like his mother; my father is a million times worse.

"It's not." He lifts my hand to his lips and kisses it tenderly, making me sway under his emerald gaze.

"Come on, let's get out of here before I fuck you in the street."

He signals for his car to be brought around, and I finally release the breath I hadn't realized I was holding.

Reed Johnson has stolen a vital part of me, and I never want him to give it back.

THIRTY-FIVE

REED

"ARE you sure you want to eat that?" I grimace at the vendor loading all sorts of precarious-looking items on top of the hotdog. Before now, just the thought of the so-called meat made me want to vomit into the nearest trash can, but watching Gia practically salivate for the food has me rethinking my previous conception.

"It's sooo good." She almost snatches the hotdog from the vendor, causing me to chuckle, then her eyes roll on a loud groan that has me adjusting my cock as she takes a huge bite out of it.

"Okay, give me one of those." I push a twenty into the vendor's hand, and he takes the cash with a laugh that mirrors my own.

Once I got in the SUV and over the fact we'd bumped into my mother, of all people, I undid my tie and threw it in the back of vehicle and could finally breathe more easily. Proof that some fucking idiot was trying to choke me with their creation.

I felt stripped bare with Gia sitting beside me. My demons

were exposed despite the one still hanging over me, but when she brought my hand to her lips, much like I'd done earlier, all thoughts of her father were banished from my mind. In that moment, all that mattered was her.

My teeth sink into the hotdog. Jesus, my mother would have a fit if she realized I was eating processed food loaded with fat and additives, and somehow, that thought makes it much more delicious.

We start walking, and I take her hand in mine.

"I figured I'd bring us back to where we started out as a family," I say, and nod toward the lake with the rowing boats. A few people are still milling around, and the odd family enjoy a picnic as the sun goes down. Each of them probably making the most of the warm evening, and honestly? It's beautiful to see. It's like an awakening. Why the fuck would I want to be in a stifled restaurant when I could be here with Gia and our family.

She smiles and drops her head, shaking it with the force of her laughter.

"You were a mess that day."

A laugh booms from my chest. "You think? I thought I was going to die from the intake of algae."

She rolls her eyes. "You're so dramatic."

I mock scoff and lay my free hand over my chest. "I couldn't google quick enough. I even had Mase research it for me while I made my way over to you."

"What did he say?" She smiles brightly.

"He must have told Tate, because the fucker called me up telling me I was going to be choking up tadpoles in my sleep, it's why I laid on my side all night."

Stopping in her tracks, she turns to face me. "I'm pretty sure you were on your back while I fucked you."

"Apart from that time." I nod.

She chews on her lip again, and I can't help but to bend down and tug it from her, pulling it between my teeth as I hold her hips in place. When I release it, she stares at me with a look of awe. "Tonight's been perfect, Reed." She pants out heavily.

I step back and eye her skeptically. "Perfect?" It's been a lot of things, but I wouldn't call it perfect. My mother helped put a stop to that. "It's ended perfectly."

She glances over her shoulder, toward the hotdog vendor, and smiles. "It has."

Throwing my arm around her, I tug her into my side. "Come on, let's get home and relax." When she bands her arm around my back, something settles inside me—a sense of peace and belonging.

I feel at home.

THIRTY-SIX

AS SOON AS we got in the SUV to return home, it started to piss rain, but I was thankful it didn't happen beforehand. That would have put another damper on the night.

After waving Tyson off on his quest for a hookup, Gia went up to bed while I was left with making sure the dogs went out to pee. Which is easier said than done when the demon dog refuses to go outside during the rain.

Annoyance rumbles inside me, and I stare down at it, and it tilts his head as if surveying me like I'm the one with the problem. "What sort of fucking dog are you?" I tip my head toward the door. "Go on. Go piss." I motion toward the door. "Go!" I have Gia waiting in our bed, for Christ's sake. He steps forward, and jubilation fills my bloodstream, then it pokes its head outside and stops. Then he looks back at the kitchen table, and my gaze follows, where a jacket hangs on the back of a chair. "You've got to be fucking kidding me," I grumble.

My phone pings, and I pull it from my pants pocket, and when Gia's face fills the screen, her biting on her bottom lip with her tits half hanging out her lacy red bra, I almost want to kick the dog outside and leave it there.

"For fuck's sake." I spin and grab the jacket, hating the fact it belongs to numbnuts. Then I hold it over my head to shield me from the rain and step outside, but when I turn back to face the dog, it hasn't so much as moved. "Come on. What the hell are you waiting for?"

It lifts its head up at me, then a loud bark erupts from it.

"Shhh. Shut the fuck up," I whisper, then move closer to it. The thing is somewhat attached to me for some unknown reason, but it does make me feel slightly reassured that he isn't going to attack me. I bend over the furball. "Come under this, you dipshit."

When the dog steps between my legs, I'm dumbfounded. Absolutely. Fucking. Dumbfounded.

"You don't like the rain? Fuck me, you are broken." Instead of analyzing the inner workings of this animal, I throw in the towel and use the jacket as a cover for it. I need to get back to Gia; she's probably playing with her clit right about now. "If you were mine, I'd ask for a refund," I grunt down as it sniffs the grass.

The cold rain is soaking through my shirt, but with Gia's naked body in mind, I suck it up. "Can you hurry up? I need to find the other fucker next." I know where Bubbles will be, hunkered down in Bryce's room. The dog might not be a bulldog, but it sure acts like one, a protector through and through. "At least I picked the right kind of dog." I grin, and the rain lashes down on me.

When it finally finds the right spot, I'm soaking wet and livid, but eager to get upstairs. I quickly throw it a treat on the floor, and instead of placing the jacket back on the chair, I decide to let the dog use it as a comforter and place it on sofa. "There. Use that as a pillow."

The dog jumps on it, and I wince when it starts digging around like a lunatic. Oh well, not my dog, not my problem. I smile at the thought of Tyson being pissed when he discovers the dog used his jacket to sleep on, then I head upstairs.

Bryce's door is ajar, and when I poke my head inside, my heart constricts at the sight, then freefalls, pounding against my ribcage so strongly it feels like it's bursting to get out.

The sight of Bryce clutching the damn Happy Meal toy in one hand and an arm thrown over Bubbles as he snuggles up with her is almost overwhelming. A surge of what I think is love strikes me. A feeling I welcome instead of rejecting. My mouth feels like there's wool stuffed in it, and I find the ability to move is stolen from me.

Bubbles licks at Bryce's face, and the kid simply grins down at the dog as if it's the best thing he's ever encountered.

I've never been one to say a child is cute, or an animal, or anything for that matter, but I can admit my son and his dog are cute as hell.

"Did you jump in the lake again?" Bryce rubs at his eyes, and it's only now I realize how far I've stepped into his room and made my way over to his bed. Not that it was a difficult task, given his room is small and fairly sparce.

I smile at his words. "No, buddy. It's just raining heavily."

He nods, then follows it up with an exaggerated yawn. "I let Bubbles out earlier because Tyson said it was going to rain."

Of course he did. The man thinks he knows everything. What is he, a meteorologist now?

For some insane reason, I don't want to move, yet I don't know what to say to him. The little boy and his mutt have stolen my heart, just like his mother. My ass touches the bed without thinking, and I stroke over the dog because I'm unsure what to say or do.

Bryce's room is small and painted blue, with soccer trophies on a wooden shelf that make me smile with pride.

When we move into our own house, I'll build one of those courts for him and his friends to kick the ball around on, and when my best friends bring their kids over, they can play in the pool I'm going to design with the kids in mind, and we can have a games room and a soft playroom for the baby.

Bryce shuffles from beneath the covers to sit up and grabs his cup of water from his bedside table. As he takes a drink from it, my focus latches on to the photo previously housed in the hallway. The one with Jaxon, Gia, and Bryce fishing and a wooden cabin in the background.

"I don't even remember him," Bryce whispers, and points toward the photo.

My pulse rushes, and my mouth goes dry, because fuck, that's awful.

"You don't?" I choke out, trying to disguise the way my tone is laced in disappointment for him and Gia.

I can't think of anything worse than my son not knowing me, remembering me. My gut twists, and I consider the consequences of my actions, but I'm quick to banish the feeling.

He shakes his head. "My mom thought I'd like it in here." He lifts a shoulder.

"Do you? Like it in here, I mean."

"I'd rather have a photo with you and my mom and Bubbles." His words cause a tightening in my chest, and I'm grateful I had the foresight to dump the tie. "And the baby. All of us together, like a family."

"You can still keep the one with your dad," I add, not wanting to appear like I'm pushing Jaxon out of the picture completely, but internally, my bloodstream is filled with elation. He wants me. He wants me to be a part of this family.

"Yeah. I'll keep it. But I want a bigger one with us all on. The old photos make my mom sad, but the new ones will be when she's happy."

How the hell do I argue that. "I get you." I clear my throat and lean forward and ruffle his hair to lighten the mood.

"Now, come on, it's way past your bedtime." Reluctantly, I stand from his bed. "Night, buddy."

He groans his displeasure as I head toward the door. "Reed?"

My hand stops on the door handle, and I look over my shoulder, locking eyes with Bryce. "You wet my bed." He points to the comforter, and I grimace.

"It's only a small patch, buddy. It'll dry by morning." And if not, I'll blame it on the wolfhound.

"I'm pleased my mom chose you for my brother's dad." He smiles and pulls the covers up to his eyes.

Clearly, that's not quite how it happened, but still, there could be no one happier about the fact than me despite my earlier reservations.

"Me too," I whisper, and he closes his eyes, and I head out of his room.

I'm already unbuttoning my shirt as I slip into our bedroom, thankful Gia has left the bathroom light on for it to filter into the room, so I don't trip as I tug off my socks and soaked pants.

Her soft snooze fills the room, and a sense of warmth encompasses me, and when I slip between the sheets and pull her onto my chest, I can't help but share how I feel, to release my vulnerability and fears.

I place a kiss on top of her head, slide my cock into her warm cunt, and tell her how I feel. "You're my home, Gia. Wherever you are is where I want to be. Never leave me, baby."

THIRTY-SEVEN

"SO LET me get this straight. You don't want huge tits?" Tate asks Mase and scrunches his nose. Just hearing the words has my eyes darting over to my girl.

It's Eleanor's birthday party today, and when the little ones fell asleep in the nursery, us guys gathered in the living room to discuss Mase's first booking with an Indulgence girl while the women chat about pregnancy experiences around the kitchen island.

Watching Gia in the kitchen with the other women has pride washing over me. It's been one hell of a month, and I've not spent one night away from her—even Bubbles, the fucking rat-bastard, has joined me. Mainly because Shaw refuses to dog watch any longer. Turns out, Bubbles has a thing for soft furnishings. Thankfully, Bryce has taken a liking to her, and Gia was okay with her sleeping in his room so it doesn't disturb us in the night. So I'm pretty damn grateful even though the thought of the pet hair all over my son has me wanting to scrub him clean each time he leaves his room.

"You don't like big tits?" I glance back at my friend in

utter shock, because every time I look at my girl's rack, I blink in disbelief. The size and thought of the weight alone make my cock rock hard, not to mention the softness of her nipples and the way small drops of milk leak from her, and it's all entirely for me at this stage. It's like she's producing milk for her baby's daddy while she finishes keeping our baby safe.

Providing for us both.

I rearrange my cock; grateful the infants aren't around. It's not something I've ever had to consider before now, mainly because I've never been in the vicinity of children long enough to have an issue to care.

Mase's cheeks heat, and he drags a hand over his shaved head. The tattoos on his neck contract, another giveaway of his discomfort. "It's not that I don't like them."

"Tara had big tits, right? You want different." Tate surmises.

Mase's shoulders sag. "Exactly, and not anything fake either." We all share a knowing glance. Tara was fake through and through, every part of her, and I grimace at the fact I ever found that stereotype attractive, not when there're natural beauties out there like Gia.

My eyes find her again, and we remain locked in a trance until Owen nudges me.

"One girl or two?" he asks, and I blink at him with confusion. Then he gestures toward the phone in Tate's hand. "For Mase. Do you think the first time should be one girl or two?"

"One," I state. "Definitely one."

Tate clears his throat and broadens his shoulders. "So, to summarize. One girl, natural beauty, fresh faced."

I nod along to his words.

"Smaller tits, what color hair did you say?"

"Not blonde." Mase quickly inserts, and we smile at one another at his speedy response. His ex dyed her hair blonde, so I can appreciate where the comment came from.

"Okay. Anything else?"

"No. If you click on accept now, you can skip all the specifics," I add.

Tate scoffs. "Like what specifics?"

I glance over my shoulder to check Gia is out of earshot, then lower my voice. "Any additional extras like piercings, particular kinks and such."

Tate sits forward, leaning on his elbows, his eyes alight with glee, and I want to hit myself in the face for giving him ammunition for his schoolboy antics. "What kind of kinks?"

"Just click on the next fucking page," I grit out. He knows damn well what kinks are available on the app; he's heard me brag often enough.

Tate slumps back in his chair like a petulant child. Then he stares at the phone in his hand, and his lip curls into a sly smirk. "What would you like your match to be willing to participate in?"

Great, here we fucking go.

"Ass play, spit play, blood play." He scrunches his nose before continuing on. "Wet play, BDSM ..." He quirks an eyebrow toward me as if I'm the one choosing, and I look away, not willing to be drawn into the conversation any longer than necessary.

His voice drones on, but I tap out of the sixty-five questions I was once accustomed to.

Until I met her.

She throws her head back on something Ava says, and warmth spreads through me as she places her hand on her stomach, stroking over it with affection.

"I'm going to marry her."

"Do it before she has the kid. That way, you can both have the same name," Owen adds, and I only now realize I spoke aloud. "And sort fucking Fanzio out. The last thing you want is that prick fucking it up for you," he snaps, with a venomous glare aimed in my direction.

"You don't want to lose her, Reed," Shaw tacks on, and a

tremor of fear flashes through me at the thought. Of course I don't; that's the last thing I want to happen.

They're my world.

I steel my spine with determination; that's never going to happen.

The girls pull me out of my daze when Ava's panicked voice cuts through the air. "Reed! I think there's something wrong with Gia!"

And just like that, all thoughts of George Fanzio are banished from my mind.

I just wish I'd dealt with him sooner.

THIRTY-EIGHT

GIA

I'VE LOVED every minute of meeting Reed's friends. From the moment we were welcomed inside Shaw's home, I was embraced in Emi's arms. She's sweet and demure, and it's clear how she holds herself that she's been trained in sophistication; something I've shied away from over the years.

When she explained she became pregnant with Eleanor after a one-night stand with Shaw, I thought our stories would align, but how wrong could I be? The poor girl is a Mafia princess, and her overbearing brother Luca hunted Shaw down and forced them into an arranged marriage so not to bring shame on the family.

Their story is both heart-wrenching and endearing.

Ava—Tate's wife—is a bubbly, smart, young woman. She's recently given birth to their son, Sonny. He's adorable and an image of his daddy. She explained that she first met Tate while she was a foster child and slept with him on her eighteenth birthday, unbeknownst to him. Years later, she became an intern at their company STORM Enterprises, not realizing Tate was a co-owner. Her life sounds harrowing, and she's a testament to her strength. The connection I feel with her when I look into her eyes tells me everything I need to know, and the way her eyes soften when she looks at me tells me she sees a reflection of herself.

Owen's wife, Laya, is Tate's sister, and she's also been through her own trauma. Her first husband was involved in shady activities that brought his demise. Owen rescued her from a terrible situation, then he adopted her infant son, and they were married within days. Their adorable baby boy, Lowan, is only a few weeks old. Laya said Owen is a hands-on father, and it's made life a hell of a lot easier than if he wasn't, given her little ones are both under two years old.

"Next time we meet, you need to bring Bryce," Ava declares while pushing another chip into her mouth. "The guys will entertain him."

"Reed wanted to bring him today, but he had plans to stay over at his friend's house."

"Reed talks about him a lot!" Emi smiles whimsically. "And Eleanor talks about Reed a lot too." She giggles, making me laugh at the thought of how annoyed Reed gets about Eleanor's obsession with him.

"I think we need a spa day. Leave the babies and kiddos with their dads," Laya suggests, and I nod in response.

"Yes! This!" Ava holds her hand up for Laya to high-five her, and I giggle at their camaraderie.

My gaze lingers to Reed, and I find him watching me. His green eyes are trained on me as if he doesn't want to miss a thing. A smile tugs at his lips before he trails his eyes slowly down my body and licks his lips when his perusal meets my chest. Heat floods me. I fidget from side to side as I imagine him becoming hard at my heavy breasts.

Knowing Reed gets so turned on at my body has an incredible effect on my self-esteem. I'm not stupid. I look nothing like the thin fake-breasted women he paraded around at the community event, and given his previous bachelor life, I can only imagine what the women he's been used to look like. But he's never once made me feel anything but adored, like he craves every inch of me.

"He's so in love with you. It's so stinking cute," Emi whispers in my ear, and I crinkle my nose.

My heart does a silly flutter, because as surreal as it feels, having someone else confirm my suspicions feels almost too good to be true. "You think?"

"Girl, he is obsessed with you!" Ava is animated as she speaks, making me laugh at her dramatics.

"I've known Reed since I was a little girl, and never, ever, ever did I think he would become attached to one woman. Ever," Laya tacks on.

My heart soars at their words of encouragement; it's everything I wanted to hear and so much more. It cements the way I feel, and a part of me bubbles with excitement at the prospect of our future together. Maybe we can make it as a family. Maybe I can have the family for Bryce and this baby that I always dreamed of having.

A surge of pain flashes across my stomach, and I wince and bend over to grip onto the counter.

"Reed! I think there's something wrong with Gia!" Ava screeches, and I close my eyes at her words, knowing how panicked Reed is about to become about what could potentially be Braxton Hicks.

THIRTY-NINE

REED

MY LEG BOUNCES uncontrollably as we wait for news from the doctor. Owen has flown in the same obstetrician who he and Laya used, a world-renowned specialist, and I couldn't be more grateful for his connections.

Our friends, also known as our family, have gathered in the waiting area to offer their support at what will be an induced labor at almost thirty weeks due to preeclampsia.

My heart thuds rapidly, and I push one hand through my hair while the other remains tightly wrapped around Gia's. Her emerald eyes remain locked on mine, and the doctors work on safely delivering our baby. I have the sudden urge to tell her exactly how I feel. My throat is already dry, and my chest heaves with anxiety from the day's events. "Gia. I-I …"

The commotion at the end of the bed has me lifting out of my chair to glance over the top of the operating divider. Each heavy thud of my heart makes me feel like my world is sitting on the edge of a cliff, hanging precariously over the side. This moment is going to determine our baby's future.

"Safe delivery. We're moving baby into NICU," one doctor

calls to another, and my heart falters, and Gia's hand tightens on mine. "Safe delivery."

One of the medical team approaches us, and I stand with Gia's hand still in mine. "Congratulations. Your little one was delivered safely. The next step is to get momma stitched up and baby on oxygen while we determine his medical needs. As soon as he's stable, we can offer skin-to-skin contact and try to induce your colostrum."

"Gia already has colostrum. She's producing milk already."

"Oh. That's perfect. I'll let the doctors know." She glances from me to Gia and back. "Will you be joining baby in NICU?"

My palm becomes sweaty at the thought of leaving Gia. "I want to stay here." I shake my head.

"Reed. You need to go with him."

My head snaps to Gia's. "I'm not leaving you here." I glance around the room, and frankly, it looks terrifying. It's clinical and buzzing with medical activity. There's no way I'm leaving her here alone; what if she needs me? What if there's a decision to be made and I'm not here?

"Please." Her bottom lip wobbles, and tears stream from her eyes. "He needs his daddy, Reed. He needs someone, and I don't want him to be alone."

My chest squeezes at her words. Our baby needs someone. He needs his daddy; otherwise, he's going to be alone. There's no fucking way I'll allow that.

Reluctantly, I gift her with a nod, then lower my head and kiss her forehead while swiping away her tears with my thumbs. "I'll send one of the girls in."

"Thank you."

The words linger on my tongue to tell her I love her.

Just fucking do it.

"Sir, are you ready?"

I'm snapped out of my daze and away from Gia, and as I

turn on my heels to follow the stream of medical staff and our incubated son, I feel a heavy tug in my heart. Something I never want to feel again for as long as I live.

A longing so powerful it feels like someone is tearing me in two.

FORTY

WATCHING Reed have skin-to-skin contact with bubba is my new favorite thing in the world, and better yet, when Bryce is a part of that, my heart swells with an overwhelming force of love for the men in my life.

Bryce is sitting between Reed's open legs on my hospital bed. Both of them shirtless while Reed's strong arms are wrapped around Bryce, and he holds our baby while Bryce has him resting on his small chest.

Tyson has been incredible at holding down the fort at home, taking Bryce to and from school. Remaining at home as his primary caregiver has allowed Reed and me to be at the hospital with our newborn son.

Reed turns his head to look at me. "I've been thinking about names."

"Hmm," I muse. Every name I suggest, Reed screws his face up over.

Reed straightens a little and swallows hard.

Oh, sweet Jesus, I'm not going to like this suggestion. I can feel it, but I need to hear him out because he hasn't so much as made a single one, and bubba is a week old now, and I can't keep referring to him as bubba.

He clears his throat, and Bryce cocks his head back to scan Reed's face. "I was thinking we could honor your dad and name him Jaxon."

My chest expands with the affection behind his words. Whatever was about to come out of his mouth, I never in a million years expected that.

"I've been thinking about it for a while, but wasn't sure if you'd both be okay with me suggesting it." He shrugs, then swallows again.

"You want to name him after my dad?"

Reed locks eyes with Bryce. "Only if you want to, buddy. If you and your mom are comfortable with it." He glances toward me, and I push away the tears sliding down my cheeks and try my best to stifle the sob threatening to bubble out of me.

"Can we call him Jax for short?" Bryce asks.

Reed's lips curve into a smile. "If your mom is okay with that." As he glances at me again, I nod. Our gazes fix on one another. His is an outpouring of love and gratitude, and mine is one of strength and resilience, a look of appreciation and love. My heart becomes heavy as I consider the gift that Jaxon left me with. A beautiful son, and now with Reed by my side, I've been given the gift of a new start, one I wouldn't change for the world. One I once dreamed of, but now I realize what was missing all along.

It wasn't Jaxon.

It was Reed.

This beautiful, broken soul, who, despite his flaws, has done everything in his power to put me and Bryce first. He's become the backbone of our family. Someone I can rely on, a perfect father figure for our boys. A man I love more than the one I longed for.

My everything.

I love you, I mouth to him, and his breath hitches.

"It's like my dad gave us him. Isn't it?" Bryce muses and smiles down at his baby brother in awe.

"He did. He gave us all the best gift ever," Reed agrees, and strokes Jax's hair while he places a kiss on top of Bryce's head.

Bryce tilts his head back to fix his gaze on Reed. "He gave us you too. I know it."

Reed's eyes fill with tears, an outpouring of gratitude to the man I once loved most in the world. Then he turns and stares deep into my soul. "I think he did too, buddy. He gave me everything."

FORTY-ONE

FIVE WEEKS LATER ...

WE'VE BEEN HOME for a week now, and it's official. I want to move to a new house.

This little home was ideal for me. It was mine and Jaxon's dream, but it's no longer a fit for us.

It's a dream that never fully transpired, and it's also too far from the city center; Reed has had to spend the occasional night away from us and at his apartment because of late meetings and early morning starts, and to say he was beside himself was an understatement.

He hates being away from us, and as much as I try to remain strong, I can admit I want him here. I miss his heavy arms wrapped around me, the way he looks longingly at me when he places Jax on his chest and gently strokes over his dark head of hair. The way he insists on waking Bryce up for breakfast and feeding him a concoction of the organic shit he keeps attempting to persuade him with, only to then give in and offer him the Chunky Chips Cookie cereal my son is obsessed with, and the way he calls Bubbles every swear name possible but then smiles affectionately at the connection Bryce has with her.

The birth of Jax has been difficult, due to me also recovering from a C-section, and throw in my emotions being all over the place, I miss Reed terribly while he's at work.

I swear I have some sort of dependency on him, something I swore to myself after losing Jaxon I would never let happen again, yet here I am, counting down the minutes to his return.

The girls have become an extension of my own little family. Their support has been incredible, and again, another reason I want to move closer to the city, somewhere halfway, maybe. That way, Bryce can remain in his current school, and give us the security of our found family. I can also commute to the community center and continue to fulfill my ambition of helping those within the community I so desperately want to support. My little way of giving back something from the way they welcomed me.

My mind floods with ideas about towns within close proximity to the city while I stir the pasta sauce, and I smile at how excited Reed will be at the prospect of us having a house together, one we choose and build our future in.

He's not mentioned another word about moving since the day we had an argument, but something tells me he's itching to make his original plans a reality.

The doorbell rings, snapping me from my thoughts, and I move the sauce off the heat, glance at Jax asleep in his travel crib, then head toward the door.

I make a male silhouette out from behind the glass, and when I open the door, anger flashes through me at the sight of Kevan staring back at me, shifting from side to side.

Great. Now is not the time to be dealing with this shit, especially with my emotions all over the place. I grit my teeth.

"You can't be serious!" I snap and step back to close the door in his face.

"Gia. Please wait. It's important." He wedges his foot in the door, and I still, but when I glance up, looking for a sign of a threat, I find none. Instead, all I find is remorse. "Please, just a few minutes of your time." His eyes implore mine. I'm not sure what it is in his tone that has my body on high alert, but something about the way he speaks, almost a plea, has my body stilling and my mind complying. I take a deep breath and hope I'm not about to regret my decision. "Okay," I whisper, and open the door farther to let him inside.

He stops in the hallway, and I motion toward the living room. When we walk inside, I wince when I consider him witnessing the mess of a newborn and young boy in such a small space.

"How are you feeling?" he asks pensively.

I clear my throat. "I'm getting there." Casting my eyes over him again, I take in the envelope in his hand, but he's unable to meet my eyes. Something he's never struggled with before. I swallow back the nervousness in my throat. "What are you doing here, Kevan?" I gesture toward the cryptic envelope.

He takes a deep breath, and I know whatever he's about to say I'm not going to like. Scrap that, I'm going to hate it. It's going to destroy me.

I know it.

For weeks, my life has been incredible, and that envelope holds something that will obliterate it.

He clears his throat, and the guilt rolls off him in waves. "I'm doing this for the right reasons, Gia. Once upon a time, me and Jaxon were friends."

"Before you tried it on with me in a bid to break us up, you mean?" I snap.

He blows out a breath and swallows. "Yes. It was wrong of me. I've been controlled by your father for a long time."

"And before you tried to get me drunk and follow it up with a kiss?" I continue with my little tirade, delivering blow after blow of all the stunts he's pulled over the years in an effort to follow my father's instructions and win me over. "And when Jaxon got the job at the hardware store, and you complained he'd been abusive, and the manager let him go? We needed that job, Kevan." I exhale.

"That wasn't me!"

I glare back at him, and he winces. Then he holds his hands up.

"It wasn't, I swear it."

I shrug. "Whatever. What are you doing here?"

He glances away again before bringing his eyes back to mine. "I'm sorry."

"About?"

"Everything. The past, the present, and more importantly, your future." He holds the envelope up, and a feeling of dread sits in my stomach like a lead ball. "This is a contract that Reed signed with your father."

My heart hammers precariously. "What contract?"

"He agreed to fight for custody of your son unless you signed the shares over to your father. That way, Reed can purchase the community center land."

A crushing feeling takes over my lungs, filling my body with a poison that threatens to bring me to my knees. He wouldn't, would he?

My throat becomes dry, and I tremble as I contemplate his words while I try to maintain the man I love would never do that to me, to our son. I shake my head and stare at the envelope. He wouldn't use us as pawns in his quest for money, would he?

"It's true, Gia. Look for yourself."

"Why are you telling me this?" My voice crumbles as the words come out of my mouth like ash on my tongue. The bitter truth of Reed's lies burning through me like gasoline.

"Because I want you to know his true intentions."

"Why?" I snap, then wince at the cruel tone behind it, but I straighten my spine, determined to remain the strong, independent woman I became, yet feeling anything but. "So, you can step in and marry me? Take the shares from me too?" I shake my head, and tears stream down my face. Another broken home, another betrayal, all by the men meant to love me above and beyond anyone else. None of them can be trusted. Not a single one. "You're power hungry and heartless. You cheat, steal, and prey on those who are vulnerable." I stab my finger into his chest. "You're cowards. You're all goddamn cowards!" I scream as my hands ball into fists, and I hammer against his chest.

His arms band around me, and I sob against him. "I'm sorry," he whispers brokenly. "I'm sorry."

His words are my undoing and bring me back to my new reality. He's sorry? Well, I'm sorry too. I'm sorry I ever met Reed Johnson and allowed him into our lives.

I step back with renewed vigor, and as I swipe the tears from my face, I stare Kevan in the face. "He can have the shares, but he'll never see our son again."

Kevan shakes his head. "That won't be necessary."

My eyebrows knit together.

"I came here to give you this." He holds up the envelope, and I take it. "It's a copy of the contract and a copy of the shares I own, signed over to Bryce from today."

My eyes widen.

"It's what I came to tell you. You have the power as Bryce's guardian to have full control over the company. I don't want to work with George Fanzio any longer. He's gone too far, Gia. I'm only sorry it took until now for me to see it."

Shock reels through me, a wave of emotions hitting me one after the other, but not a single one of them as powerful as knowing the man I love betrayed me and used our son as a bargaining tool to get what he wanted.

He's not the man I thought him to be; that man doesn't exist. He never did. I swipe at the lone tear trickling down my cheek. It was all a performance, a way to get what he wanted. He played me, played with all of us, and that thought sends a tremor of devastation through me. An animalistic sob rips from my chest, and I grip onto the living room chair to hold me up as the room spins.

Kevan steps forward, and I shake my head. "Can you leave now?" I whisper through racked sobs. Leave and never come back, I want to say, but I no longer have the power to utter a single word.

Kevan nods, then swallows thickly. "I'm sorry, Gia. Truly, I am."

As he closes the door behind him, I sink to the floor and stare at the contract in my shaky hand.

How could he do this to us? He promised. My lip quivers as a deep-seated stabbing, like a knife is being twisted inside my chest, causes me to suck in sharp stuttered breaths, yet I still don't feel like I'm breathing. One attempt after the other as a sickening wail lodges in my throat, and the feeling of it tightening has me clutching at it.

"Pl-please, no." My tears fall freely now, and I will them to come.

The soft sound of our son cooing has nausea rushing through me, and I snap my gaze toward him.

Oh Jesus, he was going to take Jaxon from me. The man I love was going to tear out my heart, my reason for living. He was willing to destroy our family for a piece of land.

For money.

Betrayal, hurt, and devastation ravish my crumbling heart. He lied. It was nothing more than a lie.

FORTY-TWO

REED

THE VOICES around me drone out as my mind wanders to how beautiful Gia looked when I left her this morning.

Watching her feed Jax makes my chest fill with indescribable pride. My little man is the perfect blend of both of us, and I couldn't be prouder. His little bow lips are just like his momma's, and he's delicate, his hair silky to touch and dark like both of ours. Gia is convinced he's a mini me, and I smile each time she says it.

We've not had any sexual contact since Jax's birth, and it's killing me, but I'm determined to wait until Gia is healed. She's made moves to suck my cock, and she's literally offered her tit to me to suckle from, but I refuse to do any of that until I can put my cock where it belongs, in my woman. Only then will I take milk from her as her pleasure slides down my shaft.

"Reed, are you fucking listening? I said I need to go to LA!" Mase snipes out.

I glance around the boardroom table; all the guys are staring at me as if I've missed a vital part of the meeting, so I sit up straighter and drag a hand through my tousled hair. "Who? What?"

"Jesus." Shaw chuckles and shakes his head. "Your head's at home, isn't it?"

"Wait until Jax starts cutting his teeth. Believe me, your head will be back at work pretty damn quick." Owen inserts on a belly laugh.

"Back to me," Mase snaps, which is completely unlike him. "My father died. I mean halle-fuckin'-lujah. But now I need to go to LA so they can read the will."

"Okay," I mumble, unsure as to why the fuck he's so disgruntled about a man he hates passing away.

His jaw drops slack. "Okay? Okay? So, you'll book us flights?"

I jolt. What the fuck did he just say, us?

"Absolutely fucking not," I clip back, and face him head-on, and anger rears its ugly head.

He scoffs obnoxiously. "Reed, you're my damn lawyer and I need you."

I wave my hand toward him. "You'll be fine." Does he seriously think I have the time to fly to the other side of the country right now?

"Dude, he needs to make sure he isn't getting screwed over," Tate adds, and I want to kick the fucker in the balls. There's no way he'd leave Ava and his baby; no fucking way, and I refuse to ask her to travel in her condition. Can newborns even travel? No. He's going to have to suck it up.

I cross my arms over my chest. "No."

He sits forward. "No?" His nostrils flare. "Seriously?"

"Your mother made sure your father couldn't screw you over in her will. What could possibly go wrong?" I lift my shoulder.

Mase throws himself back in the chair and pinches the bridge of his nose.

Tate's eyes light up, and he sits forward, the excitement in his eyes childlike. "Maybe you could look at properties while out there for us to expand."

Mase's head snaps toward Tate, and he glares daggers. "Are you fucking serious right now?"

"You're very angsty." He grins back at him. "I thought you were getting serviced last night?" He wiggles his eyebrows.

Mase's cheeks color, and his chest rises. He looks like he's about to explode. Then he pushes back on his chair and begins pacing the room like a caged animal.

"You fuck anyone since the first girl?" Owen throws out, and Mase spins to glare back at him.

"No," he clips.

"She broke you." Tate chuckles.

Mase's nostrils flare. "Shut the fuck up!"

"What was the problem? You said she was amazing, best night of your life, blah blah blah," Shaw drawls.

Mase's shoulders sag as he drops his head forward, and his Adam's apple slowly slides down his throat while we wait on tenterhooks for him to speak. "That was until the end. The bit I keep trying to block out but fail. Every. Fucking. Time."

"Was she really a man?" Tate chuckles, and I'm pleased when Owen reaches out and smacks him on the back of his head.

Slowly, he lifts his head, and his pale face has me sitting forward with concern. "Nope. A schoolgirl."

You could hear a pin drop.

"That's not possible. Oscar has rules that the women have to be twenty-one or above," Owen interjects.

Mase rubs at his forehead, and a pang of sympathy hits me for my friend. He has no fucking luck with women, and if he thinks he's slept with someone so young, no wonder he's not in a rush to do it all again. If Owen is right, someone in Indulgence has seriously fucked up.

Shaw turns to me. "Sounds like he needs a lawyer." He winks.

I blow out a deep breath. Great, another fucking job to add to the list. At least this one is in New Jersey, not fucking LA.

"Are you coming to LA or not?" Mase asks, his sudden change in conversation a welcome relief. Let's face it, who the fuck wants to deal with that and the extra workload it will bring?

"Not," I state.

He exhales theatrically. "I'm out. Looks like I'm going to LA *alone!*" He huffs and slams the door behind him.

"What's gotten into him?" I ask as my eyes narrow on the door.

"Oh, I don't fucking know, Reed. You're meant to be his damn lawyer, and you just threw him to the wolves to stay home and play house. Not to mention, he thinks he slept with a teenager and can see a lawsuit coming."

I scoff back at Owen. "Like you wouldn't have done the same."

His lip twitches and he shrugs. "Probably."

"Besides, the teenager thing won't be a problem. If what Owen is saying is right, I could sue the company for not following through with their own safeguarding and rules." I grin widely.

"You're going to sue the Mafia?" Owen asks with a raised eyebrow.

Yeah, probably not the best idea, and I wince.

I drown out of the rest of the conversations while my mind wanders to why Gia hasn't messaged me back yet. She usually lets me know when Jax has his afternoon feeding and nap. Something isn't right. Gia always sends me messages throughout the day. I pull up the tracking app I have on their phones, and when they both signal being at home, an ominous feeling deep inside me twists, making my blood run cold. She always messages me and tells me Bryce made it home safe.

Something is wrong.

FORTY-THREE

REED

A SICKENING FEELING swells inside my stomach as I pull up outside Gia's. Her car is parked outside the house, but Tyson's truck is missing. He was supposed to be collecting Bryce from school and should be here by now. I glance at my phone again to see no missed calls or messages. Surely, she'd have called me if it was something to do with one of the boys, right? My heart flips at the thought. She would have.

I swallow back the bile gathered in my throat, switch off the car, and rush up the steps with my heart hammering in my chest and my fingers trembling. I dig into my pocket for the spare key she gifted me recently and unlock the door.

Silence greets me, which is rare. Due to how small the house is, every sound is heard, and I've become accustomed to my shattered peace, and I've grown to love the chaos of the small house. I glance around the hallway, and nothing looks amiss, but as I step into the living room, I notice Jax's portable crib is missing, causing a pain to lance through my chest. I spin on my heels and dash up the stairs and into Gia's bedroom. Her bedroom drawers are pulled out and empty, and when I throw open the bathroom door, her toiletries are missing.

What the fuck?

Sickness wells inside me, growing thicker and thicker by the second, and I almost stumble over my feet to get to Bryce's room, where again, his drawers are bare.

Oh Jesus. I feel like my chest is caving in and the ability to breathe is gone. I swallow hard and push myself forward.

Next, I make my way to the room that has been working as a small nursery for Jax. Although he's been in our bedroom every night, this one is to house his clothes and diapers. It's a room I've suggested numerous times we paint and stick those cute zoo animals up that Bryce suggested, but Gia has halted my plans every time. I won't lie; I was hoping it was because she didn't want to put down roots any more than she has already here, and was finally coming around to us moving into our own place together.

Jax's room is just as bare. The clothes that fit him are gone, and when I open his closet, the next size up are missing too, causing a shudder to rack through me.

Holy shit. Oh Jesus, she left.

She left me.

I grip onto the doorframe to steady myself; my lungs feel like they're being crushed as I struggle to breathe. Panic rushes through my body, but my brain cannot compute a single action, forcing me to close my eyes to try to regain composure.

Please don't do this to me, baby. Please.

My world tilts on an axis, and I know deep in my heart.

They're gone.

My entire world has disappeared.

I snap my eyes open and fumble in my pants pocket for my phone. My fingers shake as I somehow call Owen.

"Yeah?" His gruff voice filters through the line.

My throat seizes up.

"Reed?"

"O-Owe—" I clear my throat and attempt to speak again. "Owen, Gia is gone. She's gone, and she's taken the boys." I fall over my words as I struggle to get them out.

"What? Reed, you're making no sense. What are you talking about?"

I pinch the bridge of my nose. "She's gone, Owen!" my voice booms off the walls. "She's fucking gone!"

My legs threaten to give way.

"Listen." His sharp voice cuts through the air. "Calm down. Think logically. When was the last time you heard from her?"

My mind whirls as I consider the hectic day I've had. When I messaged her at lunch, I assumed she was napping with Jax. In fact, I remember thinking about how adorable they look when they nap together. Both of them have the same bow lips that flutter when they're sleeping. "This morning." I swallow hard. "The last time I heard from her was this morning."

"Is her car gone?" I can hear him tapping away on his laptop. "Are there any signs as to why she left?"

I squeeze my eyes closed, trying to answer one question after the other. "Car is still here. I-I don't think there's a reason why she left." My voice wobbles, and I hate the vulnerability behind it as I drag my hand through my hair. I'm already telling myself I deserved this. I'm not good enough for them.

"Search the house, Reed. Did anyone break in?"

A new panic flashes through me, and I rush down the stairs so quickly I almost fall, then I stride into the kitchen to check the door. "No. The door is secure." I glance at the windows. "Windows too."

As I enter the living room, my eyes latch onto an envelope, the letter discarded on the floor. I pick it up and one name has my inside twisting. "Oh shit." What the hell have I done?

"What?"

Panic hits me like a truck. "Oh, fuck no."

"What is it?" Owen snaps as my eyes scan the letter. "Reed, fucking talk to me, man."

A prickly lump gathers in my throat, and I struggle to swallow the vomit rearing its ugly head. "Oh God, Owen. It's bad." A sob lodges in my chest. "So fucking bad."

"Reed, fucking speak to me now!"

"She's seen the contract with Fanzio," I cry out, and a stabbing sensation lances through my chest. She thinks I wanted custody of Jax. That I was going to take him from her.

"What?" Owen booms back. "What the fuck? You said this was under control."

Despair ravishes through me, and I sink to the floor. My body shudders as an icy chill takes over me at the way I've betrayed her when I promised her the best of me. "I know." Realization that I've destroyed her, destroyed us, flashes through me, and I struggle to breathe, knowing how badly I fucked up. I hurt her, and ultimately, Bryce and Jax too.

Oh shit, my heart squeezes tightly, and I rest my palm over it, willing it to slow down as I squeeze my eyes closed.

My son will grow up hating me. He will think I'm a deadbeat like my father and won't know how much I love him and his brother. How his momma is my world. He's going to fucking hate me.

Jesus, what the hell have I done?

"I know. I fucked up. Please fucking help, me, Owen." I swipe the snot from my nose as I hiccup through my tears. "Help me figure this shit out." It feels like someone has stamped on my heart and ripped it from my chest, leaving me open, exposed, and ultimately, useless. "Please," I beg.

He sighs heavily. "I got you, man."

I can hear him moving around and the sound of keys as I

stare at the paper in my hand. The same paper I willingly signed not so long ago.

Just what the hell was I thinking? What sort of person was I to do this? She deserves better than me, they all do. Maybe they're better off without me in their lives. A dull ache throbs inside me as my emotions flow from me like a river. Devastation isn't something I've ever felt before, but this has to be what I'm feeling now.

Jesus, what I would give to hold her in my arms and tell her I'm sorry. I want to tell her I love her and our little Jax, that Bryce is the best son in the world and I love him like my own because he is my own. He's a part of me because he's a part of Jax and her.

I love them, and I never got to tell them.

Such a fucking dick.

I stare down at the floor, and memory after crushing memory hits me.

My son opening his eyes for the first time, and the way his small hands ball into a fist as he feeds from his momma.

The way Bryce snuggles up to me at night while I cradle Jax, and the way Gia rests on my chest, stroking over my heart while I tell her she's my little thief.

"Fuck," I choke out, and push away the tears.

Will my sons hate me like I spent years hating my father?

Somehow, I push off the floor and make my way upstairs and into our bedroom. As I slip inside the sheets, I inhale her peachy scent, then close my eyes, curl up in a ball, and let myself cry like a damn baby, wishing for nothing more than to turn the clock back. An animalistic wail erupts from my chest, and I cling to her pillow, wishing I could be the man I wanted to be and the one I became, if only for a little while longer.

FORTY-FOUR

REED

"DUDE. You need to get the hell up; you can't stay in here forever." Tate's voice cuts through the blurry haze I'm living in. It's been three days since she left, three days I haven't seen my son, not even on FaceTime. Not so much as a damn text to tell me they're all okay, and while I should be mad at that, I don't blame her.

I miss them and the chaos of the house. The familiar smell of peaches surrounding Gia and the way Jax's soft hair tickles my nostrils when I bury my nose in his hair, committing his scent to memory. Yet all of it feels like so long ago already, and I can't smell either of them anymore. No matter how hard I try, they're not there. It's like they never have been.

The pain of their absence is paralyzing.

"I just want my babies back, Tate." I sniffle, and he shifts from side to side.

Owen tracked Tyson's phone to the airport, but only he boarded a plane back to his base, while Gia and the kids are fuck knows where.

"I know, man, come on. You need to eat something at least and shower too. You fucking stink." He scrunches his nose. "She can't stay away forever. She's pissed."

"I know that," I snap. "I fucking know that because I did that. I promised I wouldn't hurt her, and I destroyed her." I shake my head and stab my finger into my chest as I become louder with each word.

His face softens. "Then maybe you should just give her some time."

"Like you did with Ava?" I grit out, then guilt lances through me at his solemn expression. "My son is growing without me." The thought feels crippling, like hot knives piercing through my skin and flaying my heart open, forcing my blood to run cold and causing me to tremor. "I need to tell her I love her," I whisper through tears, the pain so intense inside me I don't feel the effect of those tears sliding down my face, one after the other, I only know they do when they splash onto my hand.

Tate licks his lips, then he nods. He maneuvers to sit back on his haunches and surveys me from beside Gia's bed. "Well, where would Bryce like to go? Because if I was her, I'd be keeping the kid happy."

I shake my head. "I've already thought of all of his favorite places, Tate." I shake my head as I consider the parks, the soccer games, and the community center. "Both of their favorite places."

He nods and watches me closely.

"I don't deserve them. He was always better than me."

Tate frowns. "Who? The husband?"

I flinch at the word *husband*. "Yeah, him." I point to the upturned photo lying on her bedside dresser. The one she'd put away in the drawer to appease me.

Tate picks it up and turns it over, and something sparks in my mind, causing hope to flare in my chest. I quickly snatch it from his hand and scan the photo.

Holy shit.

My eyes widen as I take in the scene in the photo, and I spring up from the bed.

"What is it?"

"I think I know where they are."

"Really? Where?"

"Here." I tap the photo. Specifically, the cabin in the background of the image.

"Do you know where it is?" Tate asks as I make quick work of shoving my feet into my shoes.

"No, but I bet Owen can find it." I answer with a wince when I consider I should have asked more questions, but jealousy stopped me.

Tate drags a hand through his hair. "Do you think this is a good idea?"

I turn quickly to face him. "They're my family, and I want them back. It's the only option." I stare at him pointedly. "I need them to know how much I love them."

A grin breaks out across his face. "Okay, but …" He scans me up and down. "I'm not sure you'll manage out in bumfuck nowhere."

My eyebrows narrow, and I puff out my chest with pride. "I was a fucking Boy Scout."

He scoffs. "In a suit?" Then he drags his gaze lazily up and down my body. "You joined for the Girl Scouts, right? To eat their cookies?" He wiggles his eyebrows.

"You sick fuck. Get the hell out of my bedroom!" I sneer back at him.

He slaps a hand on my shoulder. "Pleased to have you back, man. But you need a shower."

I ignore him as he makes his way to the door, but when he suddenly stops, he draws my attention. "Don't forget to pack bug spray."

Bug spray?

I've more important things to consider.

Like making the woman I love take me back and keep me forever.

FORTY-FIVE

GIA

MY HAIR BLOWS in the breeze as I take in the sounds of the forest. I've been coming out here for years, and when I'm here, I feel at peace. I feel like Jaxon is here with me; his support throughout our time together brings a sense of solace to the cabin and the surrounding area.

It's off the beaten track, secluded, a little piece of heaven wrapped up in a small wooden cabin that's seen better days and in serious need of renovation.

The wooden dock I sit on is where I've spent much of my time watching Bryce grow from a toddler in floaties to a competent swimmer able to enjoy the lakeside setting. My only wish was to have a cabin raised higher so you're able to view the lake from there. Instead, it's quite a walk down the rugged path to see it.

When I close my eyes, I see Jaxon telling me everything will be okay. He snuggles into me, and I mimic the action, pulling the blanket tighter to keep the chill out.

The dreams and hopes we had as teenagers in love to the here and now are so far apart, nobody could ever have predicted it, and what's more, if I'm being honest with myself, I wouldn't have changed it neither.

"You shouldn't be down here by yourself," a deep voice growls, and I close my eyes at the pain the familiarity brings.

"I'm perfectly fine. I'm used to doing things by myself," I snipe out with venom. I tilt my head to glare at him, but I'm taken aback by the man I see before me.

Reed's not the perfectly put together man I know him to be. His hair is disheveled, his five o'clock shadow now replaced with unkept facial hair, his eyes are red and puffy, and his clothes look like they haven't been changed in days.

I'm not sure why it hurts so much to see him like this. It shouldn't.

His eyes soften as he stares at me, but I glare right back. Then he shifts them away, the guilt swims in them. He glances around him. "Are the boys okay?"

"They're fine," I snap, and glance down at the baby monitor beside me.

He swallows hard, then brings his gaze back to mine where he holds it. "I missed you." My heart skips a beat at his admission. He chokes a little, then clears his throat. "I missed the boys. Missed you all so damn much, Gia."

Tears well in my eyes at the emotion pouring from him.

"Please let me explain." His solemn eyes bore into mine, and anger surges through me. Why should I let him explain? How can he try to explain this away?

I lift my chin higher and grit my teeth.

"Please," he begs, and the sound has my heart squeezing tightly in my chest, threatening to burst. I want to hate him. I want to pound on his chest and tell him he destroyed us, but I want him to tell me something I don't know. I want him to make me understand and make everything right, and I cling to the notion that there's more to this than I've been told. As much as I have the evidence proving his guilt, I know Reed. I feel him deep in my soul. I'm not just his little thief, he's mine too, so I nod.

His shoulders sag, and relief floods his face. It's obvious he didn't think I would let him explain. But when our son comes of age, I owe him an explanation as to why his father is not on the scene, why I did everything I can to protect him against the men who think they can rule the world with greed.

Reed brushes some dirt away with his shoe, then sits down beside me. My lip twitches at the thought of him muddying his ass and how he thinks kicking the dirt will make a difference.

He pulls a wad of rolled-up papers from inside his pocket and holds them out for me to take.

"What are they?"

He shakes them. "Take them and see."

I shake my head with a heavy sigh. "I'm not interested in your games, Reed. I'm tired. So fucking tired."

His face softens, and guilt mars his handsome features.

He places them in my lap, but I make no move to open them. "When you walked into your dad's office..."

I flinch at the term of endearment that man doesn't deserve.

"I was a different person that day. I was ruthless and controlling." He shakes his head. "I was hellbent on getting the deal I've been trying to get for years." He swallows thickly. "I don't allow myself to open up to anyone, Gia, and you know what? I'm grateful I didn't. I'm grateful the first person I opened up to was you." As he rests back on his hands, the evening sun beats down on us both, but it's still cold in the air despite the feeling of warmth his presence brings.

"I didn't like kids, hated fucking animals." He shudders while my eyebrows shoot up. "The lengths I've gone to make you like me. Make all of you like me." Releasing a humorless chuckle, he shakes his head. "When I knocked on your door, I'd signed those papers thinking all my Christmases had come at once. You would get to keep the baby I never considered, and I'd get the land I'd always wanted." His Adam's apple works, and his chest rises while he takes a moment to look away as if to compose himself.

"I don't know what the fuck I was thinking. How I thought I could ever not fall in love with you and my boys." My heart skips a beat and leaps in my chest so hard I have to suck in a sharp breath of air to keep breathing. "That moment in the kitchen. The one where I ..." He means when he came in his pants, when we shared something more. "I realized then I was never letting you go. All of you." He shifts a little. "I went back to the office and put a plan in motion." He gestures toward the documents. "I made sure that when I got the land, it would all be in Bryce's name."

I'm stunned. My mind struggles to play catch up.

"Bryce owns the land now. From that day forward, I wanted it for him, not myself." He shakes his head. "From the moment we were in the kitchen together, I knew I wanted to make sure it was Bryce who would benefit from our relationship. That he would get the legacy he deserved in honor of the man who gave me the most precious gift in the world."

"But you still fought for the land. You could have told me and put a stop to it, and you didn't," I whisper.

He turns to face me, then cups my chin in his palm, and for the first time in days, I feel warmth spread through my body. "I don't care about the land, Gia. It's Bryce's, put it in a trust, expand the community center, give it Jaxon's name, and create a legacy. I don't give a fuck. All I care about is you and my boys."

A tear slips down my face, and he leans forward, pressing our heads together, much like when we were in the kitchen months ago. "I love you, Gia."

I hiccup on his words.

"I love you so damn much, baby. Please tell me I can make this right."

"I want to," I admit softly, and when his lips touch mine, I lose all coherent thoughts as he slowly pushes me onto my back and climbs over me.

Chest heaving, he stares into my eyes, his body is resting on his forearms, and I long to feel his weight against me.

His breath whispers over my face. "I've been so lost without you."

I cup his cheek in my hand. "Show me."

FORTY-SIX

REED

"SHOW ME." Her tender tone sends a ripple down my spine, and I close my eyes at the thought of never being given the opportunity to touch her like this again. How I want to.

When I open my eyes, it's with a renewed sense of determination, one to make her realize how much she means to me.

This moment isn't about getting my rocks off, or treating her roughly, it's about me showing her how much I love her. How much I want her, and more importantly, how good we are together in the hope she will never leave me again.

I slowly unbuckle my belt buckle, my eyes never leaving hers. "Are you okay with this?" My gaze roams over her, and she nods.

"I stopped bleeding. I'm okay."

"We don't have to." *But fuck, do I want to.*

"I want to."

My body sags in relief because thank fuck for that.

I slide my zipper down. My balls are heavy with need, and I already know I won't last long. "I'll go slow."

She bites into her bottom lip and nods. Then my hand trails up her skirt, and the moment I touch her smooth skin, arousal thrashes through me. She's a drug and I'm the addict, desperate for a hit of her, completely enabled, and I withdraw the moment I'm without her, causing me to buckle under the pressure.

Her panties are soaked, and I finger the lacy fabric between my fingertips, loving the feel of her wetness and need for me. My balls draw up, and I bite into the side of my mouth.

"I'm not going to last long," I admit. "I'm sorry."

"Me neither. I've been craving you."

Her words make my chest fill with pride and satisfaction. She's been craving me.

I bury my head in her neck and breathe in her scent, filling my soul with her presence. If I have to spend the rest of my life making it up to her and my boys, I will. I'll prove to them I'm the man they deserve.

My fingers tremble as I push her panties to the side. Her hips buck when I graze over her swollen clit, and I revel in the reaction as sparks of arousal flare inside me.

As I pull my cock from my boxers, pre-cum coats my hand, dripping between us, and I use the head of my cock to rub up and down her slit.

The small gasps and moans of encouragement spur me on, and she bucks beneath me.

"Please," she pleads so epically. "Please, Reed."

I rear back and scan her face. "Tell me you love me," I beg, hoping she can see the truth and desperation in my eyes. Hoping she can see into my broken soul as I plead with her to fix me. Fix us.

"Tell me you love me, Gia." And everything will be okay.

I wait with bated breath as she swallows, her eyes swimming with unshed tears, and I suck in a sharp breath when she cups my jaw with her palm. "I love you, Reed."

"I fucking love you too." I slam my lips against hers and slowly push inside her, filling her to the hilt as our tender kiss becomes feverish. Both of us swallow back our groans, our longing.

My hips work at a steady pace, determined to make it last. One thrust after the other in calculated moves that send waves of pleasure through me.

I move my fingers over her swollen bud, grazing and toying with it in circular motions. Her heavy pants spur me on with each touch, and her pussy tightens around me. She comes undone in my arms, and Christ, she's the most gorgeous sight I've ever seen in my entire life.

"I love you, my little thief," I repeat as my release floods her, and I will her body to swell once again.

FORTY-SEVEN

REED

I SPENT the night stroking over Jax's soft head of hair, loving the feel of his warmth against my bare chest. How I could ever willingly be apart from him, I'll never know. I may not have liked children before I met Bryce, hell, I don't think I like any other than my own, but now I can't imagine them not being in my life. I wouldn't survive it.

They're my everything, and I can't wait to fill Gia with more. So many fucking more.

His hair felt softer than before, and I'm positive his face has filled out, and I despise myself for the time I've missed; the pain is immeasurable and not something I ever want to endure again. I'll spend a lifetime proving my love to them.

When we returned from down by the dock hand in hand, I was surprised that Gia offered for me to stay with her and the boys. I was hoping we could work things out slowly, but given she all but jumped me again, I had little to no choice but to stay the night. I've spent what little time I've been awake thinking about our future together. Fuck going slow, I want us married as soon as possible.

Bryce was asleep when we returned, but I checked on him and gave his messy hair a kiss. Bubbles, the psycho dog, was curled up beside him, and it made my heart swell at the sight.

"I don't want any more secrets between us, Gia." I toy with her hair as she lies on my chest.

"Me neither." Her finger trails over the small smattering of hair along my V line, and the action makes my cock thicken beneath the sheets.

"I bought the damn dog, hoping to win Bryce over." I glance down at her, and she chews on her bottom lip, but I can still see the small smile playing on her pretty face. "I didn't know it wasn't a bulldog or a boy, and I didn't care. I just wanted to make you both like me."

"He loves Bubbles." She admits with a giggle, then she shakes her head and turns to face me. "You're an idiot, Reed."

"Tyson has a dog." I shrug, and I'm pretty sure she can read between the lines. I needed to outdo the fucker.

"Tyson is …"

"Not competition?" I lift my eyebrow.

"Exactly. Not competition."

"You still slept with him," I remind her.

She rolls her eyes, and I bend and swat her ass playfully. "You slept with the whole of New Jersey," she quips back.

"I didn't let them sleep over. They were not fixtures in my personal space after I fucked them. We were done."

She eyes me skeptically and scans over my face. "If it makes you uncomfortable him staying over, then he won't anymore."

Her words surprise me, but honestly, they shouldn't. This is Gia, and she's simply amazing. Always putting other people's thoughts and feelings first.

I blow out a heavy breath. "It's fine. He's grown on me. Anyway, he's good with the boys." I hate to admit it, but he is good with the boys, and I trust him with all of them.

She nods, and her smile grows wider, then something

flashes in her eyes that I don't like. She shifts and turns away from me, but when she rests her head back on my chest, I relax slightly despite there being an odd change between us. Maybe she was thinking about all the hurt I caused. My stomach rolls at the thought and my arm tightens around her.

"I love you, Gia." I'm not sure who I'm saying it for, her or me, but I need her to hear it again. I'll never fucking tire of telling her.

Minutes pass between us, and if it wasn't for the change in her breathing, I would've thought she fell asleep.

Her finger draws soothing circles on my stomach, and she trails a path along my abs and back again. "When my mom died, my father changed."

I nod, because she's told me this already, but the way her chest hitches tells me she's going to maybe divulge more of their feud and his clear hatred for his daughter.

"He wanted me to become a replacement of my mom."

I find her words odd but don't ask more, and when she turns to face me, I see it written all over her face, and I hate myself. How did I not see it before now.

"In every sense."

Vomit builds inside me, followed quickly by a burning anger that has my entire body pulling tight. "He abused you?"

She licks her lips. "He did," she says.

A pang of pain grips my heart in a viselike grip. "Jesus, Gia."

Her tears don't fall, instead she remains steadfast. "I became pregnant, and I didn't know who the father of my baby was." She closes her eyes as if it pains her to remember, and I wince. When she opens them, I see the torment in them, the pure self-loathing she has no place feeling. "I had to admit everything to Jaxon. Just in case." Bile swirls in my stomach for her.

She's the strongest woman I've ever known. But just how the fuck do you ever deal with that?

My throat is dry, scratchy when I try to speak. "I'm so damn sorry, baby."

She shakes her head. "He didn't care. He said he'd put his name on the birth certificate either way. Protect us, no matter what."

My eyes fill with tears, with gratitude for the man he was, and it makes me prouder than ever that my son holds his name. "He was an incredible man, Gia."

Her tears fall as she continues to play her finger up my stomach and along my chest. "He didn't want a DNA test." She looks up at me through damp lashes. "But I insisted. I needed to know. Bryce is his, thank God. We thought we'd gotten our happy ending, but then he left us."

My chest rises uncontrollably as I struggle to fight back the tears now falling. "I'm sorry."

Her head snaps up, and she meets my stare. "The funny thing is, I'm not. I love you, Reed Johnson, and if I had the chance, I'd always pick you."

My heart skips a beat. It's everything I could have asked for, hoped for, and as much as I don't feel worthy, I'll fucking take it, cherish her words, and never let them go. My lip twitches. "Yeah?"

She nods, and I tangle my fingers in her hair and pull her toward me into a scorching kiss. One that promises her a lifetime of love and security. One that promises a lifetime of everything.

FORTY-EIGHT

REED

A GROAN ERUPTS from me as I throw my legs over the side of the bed and ruffle my hair. Jesus, after not sleeping for days on end, I've done some serious making up for it. I can see why Gia and Bryce like the cabin so much; it's a little piece of solace in a ramshackle, bug-infested roach motel.

I wonder how she'd feel about me flattening it and rebuilding? Or if the subject would be too touchy for her right now. Given how I wanted to flatten the community center, it's probably best I keep the thought to myself for the time being.

Reaching over the dresser, I grab my cellphone and switch the silent mode off, then grimace at the number of missed calls from Owen. Numerous messages pop up on the screen one after the other.

Owen: Call me now.

Owen: Call me ASAP.

Owen: This is an emergency.

Owen: Fucking call me back, Reed!

"Shit." I quickly press Owen's name and dial him back.

"Finally! What the fuck are you doing going radio silent on us all?"

"I—"

"Shut the fuck up and listen. You're in danger." My spine snaps straight. Surely, I didn't hear him right. "Where's Gia?"

"D-downstairs." I stand and quickly move through the small room.

"Go to her and put me on speaker." I rush down the stairs, and relief floods me when I see her chopping fruit for breakfast in the small, ill-equipped kitchen area. She turns with a beaming smile that falls from her face when she sees the panic on my own.

I hold my phone up. "Owen." I nod toward the phone.

"Gia. Listen to me. There's no way to tell you this, so I'll just come out and say it."

"Okay," she whispers and wraps her arms around herself.

"I've researched Jaxon's death. It wasn't an accident, darlin'. Men were hired to kill him." She jolts at his words while I move to comfort her, and she simply nods as if not surprised. "Your father ordered the hit, Gia."

A sob catches in her throat before she clears it. "Okay." The strength and resilience of her makes my nostrils flare. No woman should have to go through this, ever.

"It gets worse. According to my sources, George flew into a rage when he discovered Bryce is one of the majority shareholders of the company and now also owns the land."

"Oh God." She throws her arm over her chest and her legs almost give way, but I hold her still. I become her strength, like she is mine.

"You're in danger, Gia. Bryce is in danger."

"What the fuck?" I snap out.

"Get the place locked up tight. I'm on my way up there with the best men I know to bring you all to safety."

"Owen. Does he know where we are?" I grit out as pure rage surges inside me.

"Yeah, man, he does." I hear the defeatism in his tone, and a pang of fear flashes through me. I detach from Gia, hoping she can't sense my inner turmoil.

"Fuck!" I grunt as I pace the cabin floor.

"I'm twenty minutes out, but I called in some favors, and a couple of my guys are already ahead of me."

"Reed?" I spin on my heel toward Gia, and her face has blanched with fear. "Br-Bryce is fishing at the lake."

Her words send a shudder of panic through me, and I hurry toward Jax's crib, lifting him into my arms. "Take him and get in a closet and lock every fucking door, Gia. I'm going to fetch Bryce."

"But what if …" I shake my head while pushing a knife into her hand.

"I'll bring him back, I promise." I kiss the top of her head and bolt toward the door while continuing to speak to Owen. "Did you hear that?"

"Yeah, man, I heard."

"Hurry the fuck up, will you."

"I'm on my way brother." I cut the call and head out the door to find my son.

I only hope I'm not too late.

FORTY-NINE

REED

I KICK up the dirt as I run barefoot down the trail that leads to the fishing dock. When Bryce's silhouette comes into view, I feel an overwhelming sense of relief ravish my veins.

Thank fuck.

"Bryce!"

He turns to face me, and his sparkling green eyes light up as he holds up his fishing rod. "Reed! Look what I caught." He holds up a fish, but his smile falls when he sees the worry laced on my face. "What happened? Is Mom okay? Jax?" The way he asks about his mom and little brother makes my love for him soar. "Bubbles?"

"They're fine, buddy. But we're in danger, and I'll explain soon, but we need to leave right now."

He drops his fishing rod to the ground and heads toward me, but the sound of rustling in nearby bushes has my body tensing, so I lunge toward him. The sound of a bullet whizzing through the air causes me to throw myself in front of him and tug him toward my chest, and an agonizing pain unleashes in my back. "Fuck," I grunt, hitting the ground with Bryce beneath me, careful to cradle his head as we fall.

I glance down to find his startled eyes burning brightly, boring into mine and making my heart flutter with relief. "You okay, buddy?"

"Yeah. B-but Dad, you're bleeding." He glances down my chest toward my stomach, but I register nothing other than one word. Did he just call me dad?

Movement catches my eye, and I brace myself above Bryce, but when a man with a gun appears, all I can do is cover my son's face with my hand and tuck him beneath me.

The man raises the gun, and I kick myself for coming out of the cabin unarmed.

As I seethe with a burning rage at the injustice of finally having the love of a family for it now to be torn away from me, I contemplate my next move while also considering that I don't really have one. I wanted to protect my family, and I let them down. But I won't go down without a fight, that's for sure.

A man appears behind the other, and my stomach sinks, knowing how outnumbered I am. Then he sends a wink in my direction and spits out the toothpick hanging from the corner of his mouth, and my eyes widen as they latch onto the blade that appears at my enemy's throat.

He moves quickly, holding the man in place as he creates a sea of blood in his wake, then the man's body falls to the ground with a heavy thud.

My avenger steps forward, and I jump to my feet, pulling Bryce up and shoving him behind me.

"Name's Finn O'Connell. Owen sent me." I take in his open combat boots and ripped jeans and try to find a sense of resemblance compared to his brothers I know of, but I find none. Other than the bright-blue eyes.

The O'Connells are a Mafia family, a family full of secrets

and lies, but they're good people, nonetheless, and I couldn't be more grateful for their input.

"Reed." I lift my chin in his direction, and he takes another toothpick from inside his leather jacket pocket and places it in his mouth.

"Know these fucking trees like the back of my hand." He shudders, and my eyes narrow. "Had a family member go rogue once. Oh, and another time, Oscar took an axe to the fucker who tried to destroy my family." He grimaces as he motions with his finger across his throat, letting me know that his brother Oscar decapitated someone who threatened their family.

Oh, fucking goody, they're all insane, and they've been sent to rescue my family.

"You go ahead. I'll cover you." He motions toward the trail, then disappears back into the undergrowth.

"You're bleeding, all down your back," Bryce whines.

"It's okay, buddy. It doesn't hurt," I lie. With each footstep, it's like white-hot pokers searing through my flesh.

The cabin looks untouched, but I'm not stupid enough to think there might not be intruders, especially when I walk through the door and see Jax's blue lion softie on the floor. I know without a shadow of a doubt that Gia would not have left the room without it. Our boy finds comfort in that little soft toy, shoving it in his mouth and suckling until he falls to sleep. There's no way in hell she'd risk him stirring and alerting someone to their whereabouts without it.

I push Bryce farther behind me, blocking him from view, then reach over the counter and grab the meat cleaver. Even the movement of stretching hurts like a bitch, and somehow makes my chest pull tight, causing my lungs to seize in agony. "Fuck," I grunt out with a wince when I straighten.

"Drop the fucking knife, Reed." George's voice cuts through the air, and when I hear Jax's whimper, I turn to face the man holding my girl by her hair as she clutches Jax against her chest. Her face is teary, and she has a split lip that sends a red haze over me. He touched her, hurt what's mine. He holds the knife Gia had to her throat; her neck elongated so savagely I can see her pulse racing against the metal.

"Drop the fucking knife," he repeats, and somehow, it sounds clearer this time, as if the threat is all the more real now. He holds my world in the palm of his cruel hands. A tyrant through and through. A monster.

How the hell did I ever choose to do business with this monster?

GIA

As soon as Reed leaves to fetch Bryce from the lake, I spring into action, grabbing Jax's softie and clutching the knife I'd been using, and my heart hammers. I knew my father was a monster, but killing my husband to get to me and my shares is unfathomable.

Jax makes a soft cooing sound, and my hold around him tightens, and I can feel his soft breath against my chest. "Momma's got you, Jax," I say, and kiss the top of his head.

I reached the first stair, and a flash of pain hits my face, causing the back of my head to bounce off the wall, and I struggle to remain upright as dizziness overwhelms me. Oh Jesus, that hurts. My vision is blurry, and I hold Jax tighter. "Please," I beg, knowing it's hopeless.

Then my hair is pulled so hard my head is yanked back, causing tears to flow from me in waves. Oh, fuck, that hurts. I drop the knife and Jax's soft toy as I'm dragged from the room with no consideration for the small baby crying against my chest. My only priority right now is to protect him. "Please." I try again, but my assailant ignores my pleas.

Then he spins me around to face him, with the knife I'd carelessly dropped in his hand, and that same evil gleam in his eyes that I'd become accustomed to growing up under his cruel reign is back in full force, making me swallow the bile rising in my throat.

My father looks like the deranged animal I know him to be, his face red and eyes bulging in anger. The usually carefully composed man to the public has let his guard down, and he's showing me the man I know and fear. The one who sent me to school sore between my legs so badly, I held my pee in a bid to stop the pain.

He licks his lips like a predator, and I'm his prey, and what I fear the most is the little baby boy I desperately cling to in hope we can survive this. There's not a doubt in my mind that my father will kill again to get what he wants.

"Where's the boy?" he bellows, and I flinch at the power of his tone. Jax cries louder, and all I can think is that my father didn't even use Bryce's name.

I blink hard, trying to remain in the present. My vision is cloudy and I'm struggling to think straight.

"The fucking boy, Gianna!" he yells, causing my head to throb.

"I-I don't know," I whimper as my mind races, hoping and praying Reed has located Bryce and they're both unharmed and safe.

"Lying little bitch!" My father backhands me, and my head whips to the side, and I'm grateful Jax had slid lower down on my chest.

The pain doesn't come, not how you'd expect. I don't know if I've become accustomed to it over the years, or if the dull throbbing at the back of my head is taking away the worst of it. I can taste blood in my mouth, and I'm pulled back in time as I close my eyes with dizziness.

"Sir, how did she lose her tooth?" the doctor asks as I stare up at my father and wait for him to respond.

The doctor's kind eyes flicker back to me, and I jolt.

I don't like people being too nice, that means they'll pry, and when they do, my father gets meaner.

"Do you know who I am?" My father's eyes bore into the doctor's, and he swallows harshly.

"Yes, sir."

My father's chest puffs out, and a sinister smile encompasses his deranged face.

"Gianna!"

My eyes snap open in time to witness him lunge forward. My heart skips a beat as he takes a hold of my hair in a brutal viselike grip and turns me so my back is to his front, giving him the perfect position to hold the knife to my throat. All I can think about is how I hope Reed and our sons survive this.

Our sons.

Because despite Bryce's DNA, he's Reed's son.

He's a devoted, loving, caring father, and I couldn't have wished for a better one than him. I just wish I'd gotten to tell him that. To tell him how much I love him.

Approaching footsteps can be heard, and my body locks up in fear, whereas my father's pulls tight in glee.

Oh God, please don't be Reed and Bryce.

Please.

FIFTY

MY FATHER SHUFFLES us into the living space where Reed stands before us, and my legs feel like Jell-O as the knife my father holds to my throat digs deeper into my skin.

The man I love looks terrified, and blood flows down the side of his torso. I can't see where it's coming from exactly, only that he's hurt, and an involuntary wail leaves me at the thought of Bryce being hurt too.

"Drop the knife," my father snipes out, and I tremble against him and close my eyes as his familiar scent wraps around me, taking me back to my childhood.

"You need to please me now, Gianna. Your mother couldn't step up to the task, so you have to." My tummy hurts when he talks like that to me, and the way he licks his lips makes me want to run. Run and never return.

My mom was sick. She didn't choose to leave me, she didn't have a choice.

I tug on my favorite pink nightdress, hoping it covers my legs more. "Please don't make me. I don't want to."

"Get your useless ass over here and suck it. Or I'll make you. You don't want to throw up again, do you?"

Jax makes a cooing noise and stirs in my arms, pulling me from the darkness. I open my eyes to the sound, but when I feel my father's stiffening cock behind me, I move without thinking, and the knife slices through my skin. Reed rushes toward me with a roar, and Bubbles leaps out of nowhere, attacking my father's ankle. Reed pushes me aside, and Bryce runs toward me while Reed is raining blow upon blow on my father's face as they both fall to the floor with a heavy thud.

I wrap my arm around Bryce, kissing his head as he cries against me, protecting him from the sight of the men scrambling on the floor.

The sound of a click has me stilling, and I glance over the top of Bryce's head to see a man holding a gun to the back of Reed's head. Only now do I take in the blood pouring down his back, and a cry catches in my throat as I realize how hurt he is.

Reed holds his hands up, and the man with the gun allows him to stand up and step back. The grimace he evokes causes my stomach to twist, knowing how injured he is.

"Let her and my kids leave," he grits out.

"They go nowhere," the man states. He's familiar, one of the many men my father had dealings with over the years, yet he looks straight through me.

"You can have me. Just let my family go," Reed attempts again. "I have money. A lot of fucking money."

"We want the boy." The man remains firm.

My hands tighten on Bryce, and he clings to me harder, almost squishing Jax.

"You're not taking my family," Reed declares as his muscles bunch tight and his scowl deepens, the determination in his eyes unmistakable. While the fight in him should reassure me, it doesn't. He's unarmed, hurt, and willing to die for us. I can see it in his eyes, he will fight to the death to save us.

"You're not in a position to argue, amigo." The man chuckles darkly, and the door creaks open, catching his attention for a split second and giving Reed enough time to spin on the balls of his bare feet, where he moves swiftly, kicking the gun from out the man's hand and knocking it to the floor. Then he grabs the man's wrist, and the sound of it snapping as he pulls it backward bounces off the walls. Before the guy can register what's happened, a knife sails through the air into the side of his neck, and he slumps to the floor almost instantaneously.

My eyes dart to the man in the doorway, and he sends a wink my way, then turns his attention to Reed. "I'll secure the premises while you take out the trash." Then he heads back out of the door, as if he was never there. "Medics are on the way!" he calls over his shoulder.

"Are you okay?" Reed rushes toward me, and his palms roam over my face as his eyes search mine for answers.

"Ye-yess."

He cups my face in his hands. "Thank fuck, Gia." His lips find mine, then he pulls back. "Thank fuck."

My eyes swim with tears, and I nod. "I love you."

"I love you too, little thief." His lips crash against mine again. "So damn much."

"Ew. That's gross!" Bryce steps back and wrinkles his nose.

"Come here, buddy." Reed places kiss after kiss on top of his head. "And don't pretend you didn't call me dad out there, I heard you." Reed grins from ear to ear, and the sight warms my heart.

"Can I call him dad too, Mom? Like Jax will?" Bryce's innocent eyes meet mine with such eagerness it has my throat clogging with emotion.

"I don't see why not. If that's what you want. What you both want?" I lift my head to face Reed, and his eyes shine.

"Damn right, buddy." He lifts his fist out for Bryce to bump, and he does with a grin to mirror Reed's.

A disgruntled moan comes from my father, and I freeze. "Gia, I need you to take the boys upstairs."

"What are you going to do?"

Stepping forward, he lowers his voice. "I'm going to have him taken somewhere he can't come back from. Are you going to have a problem with that?" He eyes me skeptically.

But the thoughts of never seeing my father again, never having to look over my shoulder or consider him breathing the same air as my children, have me shaking my head frantically. "No. No problem from me."

"Good girl." He bends and kisses the top of my head, his lips lingering longer than normal, and I melt beneath his touch.

"Bryce, take Bubbles with you."

"Okay, Dad." Bryce beams back at him while he leans down to collect the little dog whose tail is wagging triumphantly.

Bryce follows me up the stairs. "I think we should make this cabin bigger, Mom, because our family is growing, right?"

"So do I, buddy, so do I."

FIFTY-ONE

REED

2 WEEKS LATER ...

LUCA VARROS IS some fucked-up sick son of a bitch to have such an array of tools that aren't used for building products.

God only knows why you'd need a whisk in a cellar and a fucking cattle prod? I glance around the room—definitely no cows down here.

"You look appalled," Owen states with a smug grin on his face. Who would have thought my friend would have had so many dealings with notorious gangsters and Mafia men over the years? And yet, I find myself relieved at the connections he's made.

They sure came in useful for Shaw, and Tate too, when Ava's captor was making a move on her.

My eyes meet his. "I am."

He leans back on a counter covered in blood, and I grimace. What in the hell? Jesus. I will need an antiseptic shower once I leave here.

"Are you fully recovered?" He motions toward me.

"Apparently. Although I feel like getting shot deserves some sort of medal in itself. Then again, Gia spent two weeks fussing over me, so it was worth the bullet. Plus, she seems to have let the whole contract thing slip from her mind."

Owen scoffs. "You mean the fact you practically sold your first born for some land." I stiffen under his blunt words.

"Shut the fuck up. I soon realized my mistake," I bark.

He grins wider. "Just keeping it real."

"Well, keep it real with that fucker and be done with him already." I motion toward the bloodied and beaten George Fanzio swaying on a chain attached to the ceiling.

"He had his ass fucked with a cattle prod. We know a guy that has a thing for it."

I swear I can taste bile in my mouth, and I spin away from George, unable to take the image conjuring up in my mind. "Jesus." Who the fuck would do something like that? Where do they even get the ideas from?

"Yeah. We should rename this cellar, ass-fuck alley." He shrugs while his eyes dance with jest. "Fucked up the ass in a hellhole, or the den of hell, maybe …"

"Name it what the fuck you want. Just finish him already."

"You don't want to do the honors?" He lifts his eyebrow at me.

"I'm a lawyer, Owen, not a felon," I snap.

"He raped your wife, tried to kill your kid. He …"

Fury engulfs me at hearing the truth, so I snatch the gun from the counter, spin, and aim it at George. Expelling every ounce of hatred into him, I press the trigger. The bullet hits him in the throat, and he begins to gargle as blood bubbles out of his neck, and I take pleasure in watching the life leave his eyes. My wife and family are now free from the monster who was always going to be in the shadows haunting our every move.

"So much for being a lawyer."

"You riled me."

Owen pushes off the counter, and we head toward the cellar door, then a wave of peace floats over me. He's gone.

My family is safe.

"We could call it the thirsty fuckers' den. You know, with us no longer doing thirsty Thursday."

I chuckle at his analogy, because he might not participate in the thirsty Thursday anymore, but I sure as hell do. Only now it's me doing the drinking, straight from my wife's tit.

As we head outside, the sunlight almost blinds me, and I hold my hand up to stop the glare.

"Where are you heading to now?" Owen asks.

I straighten my shoulders, widening my stance. "I'm coaching Bryce's soccer team."

Owen scoffs, then erupts into a fit of laughter, bending over and holds his stomach. I struggle to find the humor in my words and lift my lip in disgust at his so-called amusement. When he finally straightens, he tries to hide the smile threatening to erupt on his face, and my fists ball with annoyance. "You should probably take a cattle prod with you." His lip twitches, and I want to unleash on the cocky prick.

"They're not going to be that bad," I snap.

His eyes are alight with glee, and he squeezes my shoulder. "They're going to be so much worse."

Then he walks away with a spring in his step, whistling as he heads toward his car while I shoot daggers at his back and scratch my head. "Probably have fucking lice in that godforsaken cellar," I grumble to myself. "And I don't give a shit what he says. I like kids now," I say as I open my SUV door.

In fact, I fucking love them.

I'm a reformed man.

A family man.

Devoted, trusted, and compassionate. I'm the whole fucking package.

Now I need to show it to those I love the most in the world.

Reed Johnson is worthy, and I can't wait to prove it.

EPILOGUE

REED

I HATE KIDS. I fucking hate them. Most of them, anyway. Particularly the ones who don't belong to me.

My day is a disaster. I gave up my valuable time as a lawyer to attend my first game as the coach for Bryce's soccer team at the community center, and it sure as shit will be the last time.

I've been spat on, cried on. I've had other people's children think it's acceptable to use my sweatpants as a tissue for their snotty noses, and worse, one child actually puked on my sneakers. If the little chump hadn't eaten so much candy before warming up on the soccer field I recently invested in, then this never would have occurred. But no, he seems to think he knows better, so much so he gave me the finger when I pointed out it wasn't wise to eat candy before warming up.

I surmised he'd figure it out the hard way, but what I didn't count on was him figuring it out the hard way and it ending up on my sneakers.

To top it off, Bubbles took a shit on the sideline, and a kid slipped in it. Somehow, it's apparently my fault, and some woman who claimed to be the child's mother, despite looking old enough to be their grandmother, started wagging her finger in my face while blowing out puffs of smoke at me. When I pointed out she can't have marijuana around the kids, she produced a slip of paper that looked like a child wrote it, claiming she was taking it for medicinal purposes. Medicinal, my ass. Besides, it doesn't mean it's okay to have it around the kids.

The past few months have seen an influx of parents taking a newfound interest in the game, which added to my anxiety, and when I noticed their phones pointed in my direction, that made me cringe all the more.

I'm going to be the laughingstock at the office when the guys see the shit I'm having to deal with.

The new buildings I've provided for the center have helped with my willingness to coach, especially the specially designed breakroom that was much needed for the staff and volunteers, which has doubled in numbers in recent weeks.

The bug spray Gia gave me doesn't work. I've literally created a circle of doom around me with it, and to top it all off, I triggered some poor kid's asthmatic issue, and the next thing I knew, the game was being cut short all because of one little kid's inability to breathe through some bug spray.

When Bryce told me he had the best game ever, it made it all worthwhile, but then he followed it up with that he'd never laughed so much in his entire life at how hopeless I am. I wanted to kick his legs from under him, despite me normally liking him.

"Maybe it wasn't as bad as you think?" Gia chews on her bottom lip as I sit on the edge of the bed feeling nothing short of traumatized.

"It was awful, Gia. Kids are pricks, even the girls." I throw myself back against the mattress dramatically.

She snorts on a laugh, and I glare at her, and she tries but fails to make her face serious.

"We didn't even get as far as the game. It was canceled before we finished the warm-up session." I exhale.

"Will a blow job make you feel better?" she asks, and this draws my attention in a positive way, so I lift my head.

"Do you have some milk left too?"

She shakes her head. "Nope. Your son drained me."

My mouth falls open. "You're fucking kidding me?"

"You might get some out of the left one."

"You should start pumping so he can feed from a bottle when you fill up and you can work on storing the rest up for me." I grin back at her. Why the hell haven't I thought of this before now?

I reach over and slap her thigh. "Come climb up here, turn around, and let me eat your pussy while your nipples play with my cock."

She glances at the door, then moves quickly to lock it before coming back over the bed and climbing onto the mattress and hovering her pussy over my face, her sweet lips inches from my cock.

"Good girl. Get my pre-cum over those nipples, and I'll lick it off after," I rasp.

"Jesus, Reed." She pants heavily, and I know my girl will enjoy every damn second of this.

"Hmm." I garble between her thighs and hold her open to lick her juicy cunt. My tongue slides through her slit and down to her hole while I bury my nose against her clit, the scruff of my five o'clock shadow creating friction for her as I devour her arousal.

"That's it, baby, lick that cock," I grunt in rapture as her warm mouth works down my cock and back up again. My fingers squeeze her ass cheeks harder when she flicks her tongue over my slit before sliding her mouth from me.

Her soft nipples graze the top of my sensitive cock before

her tongue travels down my shaft and over my balls, and I groan in delight as she starts riding my face.

"Fuck yes. That's it, baby, ride my tongue. Let me lick your little cunt clean."

She rocks back and forth over my face, and when she gags to take me down her throat with her heavy tits pushed against my pelvis, it makes me feel like I'm fucking them, that I'm in nirvana. My own piece of heaven.

I grip her hair in my fist and hold her head in place to thrust up into her mouth while she pushes her pussy down on my face, rocking back and forth against me. Then I slap my palm against her ass, causing her to moan, and when I circle, then press a thumb into her asshole, she tightens. Her body convulses as I groan my pleasure and fill her throat with my cum. "Good girl," I coo and soothe her reddened ass cheek.

She comes down from her orgasm, and I savor the way I pop from her mouth as she spins her body around to face me, now straddling my torso.

"You're pretty damn good at that, husband." She smiles so bright, she takes my breath away.

The moment I was discharged from hospital after being shot, I had a ring on her finger and Bryce's adoption under-way. I wasn't letting anything hold us back this time around. Nothing was going to stop me from taking what I wanted.

"Come up here and let me taste myself on your tits."

She lifts up and hovers her heavy tit over my face before lowering her nipple to my waiting mouth. The moment my musky arousal hits my tongue, a splash of her warm milk follows, and I grunt in euphoria, feeling myself harden beneath her.

My phone ringing cuts through the air, and I pull back with a sneer.

Gia reaches for it, and when she hands me the phone and I see it's Mase, I place it on speaker.

"Reed?"

"Yeah." I groan as Gia tugs on her nipples, putting on one hell of a show for me.

"I'm in trouble, man."

I stiffen, and Gia stills.

"Oh God. I fucked up." The choked emotion in his tone has my spine snapping straight. I've never heard Mase sound so desperate, not even when his wife …

"I fucked my sister," he quickly says.

"What?" I jolt on a strangled breath.

"M-my sister. My stepsister." He stumbles over his words. "She's the … she's the Indulgence girl."

"The Indulgence girl? You're not making any sense. I don't understand. I thought your sister was in school?" I sit up in bed, wrapping my arm around Gia's ass to stop her from falling.

"She is. It's worse than you think, man." Is he fucking kidding me right now? Worse? "So much worse because she's also …"

THE END

You can preorder Mase's book here: **PREORDER MASE**
Would you like to join my Newsletter?
Click on this **link** to sign up and grab a snippet of Owen's book.

ACKNOWLEDGMENTS

Tee the lady that started it all for me. Thank you for an eternity.

I must start with where it all began, TL Swan. When I started reading your books, I never realized I was in a place I needed pulling out of. Your stories brought me back to myself.

With your constant support and the network created as 'Cygnet Inkers' I was able to create something I never realized was possible, I genuinely thought I'd had my day. You made me realize tomorrow is just the beginning.

<u>**SPECIAL MENTION**</u>

To Jo, thank you for EVERYTHING!

Your support has been incredible this past few months, you've helped me stay sane and on target. Nothing is too much trouble and knowing I can rely on you means everything. Thank you.

Jaclyn and Lilibet, thank you both so much for all your comments and support, you keep me on my toes in the best way possible, I'm grateful for every comment, word of encouragement and suggestion. Thank you both.

Terra, thank you for jumping on board the BJ train. Next stop Daddy Vinny.

Debbie thank you for being you. You're amazing and your strength inspires me, thank you.

My Incredible ARC and Street Teams.

Thank you for every share, every comment, video and

message. I'm so grateful you find the time to support me and my books.

Special mention to Lorna for the baby name, 'Lowan'.

My Reckless Readers!

Thank you for being a part of my reading group, your support is amazing. We're building an amazing group together, and I'm incredibly proud of us. Thank you for making our space, safe, fun and above all else, supportive.

To my world.

Boys, your mum is smashing our dreams. Thank you both for all your support and encouragement, your belief in me means the world.

To my hubby, the J in my BJ.

Johnny, you are without a doubt the best. Thank you for helping build our dreams.

Without you I wouldn't be BJ Alpha. Love you trillions!

And finally…

Thank you to you, my readers.

Your enthusiasm and support is what encourages me on to the next book. Thank you!

Love Always

BJ Alpha. X

ABOUT THE AUTHOR

BJ Alpha lives in the UK with her hubby, two teenage sons and three fur babies.

She loves to write and read about hot, alpha males and feisty females.

Follow me on my social media pages:
Facebook: BJ Alpha
My readers group: BJ's Reckless Readers
Instagram: BJ Alpha

ALSO BY B J ALPHA

<u>SECRETS AND LIES SERIES</u>

CAL Book 1

CON Book 2

FINN Book 3

BREN Book 4

OSCAR Book 5

CON'S WEDDING NOVELLA

O'CONNELL'S FOREVER

<u>BORN SERIES</u>

BORN RECKLESS

<u>THE BRUTAL DUET</u>

HIDDEN IN BRUTAL DEVOTION

LOVE IN BRUTAL DEVOTION

<u>THE BRUTAL DUET PART TWO</u>

<u>BRUTAL SECRETS</u>

BRUTAL LIES

<u>STORM ENTERPRISES</u>

SHAW Book 1

TATE Book 2

OWEN Book 3

REED Book 4

MASE Book 5

<u>VEILED IN SERIES</u>

VEILED IN HATE

<u>CARRERA FAMILY</u>

STONE

AZRAEL

<u>MAFIA DADDIES</u>

DADDY'S ADDICTION Book 1

POSSESSION Book 2

DECEPTION Book 3

DOMINATION Book 4

UNTAMED Book 5

<u>UNHOLY SAVAGES MC</u>

KILLA Book 1